V,

I

INSIDE & OUT. YOU'RE ONE OF MY
FAVORITES. THANKS FOR BUYING.

— JOHNNY

L,

IT STARTS WHEN YOU STOP

IT STARTS WHEN YOU STOP

JOHNNY ABBOUD

atmosphere press

Copyright © 2021 Johnny Abboud

Published by Atmosphere Press

Cover design by Beste Miray Doğan

No part of this book may be reproduced except in brief quotations and in reviews without permission from the publisher.

It Starts When You Stop
2021, Johnny Abboud

atmospherepress.com

1

The best weather is the absence of weather. The best love is the absence of love.

'Live in the moment,' they tell you. You hear it from TV therapists and self-help authors and any other bozo proclaiming to be genuinely happy, each time worded just differently enough to be an entirely new idea for someone besides you to get rich off of. No past and no future, only right now. Well, unless you're some divinely enlightened monk or a facetious monkey playing with your own shit, I'd say it's easier said than done.

Even presently, with the fate of basically everyone and everything resting on my young shoulders, it's nearly impossible for me to not think about the series of events that brought me here. Here to this setting you wouldn't believe, not yet at least. I wouldn't have believed it before, but I'm much older now than when my story began, many weeks and months and years in fact.

Nearing departure time . . . I hear followed by a

nearly unbearable ¡SCREECH! I wince.

"What the fuck!" I say instinctively. It definitely brings me back to the present moment here with Dr. Banshee, surrounded by what appears to be the inside of some Bavarian castle frozen with a thin layer of ice.

I don't think about the dozens upon dozens of dreams I didn't understand most of my life, not while this ultra-high-pitched screeching menace is erupting, ready to burst my eardrums. If it wasn't for my heart seeming to pound through both temples, I might be contemplating my choice at hand, the choice that I just realized existed, that I don't know will work, that I wish I'd figured out before we'd lost so much already.

"My goodness, Mr. Hiro, I'm quite sorry about that. It will still take a few moments for all of the troubleshooting to complete."

Fucking troubleshooting and program updates and GPS systems too complex for even our most brilliant and most introverted nerds to have come up with. The irony of my choice is not lost upon me, even given the circumstances.

It's then that the sharp pain exits my auditory system and my mind is free to linger forward and backwards once more. First and foremost I think of the snakes, those goddamn serpents I've been seeing everywhere that I know don't belong. Trash bags and breakfast-sandwich wrappers kissed by the air to dance and slither around me and make me think of what I've never understood.

I think about a funhouse image of myself being obliterated in some big bang I probably hallucinated. I wonder where it is we might be departing towards.

The snakes are here all around me even though I know

they're not. Forces I can't see when I should and can see when I shouldn't; story of my life I suppose.

Speaking of which, we'll rewind.

PART ONE

HIRO'S YOUNGER YEARS HIGHLIGHTS

AGE: 13

2

Todd used to be an incredible athlete, apparently. I'm pretty sure his body is made up primarily of water and lite beer and lies, but on this particular front I believe him. There are photos he hung of himself in the basement where there should be photos that don't suck so hard. In these pictures of memorable glory, not to be confused with memorable glory holes, something Todd explained to me impetuously, he's holding medals or plaques or trophies with little golden self-esteem boosters shaped like footballs or baseballs or track champions.

He used to be quite the musician, too. There's more than one framed waste of space throughout that basement reminding him, and us unfortunately, of his days front-lining his band, *The Sexy Dolphins* or *The Grumpy Diapers* or something along those stupid lines. Some name he thought was brilliant, a clever innuendo that isn't an innuendo at all. The name and his looks and their sound, wow man they were really going places! Except they didn't.

I mean, technically, they did GO PLACES, like to live under a bridge or work at a McDonalds or frequent a Methadone clinic. But nothing musical besides the songs they hear in their heads while they clean toilets or smoke crack-rocks.

Todd the God even used to act in the school plays in high school. Atypical for a jock. 'Perhaps there are levels to him,' one might mistakenly think.

"Oh fuck theatre, bro . . ." he'd told me once, ". . . I was just swimming in so much sensitive actress poon I almost drowned. HA!" I wish he would have.

"What a way to go out, right? HA! Suffocating between some jumbo tatas!"

It's never too late I'm thinking, I'm sure there's a brothel around somewhere. Hell, we could ask Siri.

"Plus, everybody was always talking about how crazy-handsome I am. . . ."

How handsome you were. Smug fuck.

"Seriously everyday I'd hear, 'Oh my god, you've got to be in movies!' . . . Old broads loved me."

If it wasn't abundantly clear by now, Todd the Bod was the pinnacle of popularity. Women wanted to be on top of him and dudes wanted to be him or be friends with him or kill him and wear his skin. I imagine a fair percentage considered the murder option; the bulk of the world isn't *cool*, after all.

Toddy 'Too Hotty' ran in the game-winning touchdown against Eastern Catholic AND then took down the Homecoming King title, SAME WEEKEND! He must have crushed two cases to his face! I know this because he's not shy about telling and retelling and retelling his retellings of his glory days. I'd probably destroy in any sort of trivia contest related to the life he once lived.

He was Snow King, won by a landslide but refused to wear the illustrious *frost crown*. Typical snow king behavior. He once walked away from second base mid-game to hit a joint his friend was offering him at the fence. No one dared to say anything to the big bad wolf that he was and thinks he still is. The quintessence of badass.

What a life ahead! A future NFL or MLB all-star, he'd endorse shaving cream or protein bars or laxatives depending on the relative stage of his career. He'd have a movie-star wife and A-list kids and an award-winning golden retriever. Prize Pup Penelope, probably.

They'd travel the world on their private jet in between filming blockbusters and winning Superbowls. Upon return, there would be hordes of friends and family and fans swarming all of their known whereabouts, begging for autographs and selfies and sperm samples for later impregnation.

'Hot Rod' Todd used to be so many things, everything mentioned already and so much more. I wish I was exaggerating when I say I could recite his teenage tales of magnificence for DAYS. Days, plural. But that popular, ripped, talented, essential god that he was died or disappeared or retired right around graduation, two decades ago at least.

He's still a lot of things, I admit. . . . A drug addict and an alcoholic for example, any and all varieties of either are up his alley, don't you doubt it! Anything you can purchase for too much money and grind up or break up and snort or inject, I've probably seen him do and Blaire couldn't imagine he still does.

Where his washboard stomach used to be, seemingly

photoshopped with an absurd eight-pack, I mean who really needs that many abs, now there's a jumbo-sized pot belly equipped to hold vast quantities of piss-quality beer. He probably can't shoot a 3-pointer like he could once upon a time, but he could run a clinic on shooting dope into your arms or neck or *femoral venous sinus*.

His friends used to leech onto him and suck up any amount of bloody high-school popularity that they could. A pack of dirty dogs following him around like little puppies trying to sniff out some bitches in heat.

Well, he is still a filthy rabid animal of a man-boy, but he's the one doing all of the leeching now. The mooching, the freeloading, the being-less-than-worthless, yup, that's our guy, good ol' Todd the Tank. I'd be near okay with his *presence* and all his stupid names if he at least treated Blaire 10% as well as she deserves, as all people deserve, really.

Todd is not a movie star or musician or TV celebrity, not a professional athlete or professional anything. Todd is a big, big stinky bag of shit.

3

Blaire is a pleasantly perfect blend of racial ambiguity; she's any race she wants to be but internally she's my Japanese grandfather's daughter. A grandfather whose long and skinny, dark, silk-like samurai mustache I've never seen in real life, just a few old black and white photos. He's likely the reason my name is Hiro.

The other half of her DNA is a mystery to her which makes 75% of my DNA a mystery to me. No matter how I ask or how many times or how hard I try, I can't get real answers about the man responsible for half of my existence. If I'm honest, I haven't tried too hard. What if I find out he's worse than Todd the Fraud?

Actually, simply not possible, so scratch that. I'll just bank on immaculate conception for right now.

It's tough to see certain people in your life in a context foreign to you. Like when you're in elementary school and your teacher from 8am until 3pm becomes your server at Applebees from 5-6pm for half price appetizers in the bar area. You realize this educator is also an actual person outside of their assigned teaching establishment.

Incredible!

Your bully gets beat up by his brother. That *dummy* at the gas station is in law school. Your bully gets beat up by his dad.

A life without surprises isn't a life worth living. A person without surprises isn't a person worth knowing or loving or trusting. Variety is the spice of life; that's just science.

So, as much as I may tunnel vision Blaire as Mother Dearest, Mom Dukes, Momma Bear, and the like, supposedly she's a regular-ish person who probably would love having interests besides her angry or sad or hyperactive son. Probably.

She used to paint I think. Maybe she would start doing that again. Maybe she would get back into yoga or doing haikus. I don't know, maybe she'd start murdering people and eating their organs, I'm not a fucking psychic.

Apparently, she's quite the looker. As her son, I clearly see her as a genderless female-unit parenting machine incapable of sexual interactions. I mean, I know I exist so it must have occurred that one time, but A LOT of people believe that story about the Virgin Mary.

I see male eyes follow her wherever we go, while the eyes of the females accompanying them signifying their steaming discontent, no matter how many times they insist, 'I'm fine.'

They're not fine.

None of them are ever fine, not ever.

I'm sure my friends would tease me about having the *hot mom*, if I had any real friends, that is. You'd think from all the attention that she'd be a model or actress or some wealthy man's trophy wife, at the very least.

Unfortunately for both of us, she's none of those, and Todd's bogus disability check hardly covers half the rent. Just a hardworking woman with some silly social science degree and 2,700 jobs designated primarily to pay back the debt from aforementioned silly degree. I'm sure she would have gone to graduate school if I wasn't given life. If she wasn't given the burden that is me. She sacrificed her whole life so I could become her whole life.

Moms, right?

4

"I just wish you'd try to bond with him a little more, Todd."

They think I'm asleep. I should be, it's late, and I have school tomorrow. Santa Claus and God and Smokey the Bear would all be upset I'm breaking the rules.

"DAMMIT, Blaire, this **again**!?"

They're in the dining room and I'm at the top of the staircase just behind the open door of the linen closet. I have not yet started any forest fires.

"Oh, do NOT do that! Like we can just disregard the fact that my new husband and my only child still can't have a conversation or even just humor me!"

That's true, that guy fucking sucks. I'd rather talk to a skunk's angry asshole.

"You and that *only child* card. My troubled little guy. My special young man...."

His voice is scathing and derisive. I imagine he must be using air quotes.

". . . What you must MEAN is your spoiled, Looney

IT STARTS WHEN YOU STOP

Toon, good for noth—"

"How FUCKING dare you!" Fierce Ms. Cheetah Mother shouts to thwart the shit-talking.

They're just playing the interruptions game now. It's tough to tell who's winning, it always is. I can't make out what either is saying while they're both on full blast. It's white noise to me at this point. Like an ocean breeze and whale noises, except instead it's my mermaid mother yelling at this fish-faced slimy motherfucker.

Ugh, mother fucker.

I *know* he doesn't give a shit about me. That's both undisguised and 100% fine, but I don't think he really loves Blaire either, he just wants to *plow* her . . . whatever that means; I heard it at school.

I mean, I know it's sex but I don't know if it's performed differently. I would ask someone at school if there was anyone I trusted not to instantly make fun of me in front of my peers, and asking Todd would involve talking to Todd.

¡K'PSHH!

Their yelling tournament is punctuated by the crash of something glass or ceramic shattering.

"JESUS, babe. Don't you think I've fuckin' tried my best!? I truly feel like I've done EVERYthing I can, but he doesn't WANT to bond with me!"

I'd say he's put forth minimal effort at best but he's not wrong about that last part. Mother dearest isn't yelling back anymore. Just tears and sobs.

He's trying to make her weak. Breaking things to show that he can, to show that he will. Breaking **her** will, most importantly. He **is** making her weak.

As is the usual plan of action, the big bully routine is

followed by the apologetic nurturer drill. No more screams, he's speaking softly now. Although it's tough to hear, it sounds calculated, something like,

"Babe . . . Babe . . . Shhh . . . Sweetheart, I love you so much, so, so much. I won't lose you, I just won't. I CAN'T. Not now and not ever. Everything could be, **will** be so perfect, me and him will keep trying."

I'm sure he's throwing in his most auspicious eye-contact in at the most ideal times. Kudos for the skilled manipulation of a fragile woman. Quality stuff, shit satchel.

"It will be perfect, babe. I promise. You'll see."

He's so full of shit that literally a child knows it.

"You promise? You won't get discouraged? Promise me you'll continue trying."

Wow, Blaire, seriously though? Fucking dummy.

The crying sounds begin to evolve into kissing sounds and I decide to sprint back to my bedroom before I end up learning the fine points of plowing.

5

I remember having to take all sorts of different personality tests. They try to cram you into an exact category of person and even if you don't quite fit, they'll squeeze you in for convenience. Jamming puzzle pieces together incorrectly just to hopefully get a good enough snapchat photo for your story.

Introverted? Extroverted? Type A or B personality? Are you one to judge or perceive incoming information? They tell you there are no *right answers,* but it certainly seems like I've been providing the wrong answers.

There was a different doctor what felt like every time I needed to trim my fingernails. Psychiatrists and psychologists and certified counselors. The former are generally drug dealers with medical degrees, the middle being your run of the mill shrinks, and the latter are essentially shrinks with less years of schooling. None of them free, unsurprisingly. Dr. Herman and Dr. Aziz and Dr. Kim prescribing Lamotrigine and Venlafaxin and Pristiq. And then, of course, there was Dr. Fox Viqar.

One group of questions I've become accustomed to relates to whether you're a logical or an emotional thinker. Rational or magical. I've definitely never been anywhere near logical or rational, really. So, as the emotional magical-thought enthusiast I've always been, I've also always had a great deal of interest in concepts like witchcraft and other alternative belief systems in general. Anything that gives us the potential to be more than we're supposed to be.

One of the many things that worried my mother penguin and annoyed her shit sandwich of a bed mate was the orange and brown nike shoebox filled with voodoo dolls under my bed. Whether it's just a hobby based on an intrigue with white magic or you're studying for a final exam in black magic witch-doctoring, the result is probably the same when you're in elementary school, *talking doctors*.

Tell me more about YOUR relationship with your mother, Dr. Einat Rothstein. No, YOU'RE having irrational thoughts, Enrique Parra, PsyD.

I mean, really, a voodoo doll is just a *simulacrum*, an object made to be the likeness of something, in this case a person. You then *key* the doll, which means attempting to connect physically to the object. I'd sometimes use them as they were meant to be used, holding my momma bear doll equipped with real hair in my writing hand and looking at pictures of her while just *thinking* as much good energy as I possibly could to her or with her or at her or whatever. A conjectural theory that really gives our positive and negative thoughts significance. Simple enough.

The whole poking with needles thing is supposed to be

bad news bears and result in negative consequences for the 'Bokor.' I can somewhat speak to the backlash, although I'm not sure if it's really magic or not. I poked my Todd the Slob simulacrum where his genitals would be with a steak knife for a while. I suppose, ideally, I would have liked for his penis to have fallen off and ran away in the middle of the day with no explanation. Instead, I could still hear them have sex; the poking had just made me think of his genitals. Definitely not the win I was hoping for.

♭

"His fucking name is Fox?!"

My first encounter with Dr. Fox Viqar took place several years ago, before I gained my new understanding. My understanding via the information I've acquired and inadvertently shared and continue to receive. Back when she was ONLY worried about the dozens of other red flag behaviors. That's all, no biggy.

I'd hear Blaire and 'Hot Dog' Todd talk about me. I'm weird, not deaf. Thanks. I mean, they had some justified concerns. My complete absence of friends, serious anger-issues, depression, generalized anxiety, macabre interests, and odd illustrations. Eh, whatever. What's normal is boring . . . and lucky.

"What if I'd rather keep being sad? I mean, what if I . . . **have** to be sad?" I'd say to Lady Leader.

"Honey, don't be silly. Please, I want you enjoying your life."

Prior to knowing the ins and outs of every mental

IT STARTS WHEN YOU STOP

health facility within 50 miles, I had heard our sweet family matriarch on the phone with several doctors, receptionists, and insurance representatives, trying to set something up despite our extra-shitty, basically made up, coverage. Full patient load after full patient load, sighs and frustration and sighs and disappointment.

And then there was a name. And then another. Amongst the medical professional omelette of these first couple handfuls of names was Dr. Viqar.

"You have no idea how grateful *WE* are to you for spending some time with Hiro. I know that your secretary, Arina, said you don't usually accept our insurance but that you're making an exception for us," she says into the phone.

Blaire hangs up her primitive cellular telephone, outdated even for that time, and parks her head down on the kitchen table. I can see around the corner from the living room; I'm pretending to watch *America's Most Wanted*. You know, typical children's programming.

She takes a deep breath and wipes a tear of relief from between her eye and the bridge of her nose as she picks herself up from the dining-room table and starts walking towards me. I quickly turn up the TV two notches and focus on the serial killer being described on the screen, still roaming free. What an interesting person he'd be to meet.

Blaire, in her most chipper tone, explains to my youngster self that I'm going to go visit another special talking kind of doctor. I already know what psychologists are, developmental and forensic and clinical. I'm unusual, not naive. Thanks.

"I really think you're going to like him a lot more than any of the others," Blaire tries to assure me.

I don't say much, mostly just because I don't want to talk. Not to her. Not to Dr. Vishcar. Not to anyone. Certainly not to my completely absent father or completely horrible, replacement father figure. Although, he's already left through the front door a few moments ago without exchanging even a glance with me, so I suppose that option would be off the table anyway. Role models teaching us to be absent.

Momma Blaire made French toast and chicken fingers for dinner that evening, two of my personal favorites, which meant she knew I was less than thrilled about the news earlier. The woman tried, it's undeniable. She always tried.

7

I read about this one Haitian *vodou* witchdoctor-legend who created a zombie potion that turned the unfortunate drinkers into his applesauce-brained slaves. Apparently, people would down the Bokor's secret stuff and they'd become dead. Temporarily, of course.

They'd basically just lose consciousness and, in all likelihood, get dangerously near death before eventually waking up hurting and lacking knowledge of what happened. Some tribal acid trip. Too much Haitian cough medicine.

What really interests me about this stuff is honestly the simplicity of the ingredient list. There are no scientists in lab coats, no beakers or bunsen burners, just the hands and mind of a pretty much self-proclaimed doctor. This guy with the formula for mashed potato brains, his recipe card included dead toads and lizards and I believe the soul of a deceased human baby.

The *secret sauce* of the batch, though, is a potent neurotoxin called tetrodotoxin, or TTX. This toxin is found in certain newts and snails, but mostly in pufferfish and similar swimming sea friends. This is the type of dangerous pufferfish that needs to be specially prepared by a certified and preferably Japanese chef. It's usually enjoyed by a mixture of adrenaline-junkies and wanderlust-filled worldsmen . . . and idiots. No anticoagulants or anthrax or high-fructose corn-syrup, just fish.

蛊 or 蠱 or *GU* is another pseudo-natural but super-interesting poison, venom-based and mostly from specific regions of Southern China. What they'd do is basically create a cage match for a bunch of venomous little fellas. Snakes and centipedes and Scorpions and whatever else they could round up, placed together and left to an ultimate death match. Real survivor-of-the-fittest type of ordeal, except the hero at the end, all juicy with a collection of the losers' toxins in their belly, is ground up and turned into death juice or used in black magic spells.

Cults and Religions. Religions and Cults.

Who really needs weapons when you know what this truly dangerous world has to offer you?

There was one particular drawing I did that raised eyebrows from teachers and the principal and the mother. I drew myself surrounded by newts and snakes and scorpions, bats and porcupine fish and blue-ringed octopuses, all of them full of venom or diseases or TTX.

My army . . .

My secret army.

8

The drive there isn't long but it feels like it. There's classic rock playing on my mom's favorite station. I don't recall exactly what model vehicle we're in, something along the lines of a 4-speed automatic 95 Chrysler LeBaron in Tasman Green, certainly no youngster of an automobile, so the sound quality is on the shittier end. She's never cared much, though. She plugs along, lightly mouthing the words with a mild smile resting on her face, as always. She's sweet, really sweet. Sweet always irritated me in everyone except her. Just a dark momma's boy.

"If you're hungry after, sweetie, we can stop at Arby's, or I can make you . . ."

I can't help but mostly drown her out.

Don't misinterpret things, I wasn't making her pictures with macaroni hearts by any means. I just could never help but to dislike her less than I dislike near everyone else. She's relentlessly likable.

I've been mentally prepping. I imagine what this so-called Dr. Viqar would be like. This *alternative*, apparently far from the regular medical practitioner . . . I still imagine an ordinary man. Short and pudgy and foreign, obviously, with that name. Probably balding and old and boring, sitting there with his yellow notepad.

I bet his office smells like that restaurant Todd the Uncultured Snail hates. He'll say something condescending and I'll berate and bully him at full blast. I've always had a strength for making people's eyes fill with salty tears, proven by the copious amount of parent teacher conferences Blaire was 'asked' to attend.

Plan set. Let's do it.

We arrive in an almost completely barren parking lot, several backroads away from anywhere previously existing in my cognitive map. It's empty, like there should be a quickdraw cowboy shootout occurring shortly, tumbleweeds floating around accompanied by a beaming bright sun.

Besides us, there's only a pair of vehicles currently residing in this island of a parking area surrounded by an ocean of foreign territory. From what I recall, it could have possibly been a 2000 Kia Optima in Iridium Silver, aside of a 2004 390HP Maserati Coupe, parked crookedly enough that it appears to be done on purpose. An exact 45-degree angle.

We walk from Blaire's junker vehicle past the aggressively average vehicle and then the vehicle which looks to belong to a superhero. It's like the three Poke-evolutions of a car. Carmander, Carmeleon, and Carizard.

We walk up the two sets of four steps and walk into a surprisingly spotless office building. The other few offices appear to have names on the doors belonging to podiatrists or money managers, but it must be every single person's day off . . . except ours. It's then that I see my newest doctor's full name.

"His fucking name is Fox?!" I basically scream as Mama Bee opens the door.

"Honey! Watch your mouth!" I must be laughing out loud for at least 30 seconds before my resting scowlish expression returns.

I pick up a *Sports Illustrated* off Dr. Fishfarms waiting room table. I rip out a couple pages and throw them in the garbage for fun. I'm ruining this magazine AND I'm not recycling. Double Whammy.

I also remove a couple pages containing women in swimsuits. Those are folded and put away for private future research. No further inquiries on those pictures.

Blaire checks me in at the receptionist's desk, presumably with the same kind young female that she talked to on the phone. She has long dark hair that makes me forget for a moment what I'm here for. She turns her head toward me and catches me looking in her direction. I quickly look away but still manage to see her smile, wave pleasantly, and say hi. She seems too far out of my league to even be in my life as a medical professional. But she's young, just a few years older than I am, and she seems very sweet. Just as I manage to send a smile in her direction, out comes my new acquaintance, Fox.

Well, he is not a short man or anywhere on the chunky side whatsoever. He isn't bald or strikingly boring, not old or ugly or anything like I hoped he'd be. Instead, he's tall and fit, tan with green eyes and dark defined features to go along with a suit nicer than any I've ever seen before on any TV series, even *Mad Men*.

Frankly, he is aggravatingly handsome. And in case I needed confirmation, Blaire's instant and palpable swooning makes it abundantly obvious. I still see something very ugly in him.

He IS foreign, at least. I guess I was right about that. I'll find out at some point later he's an elaborate aggregate of exotic bloods. 25% this and 25% that but undeniably 100% pretty-man.

Blaire kneels down just a touch, puts her left hand on my right shoulder, and flutters her long black eyelashes a few times. "Hiro, sweetie, if you feel uncomfortable at ANY point in there, just come out. Ok, angel? I'm right outside."

I know the drill; I just nod my head and walk right past Mr. Fox Person into his office. He comes in and gently closes the office door behind him.

"Hello there, Hiro. It's nice to finally meet you." I stare back silently. Coldly. "Don't worry, we don't have to talk about anything you don't want to," he continues, not shaken by my scare-stare.

I look at his desk; there's a picture of him and a woman I assume is his wife. She's stunning. A straight smoke-show.

"If you'd feel more comfortable, your mother can come in for today?"

Frustrated, I shake my head. He begins to say something else and I cut him off.

"Pause yourself, Dr. Lickfart, I don't know what feelingsy shit you're gonna try to get me to share, but just drop it. We can skip doing any silly tests too. Kay, buddy boy?"

Dr. Fog McBarf stands up and smirks a little. I continue to not smile at all. He walks towards the window and asks, "You ever smoke weed, Hiro?"

I have not. Not because of lack of interest. I just believe in grammar school, as the saggy-skinned walking skeletons would call it, having a friend group greatly improves your ability to acquire such goods. I am lacking said friend group.

"Not really any of your business, Dr. Skidmarks."

He opens the window just a crack and starts laughing out loud. He pulls out the first joint I've ever actually seen from a metal cigarette case in his pocket. I can't help but to feel a tinge of excitement.

"Yeah, I heard you were quite the little shitbird. Listen, be your best shitbird self. People think you're too dark? The world's dark, toughen up."

I stare at him angrily but calmly: shitbird has always been MY word. He lights the joint. "Here, bud, not prescribing anything today, no 'feelingsy shit,' just enjoy your first high and tell me all the things you truly hate most." I hit the joint.

"Ok," I mutter as I tumultuously cough and spew smoke and saliva and some level of innocence all throughout the room.

I continue to see the Fox. I sometimes even call him by his name.

4

Being a *shitty relationship* victim is almost like being a drug addict in a lot of ways. I don't mean someone that **plays** victim, just like I don't mean someone that **plays** addict.

Some addicts don't think they're addicts, but the dealer knows. He's smiling and counting your money time after time. Purchase after purchase. Those people too dumb or too naive or too in love, they find reasons to go back to their familiar abuser.

'Can't help who you love.' A stupid quote to justify stupid actions by stupid people. They don't think there's an issue, but their friends know. They're there, picking up the pieces time after time. Heartbreak after heartbreak.

Until they're not.

Other times, all parties involved are fully aware of what's going on. You've got your 6-month chip in your pocket and a needle in your arm. Regret and bliss and depression and ecstasy. The ex that is NOT the one that got away, more like the one you can't shake.

IT STARTS WHEN YOU STOP

It **is** an addiction really. To **all** of it, it's not just the shitty love. It's the hiding and the fear of getting caught, the shame and the self-loathing, the lying to yourself, the lying to everyone else, just the lying itself.

Addicted to being helpless. Helpless to make a decision, helpless to leave, helpless to stay and be happy.

Blair's addicted to him and to the heartbreak and to all of it. Whether she knows or she's naive? I'd say it's probably somewhere in the middle.

He's gone and we've got gym memberships. ONE MONTH CHIP.

He stays gone a little longer and we're ahead on our bills all of a sudden. My dearest provider has a Saturday OFF from ALL of her jobs, AND we can afford it. SIX MONTH CHIP.

But then there he is again, the walking relapse douchebag himself. Her Heroin or Percocet or Coke. It takes a real addict several trips to rehab before it really sticks, if ever.

Unfortunately, for some of our drug using friends, there's no learning until it's too late. I just hope it's not too late for Blaire. We always hope it's not too late, usually when it is.

10

I'm young but sometimes it feels like my problems are adult size. Maybe not my problems themselves, considering I'm not old enough to maintain employment or acquire debt or fuck without being considered a god or a victim. But it's been explicitly shown that I'm old enough to be lobbed around from specialist to specialist, to be prescribed colorful assortments of SSRI's, to be told how limited my future may be, despite their claims of my own intellect.

Funny how age works. Lots of Asian cultures start life at age 1, basically they start life at conception, as soon as those little swimmers hit their mark. Score one for the pro-lifers, I guess. Stupid Asia.

Those specialists, by the way . . . I mean, I've said it before and I'll say it again, they're people. People. People just like everyone else. Well, pretty much.

They may have been *blessed* with superior intelligence, perhaps a stronger natural work ethic, could have been excellent . . . uhm . . . hell . . . they could have even just been the spawn of some complete-shit parents whom are in possession of tons of sweet green spending dinero. Usually some combination of the three I imagine, at least one or two.

But still . . . people. Men or women that worked hard and chose a *specialty* in the glorious field of medicine. So, should we trust them to do their jobs? Yes, of course, usually. My point, though, is that the same way we forget that our parents and teachers are real people, is the same way most of us have probably never fully thought of the possibility of our doctors being super hungover. Or high. Or horny.

Startling realization. I mean, it could likely be a source of some mild anxiety at the next doctor's visit. I imagine that the thought, that slim chance loitering in the back of your skull, is irritating . . . or at least it will be. Wondering if your money and time and well-being are being spent with a capable individual. They're just people, after all.

No uncertainty for me, at least. I know what my doctor is about, the only one in my line-up at the moment. He's quite the toker, and he's been far from stingy. I imagine his sharing skills skyrocketed him to the highest peaks of the kindergarten ranks.

Speaking of that lunatic does remind me, though, that I do have something to look forward to at my upcoming appointment. Besides seeing that glorious angel, Arina, of course, a real girl that actually talks to me. Usually I'm fairly iffy about our scheduled meetings. . . . Viqar's far from the regular, but he's still a doctor. Probably.

Today, though, I just can't wait for some Aloha White Widow or a nice Afghan Skunk Indica to punch both my lungs at the same time. To remind me there are other moments besides the moment that happened just before school this morning.

Blaire, no surprise, is working. Around 7:30am . . . I imagine at this time she's usually dropping off extra foamy cappuccinos to motivated, morning movers at Johnny's Bagels.

I walk out of my front door to see Man-Tit Todd sitting on his car, shirtless, smoking a cigarette and arguing with someone I'm sure I don't care about on his phone. I try to move facelessly past him, but I unfortunately see him angrily and repeatedly press the red button on his phone before hurling it into the street.

"These motherfuckers . . . they, they don't even act how they're supp—" he says with conviction. Swaying, he takes a long drag of his Newport 100, then seems to wake up all of sudden and looks right into my light brown eyes, "C,mon, kid. I've gotta . . . go do a thing, so, I . . . I uhm, 'm gonna take you to . . . thing." He's blackout drunk before I've eaten a Pop-Tart.

"Thanks, Todd, really, but I'm early anyways, plus I mostly go through the alleys, too."

He smiles and I think maybe I'm in the clear for a douchebag-free morning stroll to school. He allows me to walk a few feet down the pavement before I'm notified this won't be the case. I see him hop off his "borrowed" Candy-Blue Acura TLX out of the corner of my eye. I'm not sure exactly what's coming but I just close my eyes instinctively and brace myself.

¡CLAP! His blistered right palm meets the back of my clenched neck. Nothing painful, just the *ol' alpha male smackaroo*. Still slurring each and every word, "Kid . . ."

he looks around like the whole neighborhood is surrounding and on his side. ". . . did I say something, like..." Another unbalanced look around. ". . . with a question marks?!"

"No, man, I'm sorry. I didn't mean anything by it . . . but I j—"

"Ahhyyeeoo!" He's not here to listen. "BUTTS are like assholes, we both have them and they all stink!"

I don't have the heart, or the balls, to tell him that's not how that phrase goes. Before I can utter another syllable, he turns his volume way up.

"Get your little asian ass into those, that . . . hmph, MY car right fucking NOW!!"

So, at that point, I do what a lot of scared little kids or domestic abuse victims would do because they think it's better than the alternatives provided: I get in the car.

CLICK goes the seatbelt which I waste no time buckling. My school isn't far, just a couple minutes away. A few hundred seconds which I don't remember, a whole shit-ton of Mississippis spent in my own head with my eyes closed, pleading to a god I'm pretty sure I don't believe in to wake me up from this bad REM-sleep story. "You've uh . . . you got any weed?" I'm pretty sure I hear him mumble in my direction.

"I don't, man. I'll probably see my guy later o—"

¡BUM-THUM-THUD-CRUD-CRUM-CRSHJJPFF! The shaking and jumping and crashing of our vehicle half over the curb and through a small metal trash bin creates what sounds like dozens of old computer monitors tumbling down a flight of echoey hallway-stairs. I open my eyes to find I'm safely in one piece. Unfortunately, so is the piss-for-brains moron in the driver's seat. He's laughing like a slow toddler, drool falling from his bottom lip, until he COUGH . . . COUGH . . . GAG, ¡BLAAHHAUUGH!

Whoever this car really belongs to is not going to love that vomit explosion. It smells like cheap beer and disease and cheese curls.

As I look past this mess of a man, I notice where it is that we've crash-landed. Where we are that he's horribly embarrassing himself, embarrassing the both of us. We're surrounded by teachers with their hands covering their mouths, horrified. Peers pointing and laughing because they can either tell no-one is seriously injured, or because they don't give a shit.

"Oh, fuck . . . FUCK. Get out, kid. Frigg'n . . . HURRY UP!"

And THAT is an entrance.

So after a day filled with embarrassment and muffled laughter and multiple meetings with faculty, I'm just moments from the normal bi-weekly routine of smoking yummy Hindu Kush or Alaskan Thunderfuck and discussing *feelingsy* things with my shrink. I'm sitting eagerly in front of his desk as he closes his office door and walks over to his empire leather executive chair. He takes a long swig from a can labeled Diet Pepsi; I can smell from across his desk that the bulk of that beverage is rum.

"Hey, Dr. Viqar, I brought this Strawberry Blunt Wrap with me, you mind fronting me a half ounce or so?"

I grab the DigiTek brand scale from my black backpack, as is standard protocol. He gives me a face like he ate my leftovers or stepped on my sandcastle by accident.

"Shit . . . sorry, guy. Nothing with me at this particular

moment. Smoked a marathon last night with some Thai woman named Mutmunut or something amazing like that."

My last eight hours' worth of dreams have died. Rest in pieces.

"No worries, though." He continues. He shoots me a smile with some real sincerity. "I've got something of a self-truth serum for you today, a mind enhancer really. No need for the *lettuce* once you have this magic potion flowin' through ya."

He tosses me something small and wrapped in plastic. To my own surprise, I catch it with ease. It's a tootsie roll, nothing seemingly special about it. I look up at him, my eyes do the asking, and he answers without hesitation.

"IF you decide to ingest this glory juice, it's important for your palate to be properly prepped, we start with that."

Seems strange, but I enjoy a good chocolate treat, so why not? I'm currently undecided about whether I will be trying any of his ultra-questionable poison cocktails. I chew my little poop-shaped milk-chocolate bite; it's delicious. But then I chew more, and more, and more and more, and then I swallow it and it stops being delicious. A bitterness fills my mouth wholly. It's too late to opt out of whatever I've already sent down my oesophagus to my stomach and eventually my small intestine.

"Ugh, Doc, what did you . . . what did I just eat?" He has a dry-erase board on his desk which he seems to be having a great deal of fun scribbling circles on. He's still paying attention to me slightly, though. He looks up at me, appears to be in a state of bliss.

"Oh, that . . . that was the potion I mentioned, a psilocybin mushroom extract conveniently placed in a

Tootsie Roll. HA! A tasty treat in an already tasty treat! This planet of ours is so magical sometimes, isn't it?"

I jump forward out of my seat, my heart is beating three times faster than it was a moment ago. I hope he's joking but I know he's not. I've never taken a hallucinogen before, let alone been tricked into doing one by my psychiatrist. I did want some sort of crack in the routine, though.

"Wait, seriously? I mean, I'm not ready to g—"

He puts his pointer finger to my mouth and happily, almost innocently, interrupts.

"Shh, little Hirito. There's nothing to *get ready* for. It's fast-acting, long-lasting, and truly enlightening. Just think happy thoughts and take note of any negativity that does come to mind so we can discuss it later. I'm sending you off a bit early today. Don't worry, though! I've assembled an essentials bag for you...." He notions to the red Jansport set aside next to his desk, "This is going to be SO wonderful. Be well, Hiroshima. See you in two weeks with all the grand secrets to that brain of yours."

The bag provided by the Fox Man was . . . a bag. Ha! Wow, a thing that holds other things. And . . . zippers? I mean, **shit**. Oh! But in the beautiful bag, there were some cool cool cool things. Paints and brushes and markers, paper and pencils and cocaine. That last item was in a little vile at the bottom of the bag; it had a sticky-note attached that said 'You're welcome, Hiro-san.' Sticky notes . . . they're little pieces of paper that STICK, I mean, onto anything!

Ok, about 80 minutes into my Tootsie Experience and things are noticeably funky. I'm talking through-the-roof levels of funk happening in my brain. Markers are seriously fantastic tools, but really though, PAPER is where it's at. *PAPER GOD TREE GOD EARTH GOD*, I write over and over and over. We can just crumble up a piece of the Earth and toss it away. Outrageous. *SUN GOD WATER GOD AIR GOD* I write several times as well.

My brain is going through streaks of incredible fireworks followed by exhaustion. UP DOWN UP DOWN UP DOWN. The music playing from my phone seems to be speaking to me, the electric guitar's melody has developed its own voice and accent and attitude.

I can't make the blue click-pen write all of my thoughts down fast enough. So many synapses firing all over the place. Thoughts and thoughts and thoughts, each of which more brilliant than the last. Groundbreaking stuff here. Until all of a sudden, it isn't.

Something just changes with my brain chemistry, essentially out of nowhere. Any arbitrary thought in this state of affairs can dramatically interfere with your positive experience, or so I've been told. In my case, it's a phone call. Blaire is the name that shows on the screen as it vibrates . . . vibrates . . . vibrates. And that's all, really, except it turns into a great deal more via the ol' classic downward thought spiral.

I assume she must be calling me to tell me she's upset about what happened with Todd the Peanut-Brained Dinosaur earlier. It's probably somehow my fault, she's got to know I'm tripping hard now, definitely wouldn't believe the candy was spiked. Now all of that mental fire I have has gone from sparking engines to burning down forests. Bundles of negativity I can hardly control, that I can't control at all, really.

All of a sudden, all of the mostly random abstract drawings I've accumulated this past hour are becoming mighty dark. The bipedal blue cat and bird-person I was so proud of so recently are getting wiped out again and again by layers of black paint. I'm finger-painting obscenities in red so hard my forearm is going numb. I shove the sheets of paper away from me because they're so ridiculous all of a sudden. I'm so ridiculous all of a sudden.

Thank goodness for sinks.

While seriously struggling to gather my wits, I manage to take a first step and relocate myself to the big, empty basement sink so I can wash some of this paint off my hands. It already seems to have made it all over my old jeans and faded black t-shirt. If anything, these garments just became much more fashionable.

And holy miracle of miracles. I feel the warmth of the water on my skin; it's instantly soothing in itself, but the waterfalls of different colors dancing away from my fingertips are something to call home about. Metaphorically, of course.

Although, this cascade of red and green and black and blue liquid is so surreal that it almost feels selfish to not share with anyone. No one could appreciate this like I do, though, probably not worth it to attempt telling anyone and risk missing a second of this rapturous elation.

Little flakes of paint ride the wave down from my hands to the sink's surface, tiny pieces of myself being washed away forever, like friendships and love and everything else that starts out as beautiful and ends up dead and gone forever.

UP DOWN UP DOWN.

IT STARTS WHEN YOU STOP

Neurotransmitters going bananas.

It takes what seems like a perfect amount of infinity to beautifully and euphorically complete my sink art. When I finally turn both handles to their respective off settings and dry my hands on a fluffy blue towel belonging to the basement, it's like I'm taken back to my home world. It seems familiar, I think.

UP DOWN . . . DOWN . . .

Pretty sure my brain has used up its monthly stipend of energy remarkably early.

DOWN . . .

The battery residing in my head is way below green, just a thin red strip left, and that's being used to find my bed. My trip is coming to a grinding halt.

DOWN.

I wake up to feel my lips screaming in agony, dry and cracking and begging for water. Thankfully, there's an unopened Deer Park bottle next to my bare sheet-less bed. I twist off the cap and it falls to the floor. It doesn't matter in the slightest, I down the whole bottle. WHEW.

What a day and night and maybe another whole day. I really have no idea what time or day it is, not at first. My body is just one all-around ache, like I was beaten up last night.

Slowly, pieces from my trip to Tootsie Town begin coming together. One and then another, at no particular rate in no particular order. I begin to think, 'That was sneaky as hell of Dr. Lezbar, but it was an amazing experience, I feel as if I learned so much about myself.'

OH! My drawings and writings and paintings! The tools that Viqar said would open me up to my subconscious, to give me new insight to the inner workings of my mind. Certainly couldn't hurt to learn a bit more about that particular topic. Hmm, right, the basement! That's where I was working.

Walking down the stairs of our rented home, I'm feeling several notches above my usual self. In addition to being excited to potentially gain some valuable insight, I also realize I'm in an empty home. Blaire, I'm sure, is being the solid provider she is. Saturday at 11am is what the DVR in the living room says. I think today she's actually breaking gender norms, helping people move, proudly rocking her *Hot Guy Movers* tee-shirt. Non-discriminatory hiring practices.

Tooth Decay Todd? I don't know or care where he is, he's not here. Hopefully dead via a horse-kick to his teeth. I mean, I know that's harsh . . . which is why I said it.

The situation changes when I finish skipping down to the basement. I'm essentially stopped in my tracks. It's like I forgot the last hour of my trip, at least, and it's boomeranged back to strike me full force. All of my silly cartoons overtaken by black clouds and devil figures. Silhouettes of some mysterious evil . . . well, it's undeniably Fox. My doctor . . . laughing while everything around him suffers.

Messages that appear to be to myself say things like, **WATCH OUT FOR BAD FOX MAN**, or **HE FAR AWAY MONSTER PERSON.** I look at my visual art journal entries as if they were done by someone else. The handwriting is recognizably mine, and the dried paint still forming random islands on my skin are identical colors to those of the Fox Warnings.

FOX DEVIL FOX DEVIL NO FROM HERE DEVIL NO

TRUST.

Apparently, I must know something I didn't know I knew.

11

Some people never remember their dreams. On average, we forget about 90% of the 4-7 slumber stories we have per snooze. I, however, remember a great deal of mine. I always have. There were some recurring themes from when I was young which I recall quite well. Themes I continue to deal with.

Welcome to your first day of Controller Training.

I'm not at controller training, I don't think. I'm pretty positive I'm sitting on a bench near my school's outdoor basketball court. I'm wearing large noise-canceling headphones, off-white and off-brand with no music playing.

I can sense the eagerness in the group. That's fantastic!

The court is a shithole, honestly. One rim hangs lower than it should, neither has a net. I can tell there were 3-point lines at one point, but now they're shown just enough to have arguments about whether the last bucket was a 2-pointer or a 3.

IT STARTS WHEN YOU STOP

Don't worry, science apprentices. We'll be getting to the fun stuff in no time. Our work with localized brain alteration in Project Person subjects is proving already to be an incredible endeavor, even more so than previous study cites!

No one is playing, no one is even here, it's way too cold. I'm cold too but I like the quiet surrounding me, and the goosebumps remind me I'm human and not a plant or a statue or a goose.

With these headphones that you'll understand soon enough, it's never COMPLETELY quiet. Pseudo quiet? Sure. I'm not certain what's real exactly. Whether it's the voices that are the objective reality, or my poor, loving momma bear's worst fears coming to fruition, it can't hurt to learn what I can.

But for today, just the syllabus.

So many dreams of cold days wearing earmuffs made of silicone and rubber and mystery, playing messages I don't understand. I said I remember them, not that they made sense.

12

AGE: 14

The first-floor smells of cinnamon and bacon and coffee brewing as I make my morning walk down the stairs. It's early, I don't have school for another hour and a half. The fatty pork sizzling in its own grease paired with Blaire softly singing to herself makes for a perfect blend of breakfast reverberation. The soundtrack to an ideal day's start.

"Morning, Sweetie," she cheerfully says as I walk right past the kitchen and into the living room. I give a really half-ass wave as I basically sprint to the couch and grab the remote.

There was a new episode of *Bob's Burgers* last night that I wasn't able to watch because the Cowboys game was on. Even though they were down 48-7 in the fourth quarter, TV Terrorist Todd giving up that remote was simply not happening. The man seriously had one of those big foam fingers in the house, watching by himself. I'm pretty sure I'd been watching Sunday Night Fox TV before he got here. Back when I could pretend Blaire might allocate a fitting suitor or preferably no one at all.

Whatever, he's a prick, but I'm getting more and more used to that. That's why I got up early though. On a Monday morning, before a week of school and teachers and classmates that think I'm a freak, so that I can sit on this old familiar couch with the tiny tear in its left cushion, and enjoy my favorite animated escape from reality.

As I scroll down the DVR list, an unpleasant surprise plops down next to me. Without even thinking, he just takes the remote out of my hand and turns to channel 1547, which is ESPN NFL Network on our service provider. One of the very few extras around here that he chips in for. I'm in disbelief at first. Did this shitbird really just do that? Finally, he looks at me, but instead of apologizing, what comes out of his constantly disappointing lips is, "Can ya scooch over a few, kid? You're riding me a little close."

I do no such scooching. My eyes start to fill with that damn saltwater, but my chin is up.

"I was **watching**," I say to him or at him or to Zeus in hopes of an Ancient Greek miracle. He hardly bats an eyelash; he's not even looking at me. He reluctantly moves two or three inches away from me.

"Sorry, kid. SportsCenter is on."

He lets out a fart. This guy IS a fart. They're literally showing highlights of the game he watched 10 hours ago.

I'm boiling with rage. I wish his existence would just *end*. The world doesn't need this douchey, mentally unstable, abusive jock shitshow. I certainly don't. Blaire would be better off, at least after her initial few months of likely being an infant-level wreck of tears and helplessness. She'd adjust; she has before.

"But I woke up early JUST to watch it. Please. I know they show the same episode of SportsCenter like 30 times throughout the day. C'mon . . . **PLEASE.**"

He shakes his head like I'm such a pain in his ass, like he thought marrying my Mother Hen would make me dissipate into the atmosphere and contribute to the global warming he doesn't believe in. Nope, young rooster is still here.

"Aren't you gettin' a little old to be watching cartoons anyway? Some ESPN would be good for you. You're sorta soft."

There's my guy, my primary male influence for the foreseeable future. Typical for weak men to point out how you're weak but never teach you how to be strong.

I'm flooded with feelings that I wish weren't there, and that I can't seem to control. First of all, the cartoons I watch are meant for adults, but I keep that to myself for now. Secondly, I'm 100% not what you'd look at and consider tough or big or strong, but *soft?* Let's not keep this escalating discontent to myself this time. Let's set the tone for the rest of this relationship, for the rest of my life in fact.

He's set the remote down, he's convinced I won't touch it, that I wouldn't dare change the channel, that I wouldn't **fucking dare.**

I definitely won't change the channel. I want the preamble melody of his precious highlight reel to play while I make my stand.

Turn it the fuck up.

As quickly as I can, and for once without overthinking, I grab the remote. The side with the faded buttons is pressed sturdily against my palm. I wind up, and with every single bit of my young strength, I crack him in the nose just as he starts to look over.

My AAA-battery brass knuckles.

A trail of red instantly begins to descend from both of his nostrils. I manage to get one more similarly solid strike before he picks me up by my armpits and literally tosses me across the living room. I crash into the mosaic flowerpot and it shatters along with Blaire's hope for a pleasant family breakfast.

"You ungrateful little shit!" He shouts as he walks towards me.

I wish I could run but the wind has been completely taken out of me and I'm covered in thin shards of whatever this vase was made of. I'm looking down, trying to push myself up when I feel his bare foot fly into my side.

¡**BWAK!** The sound I make could most accurately be called a yelp. By now, Blaire has rushed into the room. She's screaming and trying her best to hold this grown man back from me.

"Please, Todd! Stop! He's a kid, you'll kill him!"

She's full force bawling and pulling on his arm, and just as she's finished screeching her plea, he jerks back his arm and she feels his bony elbow connect directly with her chin. At this point, everyone involved is wearing matching crimson uniforms before most people are at work or school or the welfare store.

I truly think he might kill me, until he stumbles a bit and steps right onto a high-carbon steel-blade-quality shard facing straight up into the plantar fascia area of the bastard's foot. I see him suddenly turn back into a human.

"Aaagghh fuck me!" he screams in agony. While he's

hopping on one foot in tree pose, Blaire pushes with all of her petite might and manages to send him to the floor with all of the tiny little daggers accompanying it. The term *bloody murder* sounds appropriate for what escapes his lips.

She grabs my forearm tightly and we run together for the front door, she grabs the keys to her hoopty of a vehicle off of the ring-stained side table, and we rush to its regular parking spot out front. The doors aren't locked, they never are. Go ahead and steal our borderline poverty.

She presses her worn, size 6 Nike Air Zoom on the gas pedal harder than I've ever seen before, the 96-year-old automobile can tell, and it sounds soberly surprised. She may even be pressing with both feet; it seems that way at least. As I see tears continue to stream down her face, I decide to be uncharacteristically forthright about how this mess began.

"We need a new remote, I used ours to hit Todd the Tormenter in his nose as hard as I possibly could. He's a shitbird asshole and he deserved it, but I did hit him first. Oh, and twice. I hit him twice. I'm sorry this happened," I say with snot running down from my nose, "It's my fault."

I'm not certain whether I'm really sorry or not, not completely at least, but it definitely seems like the proper thing to say. She looks at me astonished. I think at first it's because I started that UFC match back there, but she sincerely and surprisingly says, "Sweetie, the only thing you have to be sorry about is your language. We've talked about this, watch your mouth, ok?"

I just look at her. She's still crying. I nod.

"I'll handle this." She says, looking at me and traffic and me and traffic with tears falling the whole time. "He's out of our lives for good, ok, sweetie?" At me and at traffic. "Out of *my* life, and out of *your* life, I promise." I know she meant it, she really did. Or she at least tried her best to mean it.

13

Everyone, for the most part, has some visible spectrum of feelings in a day or week or lifetime, not to mention our secret sensitive feelings we hide behind our Bluto tough-guy exteriors. The ones we feel by ourselves while we listen to our personal angst-playlists in our bedrooms. Doors locked.

Sad feelings suck, this is empirical science, but they're a part of life. You get sad, you get over it, and you get sad again. Rinse, wash, repeat. 'Life is suffering,' says the Buddhist, says the realist, says the depressed person. I think about the four seasons I've watched recycle themselves while we waste their resources and kill them slowly.

Geese and orioles and Blackburnian Warblers all migrate from one portion of the year to another. They understand how to fairly utilize the natural gifts given to us by the Earth. Not us. We're greedy and we need everything all the time, so there are less cherry blossoms blooming and more Wal-Marts booming.

IT STARTS WHEN YOU STOP

Why have trees and their oxygen and their aesthetic value when we can replace them with our town's third McDonalds? The hungry don't want to drive 9 minutes away, that's a rough burger commute. There will be a playpen, at least; what a miracle for the community.

Imagine that in the beautifully paved, new superstore parking lot, there's one small frail tree remaining. Off to the side, woefully lonely with its own personal dark cloud looming from every angle at every moment. Make your best mental image of this poor tree then shut your eyelids, don't open them until you've become your imaginary plant self. Its roots are your roots, your genetics, and your upbringing. Then there's just the weather surrounding you and the parked cars and the ghosts of animals which used to live here.

During a manic episode, your branches are awakened by the warm sun and crisp air and beautiful songbirds visiting your wooden body. Children play and teenagers get high and old people walk as to not let their useless bodies turn into complete mush. You've got a gorgeous view as well as the center stage. Spring has sprung.

Pure bliss and copious amounts of productivity will gently toss you to and fro in the breeze all through Summer and Fall. The feeling of baking in the Sun's fiery rays, the joyous relief of a rain cloud bursting above. The bittersweet Sunday that is autumn. The final hoorah for our plant lives. Our beautiful deaths.

Once the glorious drug-like euphoria of your mania wears off and your formerly floating ship sinks deep down to the ocean floor of depression, that is when a wildly fierce winter arrives. All of the months before were just a flash, and in an instant we're cast to a lifetime sentence of tundra-covered sleeveless tees.

Complete beauty and rebirth or bitter cold and death. Back and forth and back and forth. Up and down and up and down. Being blessed with this incredible energy and drive for a few days only to skip two seasons and plummet back to wet cold socks, unable to perform any mundane task without difficulty and a generalized anxiety. It's exhausting.

'I go to a bad place in my head sometimes.' A whole lot of people would admit to relating to this statement. Privately, at least. Solutions for the issue seem so simple, neutralizing negative thinking or challenging negative thoughts. Tons of different, yet identical, applications of cognitive behavioral therapy. Weather-stabilizing mental antidotes. But those ideas always dissipate into nothingness, like dreams you don't remember. I decide all I can really do is dress appropriately.

14

AGE: 15

Things have been pretty tolerable recently, borderline good even. I mean, I still don't care for school in the slightest. The learning's not so bad I guess, just the vast ocean of *peers* I don't want to interact with. That I have to interact with. Group projects and desks in circles and heaps of other for-extravert by-extravert originally cliché activities.

I still haven't been nominated for prom king or voted most outgoing. I haven't suddenly become confident or talented or motivated or strong or *happy*. But there's been some degree of newfound pep in my step ever since that shitbag's been gone.

It's been several months since his screams or slaps or fake charm have been present. This means several things for yours truly. For starters, without his constant tornado of drama bullshit, Blaire is able to maintain stability the bulk of the time. Without his mooching off of her and basically squatting in our humble abode, despite bold claims of his grandiose gestures in our favor, I'm home alone whenever Ms. Birthgiver is working or shopping or cross-country dogsledding or I don't know what she does. The point is, I'm alone.

Alone.

Discreet joints out back followed by copious amounts of cereal. It's most definitely **not** that Todd the Rusty Tool would've objected on the grounds that I'm a way minor getting high and watching entire seasons of *Always Sunny* instead of studying or playing outside or developing a skill. It's just every other step of the procedure that he'd turn into an obstacle. You know, the regular, smoking all my bud or eating all the food without the intention of ever replenishing either. Ever.

Or he'd hold it over my head in exchange for *not seeing* him flirting with some waitress or dental hygienist or I think one time a Wendy's drive-through trainee. She was sweaty and gross and probably in high School. Forty-year-old fucking dirtbag.

Madre is working *one of* her jobs. It's Friday around 6pm so I'd wager she's currently slinging shrimp scampi pastas at the Olive Garden. Up-selling beverages like a champion. Single, double? Doing Grey Goose with that, right? Dealing with senile seniors and their coupons and their grandkids with their gluten allergies and vegan requests and ubiquitously judgmental tones.

So, while she's dishing out glasses of chianti to middle-class pretend-snobs to pair nicely with their bolognese sauce, I'm busy dishing out an entire bag of Doritos directly into my mouth. My lemon haze has already been broken up and placed gently into my barely beige-colored joint paper with my sticky weed fingers and rolled carefully into a perfect pearl. It's been lit and inhaled into my too young lungs and enjoyed and now there are Cool Ranch crumbs all over my lap.

Just as I'm feeling oddly content in my empty home, a barely familiar sound comes from the dining room counter. It's a phone ringing, the *HOME phone*, an ancient inconvenient device similar to a cell phone except stupid. It plays a recognizable snippet of some classical masterpiece. I don't remember the composer, but you know the one, the one you're thinking of right now, yes that one.

So it rings and rings and repeats the phone version of Bach or Beethoven or Vivaldi's timeless piece de résistance. Clearly I don't answer it because answering a home phone is roughly 100 times more uncomfortable than answering a cellphone call from a blocked number. Blaire doesn't use this phone either, not ever. I truly forgot it existed. I think it was honestly just cheaper to get the cable and internet plan that came with it. Weird. But it sang and sang and sang until it ended. But then the song started again.

I don't even know our number. I doubt Mother Duck knows either, really. I remain seated and motionless with my legs crossed on the Lark Brown classic recliner which that shitbird always bogarted while he was here. As high and lazy and comfortable as I am, it seems like this new old phone's cry may last several lifetimes, so I reluctantly peel myself off my cushiony comfort-cloud and make my way over. I pick up the dusty ancient communication device and put it to my ear.

"Hello?" I say hesitantly. I expect a machine's voice reminding me to vote Tim Collins for City Council. A programmed tool reminding me to vote for a programmed tool. Maybe a telemarketer just doing a job to earn money that I'll be rude to or hang up on even though I know I shouldn't.

But instead of either of those likely and uncomplicated situations, there's just heavy, angry breathing in my ear. I just continue to hold the phone against my cheek. I can hear a series of long sniffs and snorts and bitter breaths before I elect to repeat myself.

"Hello?"

I can already feel who it is.

"It's your fault," the voice says. My dear friend, Todd the Tub of Tofu Vomit. "It's your fucking fault, you little **shit,**" says Mr. Charming. I'm scared and angry but only briefly speechless.

"Blaire has a restraining order against you, which you're violating right now! She wants **nothing** to do with you!" I reply assertively to our antagonist.

There's a **SNIFFFF**, a **SSNORT**, and a **SNNIFF**, followed by some wild, uncontrolled, maniacal laughter. I imagine him in some shithole motel, doing lines of cocaine larger than the standard coffee table provided, losing his mind one bump or rail or pile at a time until an inevitable heart attack.

"I'm not calling for her. She doesn't matter anymore, nothing fucking matters anymore, and that's YOUR fault! Don't you get it? You ruined EVERYTHING for me, and you think I'm worried about **her** or her precious fucking restraining order? No, it's YOU that I'm calling for."

I frantically look around as if he's calling from behind the couch. I breathe away from the phone so that he can't hear the terror that I feel. If he was right here, that'd be one thing, just dealing with the problem head on. I mean, my still-developing self fighting to the death against a grown man is less than ideal, but then it's done. No more before and hardly an after. It's the stress, the waiting, that kills me slowly inside.

"So, what is it that you want to talk about?" I reply, "Current events, politics, the latest season of *Game of Thrones*?"

I'm trying to act braver than I am.

SNIFFF. SNORRT. SSNNNIF.

And again with an absurd outburst of laughter before he replies, "Aww, no, you arrogant little prick. . . ." He's annunciating his words more clearly than I've ever heard before. It's noticeable.

". . . I just called to tell you I've come to really miss you, so I was thinking you and I should have a little visit soon."

My anxiety is moving from serious to seriously crippling at a record rate. Again, fake it 'til ya make it.

"Hard pass on that, shitbird."

SSNF. SSNORRT. COUGH. GAG. COUGH.

"You really are a little cocksucker, kid. I'll see ya real soon."

Click.

No more sniffs or snorts or coughs or gags or laughing attacks. Just dial tone, and the stress of anticipation.

15

Commence Daily Depression Maximum.

I don't want to go anywhere or do anything today. I'm having some serious trouble maintaining right now. My body feels stuck to the bed. Glued or Velcroed or bubble-gummed.

"Hiro, wake up, kiddo."

It sounds as if there's some static coming from somewhere. I can't tell which stimuli are external or internal or present or absent. Real or imaginary.

Lower motivation further.

¡KUHREEEEHK! Blaire opens my bedroom door; thanks so much for the privacy.

"Sweetie, want me to make you breakfast?" There's a buzz in my ears leftover from dreamland, something about *Depression Laxatives*? I've lost track. I stare blankly at my mother dearest. Part of me tries to muster up some words. She looks sad. Worried. Scared. Defeated. She won't stop loving me, even though I'm basically incapable of reciprocating, really.

"Uhm . . ." I begin, "Commence breakfast? Ehm, yeah . . . yes, please."

Everything . . . everything is . . . fuz—

"Hmm alrighty," She giggles, "Commencing breakfast foods."

¡CRACK! The door closes and at least somewhat brings me back from my trance. I decide to put some clothing on, I believe society dictates I should do so. A pair of worn navy-blue pants and a black tee-shirt because I'm essentially a fashion mogul in Paris or New York or Milan.

How many cases are you currently invested in?

Not sure if I'll power through any breakfast today, just black coffee. Bitter and scalding hot. I'm really trying to get it together.

Three, Sir. All of which are going swimmingly.

Swimmingly. Swimmingly? Shit, I really need to start using melatonin or something.

16

I haven't mentioned anything to Blaire about the not-so-anonymous call from our friend with the *sniffles*. I don't think I'm planning on it either. She's almost surely the only person in existence that gives a damn about yours truly, so it bothers me to see her stressed or worried or upset. I can't tell if that's selfish or caring, maybe both but probably more the former.

It's the morning, something like 7:30 on a Tuesday. I'm supposed to be getting ready for school. There are khaki pants and a dark brown shirt with a collar laid out on my bed with care, but the grey sweatpants I'm wearing only have one stain and I'm *almost certain* they're not emitting an odor so changing seems like a waste of time and energy and pants.

I'm supposed to go downstairs and eat fruit and granola or eggs and toast, but there are frosted pop tarts in the bottom drawer and I prefer to eat in first period anyway. I'm supposed to brush AND floss, but seriously who flosses really, and every day?! What the shit? I haven't developed that type of committed relationship with my gums at this point in my life. I'm pretty certain that's what that colossal, value-size blue mouthwash is for.

Blaire pleasantly yells for me to come downstairs. She probably needs me to *pick up the pace* or *put some pep in my step* or some other phrase that would confuse and frustrate foreigners. Each one of her 241 jobs are equally important, after all, and punctuality is key. I think today she might be working the self-checkout at the Wal-Mart across town. Making sure no one is stealing or not caring if anyone is stealing and just pressing the red button of approval as it flashes on the screen.

I'll actually assist her by providing my complete and utmost cooperation this morning, predominantly because we're doing our federally mandated KEYSTONE standardized testing at my poorly funded public school. That means as soon as I'm finished rushing through this exam which I don't care about, I get to spend the remaining two to three hours sleeping or drawing ludicrous cartoons of lovable classic characters like Milkey Mouse or Bags of Bunny fucking each other while overdosing on prescription pills and needle drugs.

With as much pep as I can possibly muster, I make my way down the stairs only to be unpleasantly surprised.

"Hey sweetie," Blaire says, flustered and scattered as she zips around the kitchen. "I'm starting a new temp job today, it's doing data entry at a big insurance company." She puts matching plastic-wrapped turkey sandwiches and bananas into brown paper bags, one for each of us. "They offer a benefits package after two months so I want to make a good first impression. I'm running a touch late, you mind walking to school? It's gorgeous outside."

I'm worried about something slightly more serious than the temperature or humidity. Chance of precipitation 20%, Chance of me being kidnapped and tortured or murdered and disposed of more in the 70 to 80% range. Not loving those numbers, honestly. I hate rain.

I don't want to ruin her day or job opportunity or *our* wellbeing so instead of confessing my fear, "Sure," I reply.

17

Video games are seriously incredible, this is virtually inarguable. A seemingly infinite amount of options to choose from. Maybe you grew up playing *Ms. Pac Man* and you probably still hold the hypothetical high score on the machine that no longer exists at the burger spot which is actually an IKEA parking lot now. Maybe you played hundreds upon hundreds of hours of *Tony Hawk's Pro Skater*, doing ridiculously impossible tricks that lasted two and a half minutes. Regardless, awesome.

As with anything delightful, there are always those who take for granted what they have. Especially when newer versions with better graphics are constantly being introduced. Thank goodness for this fact. It luckily means I can acquire their terrific trash from the 1990s for practically pennies. I've definitely paid more than one yard-sale host with small change. Better a few decades late than never.

Some games have a clear objective. Take a well-known classic like *Super Mario Brothers*. The princess is in trouble, you pair of extraordinary plumbers! Save her by continuously moving to the right and not falling into any of the holes in the earth or getting murdered by any giant turtles or crab-walking owls.

Clear.

Simple.

Activities like that give me brief moments of *normalcy*. Both exciting and mindless at the same time.

But that unstoppable star power always runs out.

There are other games, though, that are significantly different in design. I used to play this game, *Animal Crossing*. There were no levels, no bosses, no primary objectives. No one to save, no enemies attacking, an essentially stress-free gaming experience. Your adorable character just goes fishing, decorates his or her flat, and picks fruit from the garden, YOUR garden. That's if you want to, of course.

Is it fun or boring? I honestly don't know. Completely simple and strangely complex.

Everything.

Nothing.

Lots of games were like this with some small dissimilarities. Maybe you're creating your own theme park, full of roller coasters, hotdog stands, and waterslides. Everything imaginable, all of it. The Works.

You may have preferred simming up your own unique city. Your *Zen Utopia*, or whatever else horrible people might say. As many or as few people as you wish. Big buildings? Great! One small single home per block? FAN-FUCKING-TASTIC. Your rules. You're the king of a kingdom in which the law is something far below you. Not a boundary in sight.

IT STARTS WHEN YOU STOP

¡BUT! Let's flip that switch from LIGHT to WAY DOWN DARK for a second, creating an infinite loop of Mario being stricken down by some devastating Christmas-colored shells and 'game over' screens. Being a jerk kind of *God* in those other games could potentially be fun. When a piece of the roller coaster goes mysteriously missing at the last minute . . . OOPS, endless series of winking emojis. A couple of trash cans burst into flames, then all of a sudden . . . BAM, it turns into a whole thing. Time to create a whole new park or city or person to destroy.

If you've EVER played *Grand Theft Auto*, and I do mean any of the roughly 60 of those wonderful games, then you must know that easily the best part is seeing how much destruction you can cause before you die some outlandish death. Fuck the missions. It's all about stealing the dopest car and seeing how many people you can run over, how many cop cars can you see explode? You want to get MORE stars, be WORSE than the last time. Seriously incredible stuff, those games.

So the *others*, the ones present so often in my dreams, seem to be somewhere in the middle. They aren't USUALLY *controlling* us into mass murder, but shit, they're not doing any favors for our species. We may be their source of gaming entertainment, but I'm certain they know we're real. That doesn't matter, though. WE don't matter, though. Not really. Not to them.

They're scientists, after all, or at least they consider themselves to be. We are the test subjects. They need us and they don't need us. We're just worms or mice or cats at best to these faceless fucks.

JOHNNY ABBOUD

Science.
Fuck science.

18

I'm just over halfway through my roughly twenty-minute walk to my severely understaffed educational center. Blaire was right, the weather is perfect; my iPhone informs me it's 67° Fahrenheit. I imagine under normal circumstances I'd have my headphones in, damaging my inner ears listening to *Sisters of Mercy* or *The Cure* or *Joy Division*, bands I've learned are considered important in the goth genre. I just like them because they make me . . . feel things. Am I a goth kid? Labels are confusing.

I wish I wanted to listen to Drake or Cardi B or *Florida Georgia Line*. I'd fit in more, but I truly don't. No music today, though. It's as if I'm nowhere near in control of my anxiety.

I'm walking forward at a steady pace but I swear I'm shaking the whole time, a pair of maracas in a drunk, Puerto-Rican *abuelos'* hands. Whether the clouds in the sky look like dolphins or dump trucks or if the sky is void of clouds completely is uncertain to me. The colors of the flowers growing in the garden to my left, the architectural design of the home it belongs to, what type of small sissy dog just barked at me from behind that home's screen door, I couldn't tell you any of this information. My focus is flung hopelessly from in front of me to behind me to every car driving or parked or imaginary.

Everything seems so quiet all of a sudden. The calm before the storm. It's then that I see the flood. The hurricane or earthquake or landslide personified, turned into a piece of human garbage. The sniffing, snorting savage himself sneaks out from behind the corner house before the alley.

He looks like shit. I mean, he hasn't been your typical Man Crush Monday in quite some time, but he's looking especially rough at the moment. He's got that 'been up for days but isn't tired' sort of rough vibe going right now.

I don't know why I even try to run from this former high school hero filled with rage and drugs, but I try. I try to become faster than I've ever been, to learn parkour as I go, to alter myself from lazy American delinquent to American ninja warrior. It's barely a few seconds until I can hear his footsteps catch up to mine, until I can feel him grab my tight-fitting T-shirt and use it to whip me to the ground, until my face meets the concrete.

There are always people in this neighborhood filled with cul-de-sacs, the nice area between Roosevelt Elementary and the far less nice area where my home resides. Soccer moms powerwalking, kids K-12 reluctantly on their ways to their various private or public or Catholic schools, professional men and women in suits getting into their cars to drive to their personal hells.

Except not *always*. Right now, there's no one, nothing, just me and my current personal devil.

IT STARTS WHEN YOU STOP

He's holding on to my left forearm with his left hand and gripping my neck with his right hand. He has a mechanics grip, two of them.

"FIRE!! HELP! FIRE!!" I yell as he drags me into the blue sedan he's got parked and unlocked and prepared.

I heard once that people are more likely to help if there's a fire than anything domestically dangerous, someone in trouble via another person or persons. Not surprising, fires spread, and as much as anyone likes to think of themselves as heroic, we're mostly all cowards just looking out for ourselves, watching out for our star player, taking care of our #1. It doesn't matter anyway, there's no one here to save me or put out my make-believe residential fire. Fight or Flight, I'm trying both.

I scream and kick and punch and bite and even manage to beep the horn but only once and only for a second. I'd piss and shit myself if I thought it could really get me out of here. I've never wanted to be surrounded by classmates that pick on me or the school faculty that worry about me so badly. The hairy, cracked skin of Cum Wad Todd's knuckles finds my school-age face. And then again.

And again.
And again.
And ag—

By the time the fog wears off and I can make out my surroundings again, I'm duct taped to the passenger seat, hands behind my back, feet together, lips sealed shut, and seatbelt fastened, of course.

"You destroyed everything I had," he says with moist eyes, even though I was born before he ever met Blaire. There's a lot of blood on me. "I can't even talk to her now,

I can't even tell her **MY** side." His side of why he just threw hands with a 15-year-old.

He is sniffing and snorting right from the little baggy while we're doing 90 on the highway. "I can't live without her, I WON'T. NO, NO, **NO** . . . I'm not going back to life without her, I'm NOT." He chuckles maniacally while tears continue down his scruffy, unwashed face. "But I'm taking her precious little Hiro with me."

He's *flying* through traffic. I feel like any moment could be my last. He seems to be loving it, every single second. I'm holding onto the seat below me by my fingertips as if that would change the outcome of any disaster in the slightest.

"**SNNFF** . . . *huuu* . . . WHOO! Like real life Gran Turismo baby! **SNNIFFF**."

We just broke 100 miles per hour.

"You know she fucking aborted **MY** child, right? Psh, HA. HA! You ruined everything that I did have AND could have possibly had! **SNNNNFF**. You and your goddamn pussy feelings were too much to deal with to imagine a **real** life with me."

I wonder if that's true but it's difficult to focus. It's tough to see people out of context. 110 now. Shaking his head in disgust, he continues, "MY seed wasn't good enough, but whoever or *what*ever led to your conception apparently made the cut. HA!"

What does that even mean? He keeps sobbing. Sobbing and laughing.

116. The baggy has nothing left for his nose so he's moved on to giving it a tour of his mouth with his tongue.

119. The road ahead is about to turn. The driver beside me is not about to turn.

121. As we near our fate, he looks right at me, right into my eyes, "She and I, we could have ha—"

19

A vehicle departing; I wonder if it will be like other modes of transportation. Driving or flying or roller-skating and serving milkshakes. Something completely relatable or abstractly indescribable.

Final boarding call an automated, echoey voice mundanely states, coming from some sort of loudspeaker, I think. It no longer violates my eardrums.

I reminisce about my first and only time on a plane. I was little, five or six, maybe. It was a long flight, for a kid at least. Heading from one coast to another to start again.

Please complete your currently assigned project as promptly as possible, and return all equipment to their properly designated storage locations.

There was a lack of expectations, considering I had never been on a flight before. Getting onto that thing was certainly boring, but the concept of flying in the air in a man-built machine is mildly extraordinary. Every zeroed-in moment of cloud observation blew my mind. Just, like continually, blew my mind.

IT STARTS WHEN YOU STOP

People rented the garbage airline headphones or slept uncomfortably or read novels, pretending to be the perfect protagonist in their fictional fantasy. Hours went by calmly, Blaire mostly asleep beside me, with a single serving of half-salt, half-peanut blend, served in a frustrating plastic baggy about mid-way through the trip. They're aesthetically paired with your choice of soda or juice, elegantly poured one eighth of the way full.

"You should be completely glitch-free by now, Mr. Takafuji," Dr. Banshee says gleefully. "Shouldn't be any more missing body parts or unprovoked caterwauling after this point."

I hear Banshee's words enter existence in the background while I gaze upon all of the mood machines disguised as Centipede or Galaxian or Dig Dug. *Simulation Machines* are what they're called, just a reminder what our lives mean to these Curious Georges. I've always felt my existence seemed real enough, but perhaps I'm just some creature's virtual reality.

My mind regresses quickly back to that flight, to the moment where it stopped being boring or smooth or typical for several passengers. The moment where a completely standard flying occurrence led me to learn a great deal about myself.

Right at the juiciest part of one person's raunchy erotic romance novel, or the concluding seconds of another person's sudoku puzzle, the plane begins to shake. Just a touch at first, not enough for most people to justify lifting their chins away from their chests. But the gentle whisper turned into a whine, then into a whooshing sensation all around us.

"Well, that's good news." I finally manage to say to Banshee with a certain amount of ambivalence in my voice.

More and more and more, I heard people's luggage ¡BOOM! and ¡BANG! and ¡CRASH! all throughout the overhead compartments. Everyone onboard, including Mama Ramen, is now awake and aware of this airborne obstruction. Some God or giant or mean cloud tossing us around like dice in their red, plastic, Yahtzee cup.

Blaire, of course, is doing her best to comfort me, despite being discernibly uncomfortable herself. She squeezes my little left hand tightly with her right, while her delicate remaining fingers clench her armrest as forcefully as she can.

She's not alone in her nervous behavior. Every ¡BOOM! and ¡BANG! , each ¡THUMP! and ¡BUMP! and ¡CRASH!, seems to either bring people closer together or bring about their most chaotic selves. ¡BANG! makes a father a row ahead hug his crying young daughter securely. ¡CRASH! makes a dark-haired older woman clutch the gold Crucifix pendant hanging from her necklace, while making the shape of a cross with her other hand, touching her middle finger to her forehead then chest then shoulder then shoulder.

Everyone around us is on edge, uncertain if our aircraft will return to its calm cumulus cruise, or will contrail straight into the ground, erupting into a mushroom cloud. It's then I realize why I feel so different than everyone else, here and generally: it's because I wouldn't care if this plane cannoned directly into the

Earth's crust.

¡THUMP! makes a seemingly alpha male completely tense up. Eyes basically glued shut, he grabs both armrests as hard as he can, not caring about the old gum he's fiercely digging his thumb and fingertips into. ¡BOOM! makes a large, elderly man beside him begin talking to himself at full volume. It seems like he's speaking in tongues, but it's probably Arabic or Farci or Fish-Person.

No matter how piss-poor their eclectic lives may be, they still all seem like they'd choose life over the alternative.

"Everything will be fine, sweetie. Turbulence is normal. This is just a particularly rough patch," Blaire assures me.

It's almost freeing to know I'm fine with whichever outcome. It's only for this selfless woman that I feel selfish about that sense of freedom. It's only for her that I'd fight to choose life.

PART TWO

SLEEPY HIRO'S LONG SLUMBER

20

Where The Fuck Am I?

If you've ever had to ask yourself this question seriously, you can understand the associated anxiety, but I don't feel it, not now, even though I most certainly have no idea where I am.

In truth, I can't even tell if my eyes are open. I just see drifting colors floating together harmoniously. Yellows to greens to blues to purples to reds, but all with tones of grey.

I hear the sound of waves gently crashing against the shore with just the perfect amount of breeze. Although, a concrete mixer in action sounds surprisingly alike. Two completely different occurrences creating identical auditory stimuli: similar to truth and lies.

I smell freshly baked Cinnabon but I feel the perfect amount of full. How did I get wherever it is that I am? Doesn't matter, I feel *perfect*. Did I somehow ingest something sneakily hallucinogenic?

Psh, I'll work with it. I'm up for perma-tripping so

long as the warmth of this happiness continues to radiate all through my body. It doesn't, though.

The colors all begin to turn to white and drift slower and slower until there's nothing. I'm half deaf and half blind and looking directly into a screaming sun. There are footsteps, now audibly clearer than anything I've ever heard. Like they're walking in a completely empty hallway, alone, and attached to an amplifier.

The footsteps stop.

I hear a voice but I can't make out the words right away. I know immediately, though, that this voice belongs to my loving mother. It's like a disheartened and familiar buzz until I can finally make out.

"I know you can make it out of this. . . ."

I want to respond but it's as if I forgot how to move any part of my body, including my mouth.

"Please wake up, Hiro, sweetie, **please**." The way she says please feels like a screaming whisper.

"Please wake up."

A final piercing plea and I drift off again.

21

I now feel whatever green and grey would feel like mixed together. Ambiguous I know, but it's tough to describe it any other way, and there's no way at all to describe my location. Conscious nostalgia, like I've gone through this exact situation before. Maybe not . . . something similar? I don't know.

I'm not feeling myself. Not good. Well, I mean, not well. Not anything, really; I feel like I'm having my first bad experience with mushrooms or peyote or Bufotenin or all of the above. Everything is distorted. I don't feel blind but I don't actually see anything, just these pesky colors.

Who were those voices? The faraway words hardly making sense. The leaf-green and dull-silver doors seem to be closing around me. Heaviness in my chest and unable to find the red and white Albuterol rescue inhaler. I remember a rabbit in a garden I think, a flying goat? That can't be right. I'm blacking in and out. Was there some sort of course or seminar I crashed?

¡HEEEEHMM! A murmur with the volume turned all

the way up.

Are you certain that's necessary, sir? I'm sure even under the most dire circumstances, eliminating the entirety of the test subjects should suffice. Taking out our own seems . . . problematic, sir.

There's buzzing or static or color-sounds accompanying the unfamiliar voice.

I realize this Rawzgulup, and your concerns are heard and justified. Taking out any of our own, especially avid pursuers of science, is no doubt an extreme measure. But if our work would fall into the wrong hands, the interplanetary ramifications could be devastating. You and Big Banshee aren't here in the field with me. No one outside of this room can know, understood?

It's another language that I must have learned in the past with some heavy accents that hardly seems like any language at all. It's like I understand and I don't. The noises surrounding the noises are just too much. I do the closest thing to closing my eyes that I can. Black. No more green, no more grey, just black.

22

There's feeling again, although it's tough to describe exactly, sort of just an awareness. Whether asleep or awake or dead or alive, in limbo or nowhere at all, none of this is certain.

I feel myself *floating back*, but there's still just a black void. I'm more confident than before that it's a black void, though.

BEEP . . . BEEP . . . BEEP . . . BEEP . . . BEEP . . . Everything sounds out of focus and the BEEPS are excruciatingly high-pitched. A screech and a hum. It's the tempo of a heartbeat. My heartbeat?

¡CUHRUCHK! Even in my strange state of ambiguity I'm startled by the noise. There's another noise, a buzz, but it's deep this time.

BZZ . . . BZZ . . . BZ . . . BZZZZ . . . BZZ . . . It clears up and becomes something new. I'd rather it hadn't.

"Probably for the best though, nephew. In honestly, you were always so freaking depression all the time."

I just barely know this voice, full of judgement and

grammatical errors and wasabi breath.

"Worst of all, you made us, your mother and I, resent each other."

The words make it sound like the person could be talking about a sexy type of previous relationship, but the voice-box speaking at me belongs to the knockoff Chanel bag of pretension that IS my darling aunt, Miss Jenni Takafuji, my mother's spinster half-sister that grew up in Tokyo.

I won't talk about her a great deal, partly because of her lack of relevance to our story, my story. I'm surprised she even came, honestly. Mostly though, we won't be talking about her much because she just . . . sucks. A grimy, round ball of bitchiness.

". . . a drag and a burden to all anyone with whom you did freaking made any amount of contact with."

Gee, thanks, Auntie Jenni.

"So if you plan on waking up, sad scared little boy, do it NOW. THIS MINUTE! I freaking mean it, don't play with your mom's heart, she fragile. Little like you sometime but prettier. Just . . . let go"

What a gal.

A+ Aunt of the Year Award.

Fuck it . . . I will.

I'm not sure if it's the cowardly way out or a courageous cure for another person I actually care about. Turbulence. I'm not sure if it will work, if I'll feel pain, if anything will come after, if this will be the first of many more experiences or the finale of my time, if I'll have any more conversations like this.

I do.

I'm not scared.

IT STARTS WHEN YOU STOP

I let go.

Flashing lights.
FLICKER FLICKER FLICKER FLICKER FLICKER.
First just white and yellow flashing against an infinite black screen.
FLICKER FLICKER FLICKER FLICKER FLICKER.
Then all the colors in the visible spectrum flash around like fireworks. It's popcorn in the microwave, except each kernel erupts into some sensational abstract masterpiece. A 96 pack of Crayola flavor bursts out of each salty, buttery bite. It sounds like you just opened a soda, the bubbly effervescence.

Calming.

Exciting.

The colorful explosions begin to slow down until it's just an almost lavender shade of grey. Everything felt calm until now. Loud and confused, absent of sight, lost in nothingness, all of that inexplicably felt fine, but something about now makes me uneasy. Calm before the storm, once again. If only I could move.

Suddenly, lightning begins to strike in the blurry field of fragrant lavender flowers. No more room left for melancholy, I guess.

¡SCCRREEEEEECCHHHHH!

A violent pain of a noise like a blast from a pair of airhorn earmuffs. I'm surrounded by the black and white static of a channel you don't get. And that noise. Ugh, that noise. If I'm still alive then I'd like for that to change, whatever it takes for this sensory torture to end. I try to squeeze my eyes closed tight, whatever that means when you can't tell if they're still open or already closed. I try.

I try.

It stops, all of it, and I begin to hear the voices of two individuals. *But sir, with all due respect, I believe for the experiment to remain completely error-free and unambiguous, we CANNOT do that. Please reconsider.*

There's a pause long enough for me to wonder if a response is coming at all.

Let me start by saying that if you ever speak to me like that in front of any of our colleagues, I'll fucking end you. That being said, as I respect your opinion, I'll continue to supervise in that filthy fucking place. You're lucky I get paid a seriously absurd amount, Rawzgulup.

It feels like I might know one of those voices but everything seems everywhere.

I do appreciate it, sir. It's just that it wouldn't quite be the same project with the extreme modification proposed, the subservient voice says.

Things start to sound blurrier and further away again.

They do have great drugs down here, which doesn't hurt. But perhaps I wasn't entirely clear, it was not a proposition. This is my fucking project, and you need to start understanding that.

But Si—

Don't fucking interrupt me, Rawzy Boy. There are no buts. That goes for any of your supervisors, too. Let them know. Unless I hear from Banshee himself, this is the new plan of action.

The fireworks return. Thank goodness. They're beautiful. Again, I feel myself disappear. They're so beautiful.

23

As far as comas go, although there are documented cases of men and women waking up after decades, this is far from the status quo. Most people's comas don't last more than two to four weeks. After that they've generally awoken from their slumber or are rotting deep in the ground or have been incinerated and urned. I'm certainly somewhere in between these examples.

"He'll most likely never emerge from it," doctor after doctor told Blaire. "After this amount of time without showing greater response to stimuli, we generally suggest removing patients from life support."

So, an adolescent growing regularly during a coma, following their body's normal programming, isn't necessarily impossible, it's just a matter of not living long enough to see it happen. If you're able to survive through everything physically, your brain **is** still functioning, just at its most completely basic level.

Absolute atrophy of the muscles is a fair starting point in terms of *everything physical.* Your bones and joints may fuse together after time, into a solid mass which locks your joints together permanently. Sort of a bummer.

"No, Ma'am. I would never say it's a lost cause," says some insurance demon or real demon or presidential elect.

Bed sores can be quite a dilemma while in a coma, your body is not meant to be lying down for that long. What creature is, really? Survival of the fittest dictates you should die.

Demon continues, "It's just that, Miss Takafuji, given the wildly high costs of care, coupled with the statistically low chance of improvement, we will no longer be able to continue aiding in Hiro's medical treatment. It would end up being unfair to others. I'm so sorry."

Your nervous system can end up going pretty haywire in a comatose state, forcing your body to contract into a fetal position. Your unusable hands will clench into fists, perhaps your sleepy perturbation attempting to awaken. Your fingernails will grow and grow, directly into your hands, causing bleeding and infection. Treatable with Botox and external braces, more so than the predictable pneumonia you'll acquire because of your devastatingly weakened immune system.

Survival rates for coma visitors are 50% or less, less than 10% will make full recoveries. No surprise that Mr. Demon's squadron from Insurance Hell jump ship as soon as legally permissible. Yet, even without their assistance, here I am being not dead.

"Good morning, Miss Takafuji! I'm so glad I got a hold of you before you left for work. I've got some astonishing and incredible news for you," says a woman from the hospital. Blaire avows her voice sounded like an angel. Heavenly. Divine.

IT STARTS WHEN YOU STOP

"Although we're aware of your insurance provider's decision to discontinue coverage for your son, Hiro, we received word to make his comfort and care a lasting priority."

Blaire thought this was some sort of horribly cruel joke or a mirage she'd try to stay inside of. Skeptical, she just kept listening.

"Apparently the *first of many* superfluously generous donations to our hospital was processed this morning, a truly exorbitant amount, with the sole condition of 'Treating Hiro T. well during his prolonged slumber, and not rushing his awakening.'"

Tears of happiness and disbelief and confusion gather in Blaire's eyes until they fall and fill her face. Her lips waver with the intention of speaking but she can't make words happen, so she keeps listening. Listening and crying and hoping for what she's hearing to be real.

How much of your mental cognizance is with you during your coma-cation is difficult to say for certain, and also highly dependent on the individual afflicted. Some awakened survivors describe having had *dreams* related to things they heard during their slumber, conversations spoken around them, these moments so close to waking up.

"Wh . . . Who?" Blaire finally manages to say to the wonderful giver of good news on the other end of the line. A fair inquiry.

Some of the awakened have no recollections of anything at all, nothing whatsoever. Others can hardly formulate the words to accurately paint the horrible pictures which occurred during their hiatus from our shared reality. Looping, torturous nightmares of lifetime imprisonment and murder and unwelcome sexual congress. Waking up drenched in sweat, shivering, terrified, unknowing whether this is the start of the most terrifying dream yet.

"We're actually uncertain, the party involved insisted on anonymity. Unfortunately it's beyond me, as well as illegal, to dig deeper for details. The instructions we received did have some strange symbol printed on them, though. Maybe that would help? Here . . . I'll text you a picture."

Some of my fellow, former comatose champions provide detailed testimonials about being a completely different person while in that hospital bed. What you're likely to chalk up as recurring dreams which you end up assuming as part of your identity, well, those illusions were entire lifetimes to those individuals. Some sort of wormhole to somewhere else. An odd feeling of being somewhere you don't belong. Off limits. An uncovered route to one of possibly infinite bizarre alternate realities.

¡PFVVVV! ¡PFVVV! convulses Blaire's phone. She opens the image, widens it to full screen, and stares. Trying to make any amount of sense of this foreign oddity before clearing her throat and saying, "I . . . I've never seen this before. I really don't know what it means."

A general state of consciousness depends on a nonstop exchange of chemical signals from the brain stem and the thalamus to the cerebrum, taking place all along the neural pathways referred to as our Reticular Activating System. But what if these pathways are overly talkative; could they actually be capable of taking us . . . further? Beyond our dreams and into other's dreams and then into other's realities.

IT STARTS WHEN YOU STOP

"For now, Miss Takafuji, it means we effectively treat your son like he's paying the salary of every employee in the hospital. Nothing in this life is promised, but more money than everyone else never hurts."

24

Amongst all the innumerable inventions created over humankind's existence, the wheel and internal combustion engines and fat cigars for wrinkly old men, headphones are one of my most personally pivotal must-haves. In addition to their obvious pragmatic value, they also are an interesting *representation* of privacy. No one knows whether you're listening to Radiohead or Kanye West or Volume II of your introductory Korean Lessons. If anyone asks, well, it's really easy to snub somebody when they think you can't hear them. Oh-so-convenient.

SO, imagine wearing headphones no one can see. It's at a low enough volume that you can still hear everything around you, just slightly drowned out. Not active all day, it's intermittent and unpredictable and uninvited. But it's always there, looming.

Also, pretend it's not music by any means. It's something like conversations, but not in any of the languages Google Translate has available. There are low-pitched, murky sounding gurgles and coughs, high pitched yelps and grunts.

I find myself able to understand this other . . . *language?* If that's what we'd call it. Or at least I think I do. Don't inquire how, I'd be without a proper response.

Something like a diversity poster aggregate of people screaming and panting and whining mixed with *something* speaking some foreign language that usually sounds like fatsos farting and fucking on a Brillo pad. And somehow this non-romantic language seems to make sense. More sense than Telemundo, at least. Cool.

I've been wearing these goddamn earbuds ever since I've been blessed or cursed, saved or given vision or what the fuck ever. When I should have left this place but didn't. Unfortunately, I haven't been able to turn it off.

25

The final memory or dream or hallucination I recall from my confusing and extended state of drifting pseudo-consciousness is unlike any of the others. It starts similarly, an awareness of myself, colors swirling all over, faint sounds of nature. This time, though, the colors don't move in an arbitrary manner; this time they begin to form shapes. There's black and blue and green and it feels as if I'm floating.

Suddenly, I begin to *see*, like, REALLY see, not just the color vomit I've recently grown accustomed to. I am floating. I'm in water and I'm bewildered and I desperately need to breathe. I swim upward as quickly as I can. It's getting brighter and brighter and it feels like I'm close to some actual human-style breathing.

I reach what I think must be the finish line but I'm boxed in, a thick sheet of ice traps me below. I begin to panic, I can hardly tell that the water is cold enough to freeze. I search frantically for an opening but . . . nothing.

I push and punch and elbow the ceiling of death above

me but to no avail. I should have actually worked out in P.E. I don't even think I mind not living but this isn't how I was hoping to go out.

Just then, I see something on top of the ice above me. It's a frog, and if I'm not mistaken, the nosey little fella is looking at me. What help could **YOU** be, Frog?

I'm close to giving up until I notice the surface between me and the frog transfigure slightly. There's steam coming off of my ambitious new savior, more and more, and more and more and more until there's just flames and frog bones and ash.

I almost effortlessly put my fist through the slushy ice above me. I manage to get my other arm through as well, and as I push myself out of the frigid water and take my first beautiful gasp for air, everything cuts to white.

BEEP . . . BEEP . . .BEEP . . . BEEP . . . BEEP . . .

Awareness.

Fresh awareness.

My eyes are open. This is the first I've been sure of that in a long time. It feels as if they're not used to being open, like they're holding dumbbells where my eyelashes should be.

BEEP . . . BEEP . . .BEEP . . . BEEP . . . BEEP . . .

The lights are bright, too bright, they hurt my eyes. *Hurt* . . . I haven't felt that in a while. Mixed feelings about that particular reminder.

BEEP . . . BEEP . . .BEEP . . . BEEP . . . BEEP . . .

A blurry figure moves near wherever it is I'm lying. I make my best effort to speak but it's more of just a dry grunt that comes out. Like being punched in the stomach and coughing up sand.

"**DOCTOR!!**" yells the now slightly less blurry figure. I open and close my seemingly brand-new eyes a few times; things are starting to become clearer. Open and close. It's a woman wearing a green jumpsuit or a pair of scrubs or comfy onesie pajamas. Open and close.

"**DOCTOR!!** Room 2025! He's awake!"

I continue to look around. I notice I'm dressed in an incredibly *fashion-forward* polka dot gown with no underwear. Ready to hit the town.

The beeping robot voice starting to drift into the background is attached to my chest and monitoring my heart rate. There's what appears to be a half-eaten tuna wrap on a small round table in the corner of the room. I smell the processed fish and celery and mayonnaise. *Smell.*

It's like I've never smelled anything before, ever. It's certainly not the most appealing odor, but it at least brings the now foreign distant concept of *hunger* to mind. I don't think I'm hungry at the moment, but it's tough to be sure. When was the last time I've smelled and chewed and swallowed and digested? The never-ending series of tubes and machinery and bags of clear liquid connected to my body leads me to believe I haven't actually gone through that method of nourishment in quite some time.

What in the shit got me here? Just one of the bundles of bizarre inquiries I have, but I'm most immediately concerned about whether or not my legs still work, because that's feeling like it could be a negative at the moment.

As I'm getting my bearings together, a short, stubby man in blue scrubs enters the room. He looks like a thumb with a stethoscope hanging from the little bit of neck he does have. He's probably in his fifties and has all dark features. He's certainly not a looker but the eyes under his bushy eyebrows softly signal kindness. He smiles enough so that all his straight-enough teeth show.

"Wow! Welcome back to the world, young man."

Where exactly have I been besides *the world*?

"You've been out quite some time; can you tell me your name?"

Shouldn't Dr. Thumb already know it? Oh, right, making sure I'm not a person-sized vegetable whose eyes happened to plop open. Gotcha.

"Yes, my name is Hiro." I reply. I didn't mean to stop speaking just then, I would have liked to ask some mildly important questions like **what the fuck is going on**, but at that moment another person steps into the room, the room which must have been my residence for quite some time. A familiar family member that probably just came to finish her stinky protein-packed sandwich in peace and hope her son's slumber is at least peaceful.

Hi there, Blaire.

She had a coffee but that's on the floor now; it slid out of her slender fingers as soon as she saw my rosewood brown eyes open for the first time in what I imagine has been ages now. Her eyes are open wide, her jaw is practically on the linoleum floor, her body is frozen. It's like she saw a ghost, and even though I've got little to no idea why I'm here, I'm almost sure I'm not a ghost. That would make our friendly, fire-hydrant-shaped doctor a ghost whisperer and that just sounds like a lot.

"Is that . . . are you . . . *awake*?" My sweet mother struggles to say as tears fill her eyes.

I'm not nearly as emotional as she is. I'm not informed

enough yet.

"I think so, but . . . shit. Uhm, your guess is as good as mine, I'd say." The tears stream down her face like a waterfall dropping over the edge of an ice shelf.

"My beautiful little foul-mouthed boy," she says. Her smile is complete and quivering. "I **knew** you'd wake up, that you weren't being taken from me so soon, I **KNEW** it."

She's attacking and overwhelming and smothering me with love and feelings and hugs. The tears on her cheeks are making my face wet. Yuck. I feel genuinely happy, but . . . yuck.

"I knew it." She whispers into the side of my face. Yuck.

PART THREE

FUN WITH HIRO AND THE GANG

AGE: 16

26

"Want to go get some breakfast at the diner, sweetie?" asks Blaire as I finish brushing my teeth. "They make some seriously delicious French toast," she adds. She's such a sweet and caring woman, and then there's also the brioche bread topped with powdered sugar and syrup and cinnamon. Hell of an appeal there, given my youthful appetite, but with these voices in my head popping up intermittently, I've been seeking as much solitude as possible.

"I'm really beat, Mom. I didn't sleep well at all last night. Maybe another day this week?" I reply.

There's the slightest tinge of disappointment but she just smiles sincerely. "Of course, hunny. Rest up," she says.

"Hiro! They're playing *Space Jam* on TV! I remember how much you loved that movie when you were little," she yells as she knocks on the outside of my closed but unlocked bedroom door. I'm standing up, rolling a joint above my dresser, and her raps startle a bit of the weed out of both ends.

"You used to want to watch it over and over and over, UGH, it was adorably frustrating."

I can likely still recite each of Michael Jordan and our iconic cartoon legends' lines throughout all 100 minutes of athletic wonderment.

"You wanna come watch it?" She continues, "I'm gonna fry some chicken tenders and make some mac and cheese."

I'm legitimately intrigued by her proposition. I've managed to salvage the aforementioned joint being worked on. A little comfort food with a side of the Jam would be lovely directly after smoking thi—

Thank you for the completed progress reports on the Earth division of Project Person. I'd just like to confirm some of these figures before evaluating our continued course of action.

"—oney? Honey? You awake?" Blaire asks my off-white door.

I feel like you feel when you try to think of how a song goes while another one plays on a volume past reasonable.

"Uhm, Mom . . . maybe in a whi—" I can't even finish my eight-syllable thought before I'm attacked again.

*It appears that depression rates are more impressive than ever. 121 million subjects are currently programmed with the infection. 80 percent of those humans will never even attempt to get professional help. **Pride,** they say. This has led the project's suicide sum total to reach 800,000 last human year cycle. About one every 40 seconds. That's pretty impressive stuff. Best of all, they're starting to blame it on a 'Opioid Epidemic,' when we're the reason they begin using in the first place!*

"You alright in there, Hiro?" I can only imagine what debauchery she thinks is going on in this depraved room of mine.

"Mom . . . yeah. Sorry, just reading something, ya caught me mid chapter." Her response is probably something ordinary, although I can't be certain. All I hear is the loving tone in her voice enter the atmosphere and then dissipate within an instant.

*Yes, sir. Everything contained in the project portfolio has been verified. Truly, given their medical and technological advances in the last several decades, along with their **naturally** low rate of mental illness, they'd be a surviving and thriving species if not for our experiment. ¡KAHZUM! Even with all of their silly foreign feelings. ¡HA!*

Everything's quiet all of a sudden. No kind mother's voice hoping for attention from the other side of the wooden divider. Nonchalantly pleading. No . . . *other* . . . voices giving me an Abnormal Psychology lesson that would blow your professor's socks off. All the way off.

I enjoy this blissful moment of silence as if it might be my last. Because it might be my last. Not wasting another second, I ignore Blaire's rules, or at least preferences, and light the joint that has thankfully remained intact and fall backwards onto my bed.

It's the early evening now. I've smelled the delicious aroma of classic kitchen cuisine coming from down the stairs come and go. Instead of satiating my trembling hunger fully, I enjoyed a personal-size bag of Fritos found under my bed.

I've sneakily tip-toed to the bathroom once or twice, like a ninja with a urinary tract infection. With just a bit of buzz remaining from what's now ashes and burnt paper inside of the metal ashtray beside me, and the voices being temporarily absent, I figure now is as good a time as any to venture down to the first floor.

One creaky carpeted stair at a time, I head towards the living area, hoping not to jar any voices in my head back into existence. I turn my head and see Mother Takafuji half asleep on the couch. She hears my footsteps and as soon as her dark, tired eyes begin to open, she leaps to her little tiny feet like it's the first time she's seen me in ages, like I was going to vanish from that room and from this Earth altogether.

She lights up like when your lost puppy, your best and most loyal friend, finally returns home. Her love at this moment makes me feel better than I've felt in a while. Safer, as if she fights off whatever oddness goes on in my head.

"Hey, handsomest. Feeling all rested up?" she asks. She smiles at me, so I think it'd be the proper son move to smile back. I do.

"I am, actually. Thanks. Sorry for being Anne Frank up there all day," I say in what's probably bad taste.

"Hiro! Not cool!" She says, but I catch her snicker a little as she turns her head to fake a cough. I don't say anything back, I just facetiously grin and she can't help but move forward. "It's ok. The hiding, I mean. Not the borderline anti-Semitism," she says and I chuckle fairly loudly, louder than I expected at least. She continues, "I don't mean to bug you, sweetheart. I'll just be working a ton of hours the rest of the week, that's all."

IT STARTS WHEN YOU STOP

I can tell she's about to ask me to do something, she keeps wanting to **do** things. I also know, though, that she's not so interested in dinners or mini-golf or laser tag, all of which we can't afford. Not to sound too self-absorbed, but in this case it's all about spending time with me. I choose a preemptive maneuver.

"I'm not really in the mood to go anywhere, Mom Dukes, or do much of anything for that matter, but if you wanna hang out here I'd really like that," I say before she has a chance to ask if I want to go to one of her many sources of employee-discount opportunities.

She lights up again, like a lonely ember that was seconds away from going out before being struck by lightning and erupting into a forest fire. She's so genuinely happy right now, I feel like somehow that makes me capable of dealing with the confusing and grim messages in my head. Remaining hopeful on the plummeting plane just because of the passenger in the seat next to mine.

Watching this nostalgic favorite of mine with my favorite, and pretty much only, family member, I wish my life was 50 percent animated as well. It certainly seems absurd enough to be. The *Looney Tunes* speak while a probably soon-to-be-certified Looney Tune, soon to be admitted into a looney bin, watches. Watches and giggles and smiles, forgetting for a few moments about the other nearly constant sources of confusing mental provocation.

As she walks back into the living room from the kitchen, she's holding an old-school, fake-gold British-looking serving plate. It may tragically be the closest thing to a valuable in the house—a treasure found on sale at

Target.

It's filled with more variety than a fair amount of buffets. She looks my direction and commands my eye contact. I take my eyes off the fictional, problematic aliens on the screen towards her eyes all filled with silliness and curiosity. She sets down the smorgasbord of reheated dinner accompanied by assorted frozen foods and generic brand snacks, and purses her lips, feverishly preparing for some big inquiry my way.

"So . . ." she says as she makes a face more prepped for juicy gossip than anything I've ever even seen accidentally on the E! Network. "What's going on with little Miss Arina and my baby boy?"

She's beaming with undue excitement as if I just announced an accepted marriage proposal or an, at least somewhat planned, pregnancy or a 50th anniversary with only a few dozen infidelities along the way.

"Uhm . . . what's this now, Blaire?" I respond as I bring my eyebrows closer together skeptically. I'm probably more agog than she is at this moment, suddenly hopeful she knows something promising which I don't. She's still visibly full of that nosey expression.

"Aw, sweetie, I'm your mom. I just see things in you, in others when they're around you, how you make them interact differently, how you always have. And I know you both get a little goofy around each other, it's so cute."

I wish I could really believe this was more than motherly love and support. Again I feel filled with hope. Thanks, Queen Gypsy Mother. Crushing it in your efforts, as always.

"An older girl too, what a studly man you're becoming," she adds.

IT STARTS WHEN YOU STOP

I shake my head and probably blush and definitely feel mildly uncomfortable. I want to say nothing but I know my Energizer bunny of a mother; she'd keep going and going and going, so I skip ahead to vulnerable honesty.

"If I'm honest, I wish, but . . . I don't know . . ." I look down at the carpeted floor directly between my two feet. "She's so entirely out of my league, Mo—"

"Stop that," she interrupts, "Fuck a league . . . if you knew just how special you are, sweetie. Please . . . please don't let me hear you putting yourself down." Her strength is inspiring and characteristic and annoying.

"Alright, alright, alright, nosiest person in the universe. I'll try to be more confident . . . for you." Another sheeny ray of happiness shines from my relentlessly good mother. I continue, "I definitely do like her, and there's no denying my status of scaredy cat with women, but besides that, I feel like maybe that's unprofessional? Or at least embarrassing if she rejects me, increasingly embarrassing each time I'm forced to face her in my therapist's office."

She looks at me with her eyes all the way open, not surprised, just absorbing my anxiety. There's a lot of it, though. I can't shut my mouth. "Plus, then, if I were to be rejected, there's that ambiguity about whether it was related to that unprofessionalism. I mean, should I go for it later? Or should I just respect—"

"Sweetie . . . **wow**. Really, my dearest, deep breaths for a couple seconds, okay?" She interrupts my moment of insanity; my face changes, she keeps going.

"Let's try to be mindful together and ignore the negative thoughts that aren't real. Where are you sweetie? Look around."

More mindfulness mumbo jumbo, "What do you see? What does it feel like to rub your fingers together?"

I know it will help but a part of me just always prefers being the stubborn bull.

"Deep breathes, in through the nose and out through the mouth. What do you smell? Try to move those cute little ears of yours around. What do you hear?"

Another bozo, who's had a life full of hardships and abuse and undesired but necessary overtime shifts, fighting through it all and being far happier than the average bear, and attempting to enlighten others. I imagine bears are happier on average than humans, by the way, sleeping several months a year and all.

Probably difficult giving life to what random old people continuously call a beautiful child. A dark-haired boy declared gifted by middle-aged bore-monsters wearing mismatched, and probably irregular, suits. Destined for some life of greatness by those outsiders because of his test scores. Nothing's ever felt like a gift.

Too bad about our flawed testing system, though. Examination upon examination administered mechanically to us while some of us should have probably had our adolescent depression looked into. No child left behind . . . except the sad ones, of course. Too sad, too slow.

"Feeling a little better, sweetie?" she asks, knowing now that I am.

I'm somewhere near regular breathing patterns again but my mind is in the midst of something else. Thinking about being given what you think and hope and truly believe is a perfect child. No need to try for the second when you got the first one right, right? Except for there's some sort of manufacturing error, which is especially frustrating given you're the manufacturer.

The model you expected, equipped with its natural intelligence and artistic talent and aesthetic value, well there's something detrimentally wrong with it. No matter how hard you try, how many different approaches you take, how much of yourself you give, this child you so desperately want to be happy, he or she just can't seem to find the way. Not for very long, at least.

You'll never give up; you can't. You'll love this child until your last day and then some, but how many years before you've reached the point of learned helplessness? Blaire hasn't gotten there yet.

"Eat something, ya little goof," she says lovingly.

Seeing that I've calmed down a bit from my spiraling and instantaneous anxiety whirlwind, she sits back down, relieved. I'd like to say that I don't know where that uncomfortable little outburst came from, but new *information* has kind of given me an idea.

"Thanks, Mom," I say. Remembering I'm still pretty high, I pick up some crusty macaroni with my fingers and shovel in a bite, half of it ending up on my grey tee-shirt and faded-to-grey black sweatpants. It's fucking delicious.

She shakes her head and giggles a little, "Of course, Sweetie. Always."

27

It's a Saturday afternoon around 2pm. The sun is evidently present but not harsh, only a few scattered clouds hanging in the picturesque blue sky. Kids running and bunnies hopping and squirrels being frantic little dummies.

My day is vacuous of plans, yet I feel blanketed with responsibility. I had woken up embarrassingly late in the day with a pungent half-smoked blunt from the evening prior piercing my nostrils. Taking precedence over coffee or food or morning meds, I'm finishing up a smokey walk around the neighborhood, trying to clear my mind while simultaneously fogging it up.

Small step after small step: left, right, left, right. Deep, slow drag after deep, slow drag: in . . . and out, in . . . and out. The brown rolling-paper filled with green and orange Birthday Cake burns and burns and becomes smaller and smaller as I get closer and closer to our place of residence. Left, right, left, right. In . . . and out, until it's burned and burned and become too small to hit. A final flick from my fingers sends the clip into the street and I'm footsteps from where I've always called home.

As I near the entrance of my familiar abode, connected to other buildings on both sides, I notice a large manila envelope which reads, 'Welcome Home,' placed directly in the center of the door mat in a calculated fashion. I pick it up. The handwriting looks like that of a small boy.

I look all around as if someone is playing some joke or setting some trap for me. I have no real way to know it's meant for me, but I instinctively press it towards my chest and walk the remaining two footsteps to the door. My yellow-rubber-encased front door key is already in hand and in door and turning quickly. I bolt up the stairs and don't wait until I arrive to my bedroom before tearing through the envelope.

'Mr. Hiro,' begins the letter in the same childish script; at least now I know I'm the intended recipient. 'So wonderful to have heard about your return to us. How was your trip?' the sloppily written mystery letter continues.

It must be referring to my coma, which really did feel like a trip although it was much longer, apparently.

'I've been informed about you in such great detail, upcoming friend.'

This seems pretty well-worded for something that looks like it may as well have been written in dull crayon. 'I know about the new hiccups presenting themselves in your life, as well as the angst that's always been inside you.'

My overwhelming curiosity is now fear and anger and confusion.

Recurring Severe Stress Routine activated. I hear as

my shaking, sweaty hands can hardly hold this invasive scroll full of small talk and secrets. I continue reading.

'I promise to do what I can to help, but there's something of utmost importance you need to know. He is not your friend, Hiro.'

The feeling of panic in the back of my neck awakens and it's suddenly hard to swallow.

'He's a dangerous animal . . . no, worse, friend. He's something we cannot fully understand.'

My lungs are screaming with shortness of breath, but I fight through.

'All will be revealed in time. Soon enough. You're in better hands than you've ever been.'

I know with certainty who the letter is referring to but I'm not sure why.

'Be discrete with your words, and beware of Fox Viqar.'

28

My knockoff brand TV is active. It's a deep, dusty old set that has somehow managed to survive well past its time. I don't know what's on, I'm not really watching, just zoning in and out. It seems like it's an endless series of commercials—perhaps it's the Commercial Recap Channel? A station fully devoted to advertisements for sexual male enhancement and premium-brand condoms and postpartum depression medication. Full circle television.

I'm lying belly-up on my twin-size mattress, staring at the egg-white ceiling. It could use a fresh coat of paint. Just as I begin to sink into the beige sheets below me, I'm reminded that life isn't as simple as I'd like it to be.

*You don't want to adjust their settings too rapidly or else they'll appear in need of physical sedation, and then the party's over! What you're looking to do is just slo**wwwlll**lyy increase their panic levels . . . a touch . . . and then a touch more . . . and once they **really** seem to be in need of some relief . . . ¡POW! That's when you crank it up and watch them squirm. We'll get some incredibly interesting results with this common panic attack exercise.*

This isn't the first or second or third *transmission* I've gotten today. There was one earlier about making old people forget where they live, and just a bit ago I was walked through a brief tutorial on making teenage girls vomit purposely in public restrooms. It's all so scientific, yet there's an art to it.

As I lividly clench my lumpy pillow with both hands, asphyxiating myself slightly in attempts to drown out my madness, I hear the extended sales pitches continuing to spew from the visually entertaining propaganda machine. This ad is one of many in a series of ancestry commercials. An opportunity for you to pay money to send your hair or blood to some laboratory facility in order to learn about your genetic makeup.

You can learn specifics about your extended family tree; maybe you have distant cousins in the area, maybe you're one eighth Navajo. Who knows? I begin to wonder instead about the genealogy of the group of students and teachers presently running life-altering experiments on my fellow humans and me. Can we learn all about them for $69.99 as well?

I've imagined dozens of different ways they might look. Everything from classic little green men to giant, horned chipmunk creatures to donkeys in barista outfits. I wonder if they all look similar or if their appearances are full of variety like ours. Maybe their planet is just as diverse as ours, but I wouldn't be able to tell them apart— is that racist?

I feel like I know them at this point, the way you feel like you know the characters in your favorite shows.

You've created emotional bonds. You'll yell at the screen when they return to their exes or break their sobriety streak or walk directly into a room full of zombies. You'll cry when those undead extras rip away their beautiful faces, ending your intimate, once-a-week relationship for good . . . besides reruns.

For all I know, I could provide AlienAncestry.com with my complete cloning material to find out I'm 31.5% Nylon Puppy Person from the Turbenfuss nebula. Maybe I've only been a few hundred lightyears away from some of my mixed-species second cousins this whole time. We could have been getting together to see movies and compare galaxies and have tapas.

The background soundtrack has moved from DNA discovery to phone-sex. From an informational package about your bloodline to a hotline meant to send blood to your package. All really just some variant of white noise at this point anyway. I reach over to the cluttered bedside cabinet on my right and pick up the glass-blown bowl. It's tie-dye and already packed with Laughing Buddha.

"Mmm, we're so lonely, baby. Call us so we can have some ree**aal**ly **sex**xy fun." Says one of the models pretending to actually work for this 1-800 vacuum for lonely perverts' money and cum as I reach over once more for my miniature blue Bic.

That's it. . . . That's it. Ease into their discomfort. Which one of our background speaker's excitement is more sincere is painfully clear.

I torch the fully packed smoking device in hand with one damaging inhale, a handful of hits all packed into one. I hold the delicious cloud of smoke inside my mouth and lungs as long as I can until I start coughing like a fat, congested baby. As soon as my breathing returns to normal, and before I accidentally begin to mix my Alien Ancestry and sex-line thoughts together, I allow my heavy eyelids to sink down until my next waking memory.

29

Sure, before wearing these uninvited foreign headphones, Dr. Foxy V and I got along pretty well. Before hallucinogenic warnings to myself and objectively real letters from a stalker with lovely handwriting, I was glad we were going paticnt-doctor 'steady'.

Before everything, my mother thought talking things out and sticking with one 'doctor' must really be helping me because of how calm I'd been after sessions. Neither the Ol' Fox nor I had mentioned to her the regularity in which we smoked weed during appointments. She thought it was roughly a 0% frequency, while actually it's always been at a pretty precise 100%.

The occasional bursts of new energy I'd been displaying had origin in his office as well. Viqar the Star made sure I experimented with nose candy. Against my will, in truth, but I can't say I didn't thoroughly enjoy it. Dipping a cigarette in it before sharing was his first sneaky, wonderful trick.

"Would you rather go broke seeing other schmucks?"

he'd ask me. "Just a bunch of shameless pawns working for big pharma wanting to get you hooked on some nonsense. Whatever the trendiest, priciest new drug is. Not me, Hiro. I just want to keep you comfortably fucked up until you're well."

I did talk to him too, though. Sometimes. There had been moments it seemed to help. Many other moments, less so. There were different medications involved from time to time. There was Oxazepam for severe anxiety, which was the generic form of Serax, a benzodiazepine. It went from 10mg to 15mg to 30mg. There was a smorgasbord of selective serotonin reuptake inhibitors for depression and bipolar symptoms and alien gossip queens in my cranium. Seeing as these were generally provided by Arina on my way out, I tolerated them, feeling in those moments with her that I didn't need them or anything else at all.

It was almost like he was a regular doctor a lot of times. The thing about it, though, was that he never gave me scripts to go fill at a pharmacy. He'd always have tons of 'leftover samples' to 'save us tons of *our* hard-earned money.' Mine and Blaire's he means, as if I'd saved up during my coma.

As Dr. Viqar has explained, he'd developed all types of enjoyable addictions during university and medical school, both of which awarded him the honor of valedictorian. He swears he's 100% sure what he can safely share with people. That's what makes him 'the best goddamn doctor around, and one hell of a poker player,' he says. He says this often, actually.

However he rationalizes his outlandish behavior is fine with me. I went from unable to locate and obtain drugs to making a healthy amount of green paper men selling what he gives me for free to the cool kids and the theatre kids and the gifted kids. Most of it goes to Blaire, even if sometimes I have to hide it in her purse. It's a good deal. Why ever complain?

I've trusted this stupidly beautiful, wild genius idiot for long enough at this point, but telling him about the voices that haven't gone away, that used to just be deep-sleep creations? I haven't even told him that they arrived! That'd be serious. . . . I mean, super serious.

I could deal with a pill or two per day that made me feel all silly, but I can imagine what he'll think, and I'm not looking to get spoon-fed massive amounts of antipsychotics that put me on my ass and keep my dick permanently soft. *Hard* pass.

I'm pretty certain he's drinking a flask-style martini and doing lines of fresh winter up his nose between patients right now, if there happen to be any today. But I'm also certain he's some sort of special genius savant or something fun like that. I don't know, there's some indescribable feature about him. A feeling. And I'm about 95% sure this isn't some weird subconscious crush, or *my therapist is my personal god* thing. Maybe even 98% sure! Well, no, probably more like 92%. Whatever, I'm pretty sure, really. My point, though, is that any blackmail-related attempts could prove to be a far trickier option than desired.

Decisiveness isn't necessarily the mark of an anxious or depressed person, so you can imagine how much fun I'm having deciding what to do with this new looming secret.

Looming. Blooming. Booming. Dooming.

"Hiro, sweetie. It's cold outside, I'll give you a ride to Dr. Viqar's office on my way to the store." Looks like I'll figure this all out in Blaire's comfortably unsightly automobile. The same one as what feels like both yesterday and 100 years ago.

They're running another *Controller Trainer* as my mother and I pull into the Fox Den. Recently, I've been walking or riding my bike wherever I can, but Blaire finds any excuse to come to the ol' thinkin' sessions and act giddy around the probably former Olympic gold medalist, Dr. Fox Viqar.

No surprise that she's wearing her nicer-than-average garments instead of her usual yoga pants and oversized flannel. She can't help herself. There's no reason to walk me inside, yet here she is. The hungry tigress overeagerly opens the door and enters the empty office waiting room.

Alright students, open your text screens and control panels to learning unit PRAUV 17.

Pretty Miss Receptionist, Arina, sees me take a seat on my usual waiting room chair and she checks me in. She smiles at me. I raise my arm a little bit to fake wave and make my best pretend smile for her. I shouldn't ever need to pretend smile when looking at such a marvelous creature. "Happy to see you, sweetie," she says softly. I feel frozen in happiness whenever she speaks to me. I wonder if she could know how much she means to me.

We're going to be moving onto refining delusional traits and then creating basic auditory and visual hallucinations. Did anyone have any final questions about our previous unit on adjusting anxiety levels situationally?

IT STARTS WHEN YOU STOP

Arina is easy to talk to, even for me, and very pretty. I'm *almost* always able to maintain positivity around her. She's about 5'4 with big chestnut brown eyes, dark flowing hair, and a perfect complexion. I hear along the way that her roots are of a Spanish-speaking nature mixed with some Russian Czarina and Greek Goddess blood as well. She's the most beautiful woman I've ever seen. Real life and celebrities both included. So. So. Stunning. Also, she has the ass of a gym legend or a porn star or a Brazilian volleyball player.

Actually, yes, Professor. I was wondering if we could review the direct correlation chart between sexual anxiety and depression levels once more before the upcoming examination?

I had thought my mother left, but when I took a moment to stop gawking at Arina's perfect everything, I saw that she was still in fact there, chatting and smiling and giggling with the impeccably dressed Dr. Fox Viqar. My whole life I've never seen her act so strangely towards anyone. She never made these real-life heart-emoji eyes at Todd the cremated Turkish Rug.

Absolutely! Ok, everyone prepare your human practice model so that we can run some additional test scenarios in groups.

"So incredibly lovely chatting with you, Blaire. As always." He smiles sensually at her, and her quivering knees can hardly hold up her petite body.

I give him a quiet, quite usual head nod and make my way into his office, as is the routine. This new burden between my ears, ringing or talking or texting. Everything looks the same, everything feels different.

"How have your last couple of weeks been, Hiro?"

I could tell him the truth and push to see if my inexplicable and intuitive fear of him is justified.

No. A half-truth, maybe, like that I'm doing well at school and not much news. I do generally crush school, after all. But no.

I elect to go with, "It's both grossly inappropriate and plain gross how you flirt with my mom."

I'm unsure of where I'm going with this, but I suppose I'm a creature of impulse. He doesn't react how I'd thought or hoped he would. I expected a cold stare or maybe a smart-ass, yet intelligent, remark. He's always been quite good at both of those. An overly defensive reaction would have been fine as well, as long as it distracted from the new tenants in my brain rental unit. Instead, he says, "Hiro, my friend, what's up your butthole? Something bothering ya more than the reg?" He doesn't even say it smugly, stupid, genuinely wonderful prick.

"I'm pretty sure I just made it abundantly clear," I reply as I give him my most arrogant look. I shake my head a little, like a spoiled private-school jerk after some bozo commoner attempts to correct his or her knowledge of anything, pinkies out. 'Passhhaw, bozo. You shall not!' Like that.

He just looks calmly at me and replies, "No, Mr. Fiji Takablaka, nothing about you seems abundantly clear right now, guy."

Besides his fun racism, he says it with a believable concern in his voice, but something about it feels . . . dark. Maybe I'm losing it and the reason I won't tell him is because I think I really am kooked out. But back to this pretty certain reality: I start blurting out verbiage faster than I can process my thoughts or intentions.

"You flirting shamelessly with my mother is what's bothering me. I know FACTUALLY I did zero stuttering, so maybe your English is the problem, huh, Doc? Shookraya shoorba or Quiaté tu totíng or should I keep trying to figure out what your native **FUCKING** language is?" I surprise myself with my undaunted arrogance. At least this time he gives me a bit of a shocked look. Something. Anything.

He arises and walks towards the window and just stands there for a moment . . . looking outside before taking out a pack of matches from his pocket and a joint from behind his car. He slowly takes the match from the pack labeled with some casino's logo, lights the joint in his mouth, then returns the flammable gambling memorabilia to his right pant pocket.

He takes a deep drag and blows out three perfect O's. He reminds me of the king of some fictional gypsy tribe. In no rush, he makes his way back to his desk and sits atop it. He hasn't offered me a hit yet today. Greedy prick.

"For starters, Hiro, English is my first language, fucker. But pretty sure you just said something along the lines of *Thank You Soup* and *Quiet Your Pussy*, in their respective languages. Secondly, do you happen to know how long Miss Arina has worked here?" I think for a second, but I suppose the question was rhetorical because immediately he returns, "three years, just a couple months longer than you've been coming here."

I already know this. As previously mentioned, I may have a bit of a thing for her. Why wouldn't I? She's soft-spoken but witty. Silly, but scholarly. Definitely been beautiful her whole life but somehow remains genuine and kind. She's been a perfect angel existing in my personal hell.

"Not a bad looking piece of meat, eh?" He says. I don't care for that verbiage. Not at all. "Wouldn't you love to just slip your hands up that skirt and—"

"Whoa, man!" I interrupt.

"Did you know her nipples are pierced?" He persists.

"DUDE!" I yell, "Why are you telling me this? What the fuck does she have to do with you or my mom or anything else besides handling your paperwork!?"

Does she really have pierced nipples, I wonder. If so, how would he know? Oh please, God, don't let that have happened, his big tan hands feeling up my beautiful, wonderful, perfect dream girl.

He takes another deep, contemplative breath, followed by another hit of his joint. It feels like an eternity has gone by but the joint is still lit and kicking in between his manicured fingers. My fingers, on the other hand, are just very sweaty. Pun not intended, but enjoyed.

Smoke elegantly exits out of Fox's lips; this time it's a French inhale, where the smoke leaves his mouth and enters his nose, then eventually out of his ears. Ok, the ears part is exaggerated. Got me, but really wouldn't surprise me too much.

"Well, 'the fuck she has to do with all this,' is that it's not a secret to anyone that you're madly in love, or at least lust, with that tight little thang." I give him my best scowl.

"Kiddo," he continues, "I've been finding any possible opportunity to flirt with Blaire for exactly 100% of the time I've known her, ever since we first met. Appointments, phone calls, *accidental* drop-ins to the grocery store or bank. Private, public, right in front of that bum that was lucky enough to tap that for so long, wherever, whenever."

I will genuinely always enjoy hearing anyone insult that deceased douche, but I'm still pissed the fuck off.

He continues, "She loves the attention, and buddy, have you SEEN your Mom?"

I'm gonna go ahead and assume this one is rhetorical as well.

"Mmm, she is a straight dime, and I mean she's gotta be at least a decade older than me too. I would seriously put in some serious work to . . . well, you get it, kid. Your mom is hot."

Is he going to get to his point? Or IS this his point?

"I've been openly and almost *dramatically* flirting with your yummy mama since always, you've just NEVER been able to take those peepers of yours off of our dearest Arina."

I start breathing heavier but remain silent while he enjoys the elegant sound of his own voice.

"I've literally seen you love-stare at her even when she was disgusting, Hiro. . . ."

She's never been disgusting.

". . . when she was getting over the flu, remember? Her nose was all crusty, her big browns drooping . . . less eyes than bags of wrinkly skin, really. Her lips were cracked and her breath stank; she was basically dressed in her pajamas, wrapped in sheets. A real pig in a blanket, ya know? And there you were, just ogling her, ya little sicko, you."

I remember that day. She had a grey beanie with a little ball on top, as if she were a South Park character. Her wavy brown hair was messy but still together, and she still smelled like the feeling of your first steaming hot cup of coffee in the morning. Perfect relief when you need it most. Her nose was not crusty, for the record, just red. She was adorable, and her flu-like symptoms didn't prevent her from being benevolent, inquiring about my week, or offering to make me a cup of coffee.

"Yet today," he continues, "a day where she is wearing a tight white skirt above her knees, you repeatedly look away. She's usually a little prude, but mmm, not today. Even I was mighty tempted; I prefer Blaire, though. So, why don't you tell me what's really bothering you?"

30

This isn't the first time that I recall my rocky first flight. I often visit this memory, mostly as a tool to compare my brain versus others. I think about the collectively frightened group of us, except for yours truly, that is. My darling mother, unaware that I'm currently less anxious than before any regular school day, is trying desperately to console me. Everyone I can see and hear is either freaking out or trying to calm someone from freaking out.

I admire Banshee's shiny bald head. I wonder if there's literally a shininess setting he adjusted when creating his fraud-bod.

"Careful," the giant charlatan doctor says, "it's dangerous to mess with those machines, even for the controller if not used properly."

How much could any of this matter?

It's the same type of thought contrast in a number of

dark, hypothetical situations. Tornado or school shooting or squirrel uprising. My, Hiro's, end result is never really that important, in my eyes. In my brain's depiction of these natural tragedies, I never care if I come out breathing. Unless, of course, it means I can save her from harm. Save them.

Did you know for every 20 accidents in the air, there are 5 MILLION car accidents? The odds of dying in one of those car accidents is about one in 5000. Flying accidents, however, are only around one in 11 million. Seems like a stretch, I know, but it's empirical.

Although most of us are aware of the relative safety in flying, aerophobia, the fear of flying, ranks fourth amongst all phobias in the United States. It's only beaten by arachnophobia, ophidiophobia, and acrophobia. Those are the fears of spiders, snakes, and heights, respectively.

I can hardly imagine if I had snuck in some Ant Spiders or Long-jawed Orb Weavers or an Ahaetulla Prasina. Oh boy, what a shitty mess that would have been. Everyone dizzy and nauseous and breathless. One big, high-altitude panic attack.

I study the Simulator Machines like you'd study a breathtaking piece of art or the first naked body you've ever seen. I realize that the buttons and dials, covered in their native alphabet, could dramatically enhance or completely eliminate all of the anxiety on that hypothetical nightmare flight. There's one with a yellow piece of tape covering the essential controls. I assume the script on it reads 'Out of order.' Although, for all I know, it could say, 'Treasure buried here, ya' lucky fuck.'

IT STARTS WHEN YOU STOP

Just about one in three people admit having at least a mild fear of flying, with turbulence ranking as the number one source of passenger trepidation. What they should really be worried about is the bad airport coffee, the hours of security checks, or the all-too-likely probability of your flight's second delay.

It makes sense for a person who values their existence to feel anxious upon feeling turbulence, naturally equating it to a chance of plummeting from the sky, all the way into the hard, unforgiving earth. Turbulence, though, is a somewhat broad term encompassing any air instability caused by winds, temperature differentials, or nearby storms.

It's incredibly rare for any amount of turbulence to actually cause any misfortune. The last major disaster attributed to turbulence occurred all the way back in 1966, back in the days of Vietnam and the original Star Trek and easy LSD access. An overeager Boeing 707 flew too close to Mount Fuji and unfortunately ran into some severe clear-air turbulence.

All 124 passengers and crew lost their lives that day. A terrible tragedy, but one that happened more than half a century ago. Compare that with the knowledge that your piece of shit fifteen-year-old neighbor, the one that plays music unnecessarily loud all night and litters in your well-maintained yard, he's eligible to get onto the road with you in a few months. Any and all shit-bag fifteen-year-olds are just months from that same privilege. Four wheels just like your four wheels.

"This is just one of several types of advanced

machinery designed specifically for this project, Hiro. You'll see more along the way," Banshee says as I continue to be captivated by every detail of this marvel of science designed for malintent. I feel the dry air move in gust formation as Banshee motions with his jumbo kielbasa fingers for me to follow him again. He's smiling. "Hell, I'll let you try one of these Bad Larrys once we're out in the air for a little while. We'll have a little time before we carry out the newest addendum to the operation."

My world crashes, and before I have a chance to inquire or plead, he continues his sentiment.

"Despite his clear lack of protocol and professionalism, his decision to augment the experiment's endpoint is, at least at this point, rationally correct and requisite. His outlandish behavior in your region truly has hindered the objectivity of our analysis."

For no reason at all, I mentally note the exact location of our inoperative or defective machine as Banshee's lush lips continue to jabber.

"Therefore, to avoid making so much of our effort futile, we'll simply adjust as Fox proposed. Different motivation, same play."

"But, Dr. Banshee, please! Surely there's got to be another way," I finally vocalize. I try to continue my unplanned case but he's ready with the Mutombo block.

"I'm sorry, young Takafuji. I know things may seem dismal, but for the thousandth and probably not last time, **you're safe**. As are both of your female acquaintances. Now, please, follow me," he says.

I do, I follow him. I follow him and wonder if I'm accurate in my presumptions of what our safety will cost.

31

Dr Viqar's stare seems to last forever and ever. "Well, Doctor," I finally answer, "You're definitely right about Arina today . . . sexier than ever. I guess I'm just a bit distracted."

He looks annoyed now; he puts his thumb and pointer finger against his closed eyelids and takes another huge, exorbitant breath. In a frustrated tone, he responds, "Right, but distracted by WHAT? WHAT is bothering you, or WHO?"

He finally passes the joint. Finally. I need it desperately—I'm feeling far beyond nervous. I'm trembling enough that it's difficult to grab the delicious Girl Scout Cookie-rolled goodness scenting the room. I eventually manage to inhale and focus on something else for even just one second, feeling the smoke flow in and then out of my lungs. I watch as it creates shapes and then evolves into new shapes. One beautiful distraction after another.

"YO, I see you, so I KNOW there is a person besides me

in this room!" He shouts. "Now, you're going to tell me what's bothering you or else there will be a new set of issues for you to space out and stress about. RIGHT. FUCKING. NOW!!"

I jump backwards as if his powerful lion-like roars actually moved me through the air. Like Ryu's haduken or Goku's kamayamaya coming from this animal of a person's mouth. He sits back down, fixes his Stefano Ricci diamond-plated skinny tie, and continues, "Sorry about that, Hiro, my boy, but . . . I'm serious."

I have to give him something, some sort of response at least. Lie to him, whatever comes to mind, I just know it shouldn't be the truth.

"I've been getting bullied, more than usual, ever since I woke up from my . . . long nap. People expect me to be some sort of miracle, when really I'm just all sorts of melancholy. Like I'm supposed to suddenly live life to the fullest, no more taking anything for granted. Time to jump out of planes and backpack Europe and do weird sex things in Thailand, but I still just value solitude and snack food and some quality Jamaican Dream."

The Fox is usually a hound with sniffing out my lies. Luckily, enough of my story is actually true. All of it, in fact. I'm still breathing like I'm on a cigarette 5K, while I'm trying to breathe like I'm in a yoga class. Our handsome and intimidating doctor-ish acquaintance looks me up and down for a moment. I can't tell if he's actually buying everything or maybe undressing me with his eyes, but he presses his lips together and nods a little, a TIINNNGGG sounds from his laptop signifying he's received an email, and simultaneously . . .

*Excellent work with the human models. I think

you've all got a good handle on basic human neurotransmitter and hormone configuration adjustments. I think we're ready to move on to some more complex procedures.*

Fuck. Not right now.

"Hiro, are you with me on that?"

On what? I just nod.

Who can give me some compound maneuvers using the human species brain control board?

I'm perspiring profusely. I can hardly comprehend what parts of my current experience are *real*. I ask him to specify. I don't know why I asked him to specify. Specify what? Am I asking some mysterious alien militia captain for his honest input on my made-up problem, or asking Dr. Fox Viqar about brain-control-board functionality? Do I have that mixed up? Is it all the same thing?

"How much you getting paid to babysit that joint?" asks Dr. Viqar.

"Babies?" I reply, "There are no babies."

Dr. Fox laughs deeply and shakes his head with a grin on his face.

"I mean pass that friggin' joint back to me, kid. Christ, you're high. You eat some atypical mushrooms or something today? Anything I should be jealous about?"

A normal starter serving size of psilocybin-variety mushrooms is about two to three grams. I wish I had eaten several of those servings. Anything to make me think THIS is just a phase, something that will fade out with my trip. That's what this feels like, some sort of bad trip.

"N—No, I uh, I wish, just one too many pot-cookies and not enough coffee this morning." I place my hand on my stomach and look at him, "I forgot they're not just regular chocolate chips."

He gives a half smile and grabs his prescription pad, "Ok, dummy. You're not striking me as a Chatty Cathy today, so we'll call this one extra early. I'm feeling overworked anyway, there was a truly superfluous cunnilingus session which has left my jaw feeling exhausted. Here's your script refill, hermano. You need anything else?"

He's doing almost what regular doctors might do with medicine, except I know I just exchange this piece of paper with Arina for a small package of drugs.

"No, sir, I'm good." I instantly know what I've just done.

"Sir?" Dr. Viqar repeats back to me. I'm staring blankly at the door. "Calling me sir? I swear there's something up with you."

I feel the pressure on my neck, like the actual concept of panic has come to life and is gripping my throat right now.

"You're being far less of a little goon recently, perhaps you should hook me up with some of those weed cookies."

What a Yahtzee moment. Not where I thought this was going, can't say it really makes sense either given the session's start. Not questioning it.

"Yeah," I say, "I'll try to pick up some more this week from my lab partner." He smiles, chuckles a little, and—

What about using THEIR negative emotions to drag previously happy others, especially loved ones, down around them? —Yes! Great start! Anyone else?

¡CLAP! Fox slaps his hands together, he's already at the door staring at me. "C'mon, Dodo Bird. Seriously,

IT STARTS WHEN YOU STOP

about those edibles, though, kay? Thanks."

I basically sprint out of his office. Out of his building. One moment of blissful relief, before . . .

*How about you, Kryzlovag? —Uhm, could you make them sad enough to end their own existence term? —Most certainly, the human units refer to that as *suicide*, and it's quite elementary, especially with the Asian sub-species. We'll definitely be touching more on this topic in great detail.*

What . . . the fuck? What the serious fuck am I hearing? I'm star-ting to feel dizzy auhl of a sudan. Lkie. Realy fuckang dizzzytz

32

I begin to open my eyes slowly and someone's hands are waving around in front of my face. I feel the cold air take a bite out of me, my whole body becomes one big shiver for a moment before I can start to focus on my immediate surroundings. The blurs enveloping me begin to take shape.

"Hey, you alright?"

The voice sounds familiar but I'm still uncustomarily stretching my eyes and trying to understand what's taking place.

"Should I call an ambulance?" the helpful mystery-person asks.

"NO," I immediately and emphatically reply while managing to shake my head at a rapid rate. I haven't quite gathered my wits yet, but I know for certain I'm not looking to spend money I don't have at a hospital. Just to get to the hospital, really. The kind stranger grabs my right hand and squeezes it gently. I look up.

"You gave me a real scare." She's gorgeous. A

masterpiece. I realize this perfect female stranger is in fact not a stranger at all.

"Arina?" I ask. Maybe I've died and gone to heaven. But could I have really earned a place there?

Attention all employees, please begin reporting to the conference room for our quarter-annual review of Project Person.

Nope. Definitely not heaven. As I try to pick myself up a little bit, my fantasy medic puts one of her hands on my back and keeps holding my hand with her other. I'm much more confused than usual, even recently, which is quite a statement. But, I'm ecstatic. I'd live in complete ignorance with her.

"What . . . what happened?" I ask the angel face still holding me. She seems relieved that I'm speaking.

"Well, you kinda stumbled out of Fox's office. You had both hands on your temples and you were mumbling to yourself, so I went out to make sure you were ok."

I'm horribly, horribly embarrassed.

"By the time I caught up to you, your face was almost *literally* white. Before I could even open my mouth, you started, like, shouting at yourself. A few seconds later, you were on the ground."

Let's just keep adding on to that embarrassment, I suppose. Also, shit, I yelled something? Would I have yelled out something . . . *sensitive*? I take a moment to just absorb the information. Holding my head and screaming. Fuck.

"Do you want me to call anyone to come pick you up?" She asks.

Get a hold of yourself, Hiro. You can handle a simple conversation.

"Thank you so, so much for everything, Arina. But no, I'm ok, I uh . . . I live pretty close."

She gives me a face that suggests serious skepticism. "Hm, ok . . . well, my lunch is starting right now, at least let me walk home with you. . . ." A dream coming true in the midst of a nightmare. I must be a deer in headlights. ". . . Ya know, to make sure you get there safe." Not ideal circumstances for our first *date*, but I'll take anything I can get.

"How could I say no?" I reply. I'm keenly focused on not showing my elation. So focused, in fact, that a few seconds later I hear Arina's silly laugh.

"Uhh, I'm following you, bud," she says.

Shit.

At least she's smiling. At least she's here. I try to reciprocate a goofy smile.

"Right, sorry about that. Let's go, I live a few blocks up this direction." My palms are sweaty. Stupid, cliché palms. Hesitantly, I ask Arina, "Hey, when I was . . .

shouting . . . did I actually say anything?"

She thinks for a moment about her upcoming statement, looking up in the air and away slightly.

"Well, Hiro, I kinda didn't wanna say anything until you were feeling better, but . . . it was a little scary."

I'm staring at her, horrified about what she might say.

"It, like . . . wasn't words. But it WAS something."

She pauses, only briefly, taking a deep breath as if this conversation is a physically exhausting feat.

"Nothing like any language I've ever heard. Like, maybe some obscure tribe in New Guinea or something, but probably not even that. It was like coughs and gargling mouthwash. But, not in a random order, ya know? It was

. . . like . . . something, it definitely SEEMED like that at least."

That sounds familiar. Really, unfortunately familiar.

Shaking my head, almost lost for words, I look at the Mediterranean Princess with mortified eyes.

"Wow, Miss Arina, I'm feeling SO embarrassed. I don't have any idea what that *coughing mouthwash* talk was, I wish I did. I'm super appreciative for your help already, but one more favor . . . would you mind not mentioning this to Dr. Viqar at all?"

She stops walking and puts her hand on my shoulder. I'd remain still in this spot forever if it meant she'd never remove it. She's looking right into my eyes, but breaks eye contact only briefly as if to build strength before looking back at me and saying, "Hiro, I . . . I need you to tell me everything you know about Dr. Fox Viqar."

33

How many people have to enjoy some obscure or non-mainstream artist or band or movie before it becomes a *cult classic*? How many people have to enjoy the same pseudo-masterpiece before it grows up and becomes the real deal, a *non-cult* classic? You know, a regular classic.

It's not a definitive number I don't think, it's just that the majority has to agree about it. Kind of like a religion, the major ones have enough followers that no one is questioning whether or not they're religions. You certainly don't have to believe the words inside of the Bible or Torah or Koran but you can't argue whether Muslims and Christians and Jews exist.

If, however, the group of like-minded individuals in your faith is a few dozen or less, well, then you're in cult town, my friend. Little bit arbitrary if you ask me. I mean, when you break it down, a *cult*, just like a *religion*, is a set of rules to live better, mixed with some lesson-teaching fairy tales and extremists that eventually ruin all the love and peace and togetherness for everyone.

IT STARTS WHEN YOU STOP

It doesn't matter whether you're Buddhist or Hindu or a Jehovah's witness, **you believe what you believe**, and if you're sure, you're sure.

In 1995, Shoko Asahara and the Aum Shinrikyo, or the '*Supreme Truth*,' were **sure** that releasing nerve gas in a Tokyo subway **had** to be done. They believed in their cause.

It was claimed Shoko could read minds and levitate, traits which have been claimed about David Blaine as well. I'm sure enough bozos would blindly follow his every command if he worked at it. Maybe they already are? Probably.

A year before the Shinrikyo event, 50+ members of *The Order of the Solar Temple* either committed suicide or were murdered in Switzerland and Quebec. Joseph Di Mambro and Luc Jouret were the leaders of that cult or religion or Boys and Girls Club. They spoke a great deal about the upcoming doomsday, a focal point for a lot of cults. Even if they don't discuss it, it still may get to that point.

Jim Jones took hundreds to that point in 1978. A few took some of *Jimmy's Secret Stuff* on their own; others had to be convinced or forced or filled with bullets. There are always some stubborn sailors on the ship, so be it, that's just how it is. Into the deep blue we go

34

Sitting in an oversized corner booth of the Maple Tree Diner with someone almost impossibly lovely, I take a sip of my black coffee. Volcano explosion levels of steam hover above my mug, but it doesn't feel hot enough. Hardly warm at all.

As I drift completely into the apparently room-temperature steam, Arina, my dearest, brings me back to reality city asking, "So, that's **all** you know about Dr. V?"

I love her, I think. Thankfully, I don't say that. Instead, I nod a little and say, "Completely absurd, drug addict, supermodel genius whose actual medical care sometimes seems brilliant, but mostly just warrants prison time for all parties involved. Yeah, that about sums it up."

It smells like syrup. The diner's name was not misleading whatsoever in that sense. I can tell she's looking for something more than I have, but I'm not sure what it is she thinks she already knows. She presses her full, impatient lips together before almost hypnotizing me with her words.

"C'mon, Hiro, there's **got** to be **some**thing else. ANYthing else."

Finally feeling adequately caffeinated, I reply.

"Wait, hold on, did something . . . happen? I mean, I know he's an all-around toxic monster person, but . . . something specific?"

I wait for her response but her expression is unchanging. Stern and with purpose. I continue, "Are you like . . . filing a lawsuit or something? What are you looking for exactly?"

She looks frustrated but understands it's her turn now to give me something to work with. She takes a deep and unintentionally sexy breath, and at the end of her exhale she looks right into my eyes. Her beautiful sepia-toned seeing-devices pierce me.

"It's not a coincidence that I work with Dr. Fox."

I have at least a few specific questions, but instead I elect an open-ended approach.

"Please elaborate," I reply.

"I was chosen," she continues, only adding more questions as we go. "I thought it should have been *Toasted Green Pea,* personally, but I was really honored."

Before allowing further levels of confusion, I decide to jump in.

"Ok, so, help me catch up. Chosen by whom, when, and for what reason? Also, who or what is Toasted Green Pea?"

She more than somewhat unobtrusively looks side to side, inches in towards me slightly and says, "You need to know this is highly classified information."

I thought this had been established by now.

"Of course, let's keep that a running theme," I reply to

our *newly mysterious* beauty.

She continues, "My assignment began a few weeks before you started seeing Fox. Special missions of this magnitude are designed without a specified end date. They're usually meant to take years, sometimes, like, decades. We must be ABSOLUTELY sure before moving forward. I just thought I'd have more by now. He doesn't even try to fuck me!"

Everything coming out of her mouth seems foreign from her. I guess I never knew the pretty dark-haired girl behind the check-in desk at all, even as I thought we were becoming close. That last part of her statement gives me some horribly mixed feelings. My heart surely sinks into my stomach knowing she *wants to* or is *supposed to* fuck him, not that I can be surprised. Stupid, beautiful maniac.

BUT, at least I know it hasn't happened. I don't know how I'm supposed to react to any of this, especially in this dining arena full of octogenarians. I feel like an autistic 5-year-old in need of their emotion cards or feelings chart. I just look blankly and let her continue.

"Not that I *wanted to*," she says.

Thank god.

Thank god. Thank god. Thank god.

"I was just voted or decided to be the most sexually appealing, and therefore most capable of completing the task at hand. We need to know EVERYTHING about the doctor. Everything."

I'm truly not sure if I'm any more or less confused. What task at hand? Who is *We*. All I ask at the moment, though, is, "Why?"

"We believe Dr. Fox is . . . special. Unfortunately, that's not a good thing . . . at all." My blank face signifies for her to please continue. "So, in case it was unclear, this is about something *far greater* than a lawsuit. I wouldn't NEED you if that were the case. Seriously, his office basically has a thin cocaine film covering everything and it reeks like a blunt wrap, and that's just for starters!"

This is true. Keep going, confusing angel person.

"Not to mention, I'm pretty sure the bulk of his clients are just buying drugs or sleeping with him in that so-called office. Yet he has no physical interest in me, which is making it tough to retrieve anything of value. That's part of the reason I've come to you."

My eyes open a little wider. I want no part in any weirdness she's speaking of, albeit I'm very curious. But then she puts her hand on top of mine and squeezes gently, and any and all of my doubts dissipate. She keeps going, "We think you're currently his only *real* patient. If we can figure out **why** . . ."

None of this seems like it could be occurring outside of a dream.

". . . then we think you can help us take down *The Supreme Evil Being.*"

35

It's half past time to pack my classic Illadelph glass bong with some Ghost Train Haze or Acapulco Gold, something to lift the clouds of mundane mediocrity and exchange them for clouds of skunky weed smoke. I rummage through the old, dented black filing cabinet covered in a thick coating of dust. There are green file folders with labels marked *Hiro's Art* and *Hiro's Keepsakes* but really, I'm just looking for *Hiro's Hidden Bud*.

This storage unit for paper garbage used to be one of my several secretly designated marijuana storage spaces, along with inside of my old, blue Simpsons lunchbox and my Planet Earth DVD set. Places I knew Todd wouldn't stumble upon and Blaire wouldn't try to clean between cleaning jobs. The other spots have all been dry, and after being asleep for nearly an entire solar year it's tougher to find tasty foliage-shaped drugs without going to the old source or connect or plug. The man I know so little about but feel like I know everything about. The dreams you forget about so quickly.

IT STARTS WHEN YOU STOP

It's not at the surface of either the first or second story of the metallic cabinet so I begin going one by one, file by file, hoping to find something to break and roll and cough out.

Insurance Information.
Hiro's DR. Info.
Bank Stuff.

And then my busy fingers find something which is not smokable but **is** worth revisiting. It's a blue notebook, not anything out of the ordinary, 3 for $4 at Staples I imagine. On the cover is written 'Star Level Social Studies,' because fuck the other level fourth grade Social Studies classes, obviously.

There are some cartoonish aliens with big eyes and oval heads staring at me from underneath the heading. I'm not certain what exactly about this makes me momentarily forget about my get-high mission, but I do.

I open and begin paging through notes about ancient Egypt and Greece accompanied by doodles of dogs humping and teachers cross-dressing and sharing crack pipes. In between half-completed homework assignments and half-ass chapter outlines I come across something out of the ordinary. It's not an inappropriate sketch or an actually appropriate diagram or any sort of study guide. It looks to be a sloppily written script for a commercial starring Dr. Fox Viqar, in my hardly legible handwriting of course. Fun.

On the left side there's a crude drawing of an actual fox wearing *human* clothes, the cursive script reads, "Drugs are ok if they're prescribed by Dr. Fox Viqar." It's almost like the adorably sneaky-looking illustration captures our *real-life* Dr. Fox's strange, evil appeal.

On the top of the page's right side is where it begins to read, "If you have high cholesterol, your physician will have no problem prescribing you Lipitor or Lovastatin. Easy fix. If your son or daughter suffers from asthma, what kind of monster would you be to deprive his or her poor stupid lungs from their Fluticasone inhaler?!" I envision these words coming from his masculine mask of a face.

"HELL, anything from simple physical pain to complex emotional trauma can be at least partially solved with a bit of Codeine or Sertraline or scoobydoobuline. Yet here you are, a hardworking professional or shitbird degenerate, and no one has prescribed you any fat blunts of Jedi Kush or Blueberry Headband to help you deal with your generally annoying coworkers." I don't quite remember writing this, but the verbiage is definitely my brand.

"Continuously thinking about that girl, Sally, you can't be with for whatever reason? Dr. Fox has the answer, 10 beers and $60 worth of white drugs! The prescription is pre-written!" The perfect lines for Viqar's commercial debut about perfect lines.

"Never smoked DMT in the woods to learn about your most primitive desires in this world? It's because you didn't **need** it. You don't take an anti-inflammatory if you aren't inflamed. You don't go hang out and get chemo without cancer."

I imagine him over-enthusiastically selling drugs on a television screen like a used-car or new-stereo salesman.

"And who knows your body and brain and bowel movements better than you. Other doctors might tell you not to smoke black-tar opium to forget what year it is, those Nancies don't get it. I'll *diagnose* your hard life and cheating spouse and alimony payments."

For all I know I could have dreamt this first or possibly even heard him say these actual words. I certainly didn't do it on school grounds.

"What's really the difference between Acebutolol and alcohol and Clozapine and ecstasy and Allegra. Some are more legal than others, some make you live longer or die sooner, some make you fuck like a god or a guinea pig, but it doesn't fucking matter.

"If you want it, you want it.

"If you believe it, you believe it.

"If you need it, you **fucking** need it."

I don't know what ratio of humor and intensity I had intended for whatever we'd call this, but it seems to be leaning from one to the other progressively.

"In the late 1800s cocaine was a cure-all medicinal ailment. Alcohol was illegal in the United States in the 1920s. Where's the line? Seriously, show me the line that marks cultural appropriateness. Fuck what the masses say is illegal or taboo or unacceptable. If you know you're right, fuck the masses.

"If you want it, you want it.

"If you need it, you **fucking** need it.

"Show me the line.

"Show me the **fucking line.**

"Show me the fuc—" I turn the page.

36

"It's nothing like a cult."

Arina and I have been talking the last couple weeks. Not constantly, but consistently. She's sort of all over the place. It's exciting. She makes me feel my age, a reminder of my present youth. I don't know anything about Dr. Vee being the Supreme Evil Being or whatever yet. Arina insisted that she'd said too much already. She assured me she'd get me into their next meeting so I could *experience* it for myself. It sounds like a cult; she swears it's not.

Either way, it's been feeling like this meeting of witches deep in some forest or cemetery or underground fight club is never going to happen. Maybe she's putting off seeing me. Maybe she'll never see me.

Although our talking has been almost exclusively through text, it feels like she talks to me the same way she'd talk to someone far smoother and handsomer. There's debatably even been some mild flirting but nothing like the long romantic conversations I often envision us having. I usually stare at her messages for what seems like days, taking screenshots of the ones that make me smile, trying to plan and figure out my best course of response. I'm such a Casanova, obviously.

I open our text thread, hoping deep down there's an unread message from her. Doesn't matter what it says, a *Hey* 😊 would most certainly suffice. Nothing yet, though.

There must be nobody working up there in my personal broadcasting station either. I haven't heard from any of my scientific mystery acquaintances today. It's almost like I miss them, as if I can't tell whether I'm more or less myself when they're active.

I'm standing outside of the *Java Joint,* a cliché hipster coffee shop on the west end of town. They sell weed edibles too, though, so I bought a *Space Cake.* I love the present.

My cigarette is half smoked. It's a Camel Crush, and I decide to press the little blue button which turns the remainder into a menthol.

As I enjoy my minty cancer snack, I feel my pocket begin to vibrate; it continues to vibrate which informs me it's a call and not a text. Now I'm forced to multi-task between my phone and my tiny tobacco treat. Life is laborious. Cumbersome.

I look down and see the incoming call is from Pohang, South Korea, and I almost ignore it. For whatever reason, though, I decide to pick it up.

"Pay close attention. . . ." It's Arina, and although I'm ecstatic to hear her voice, I'm wondering if she's actually a 15-hour direct flight away in the Far East. I'm supposed to be paying close attention, though. Sorry, Arina my dearest.

"Please do not say a word. You are to arrive behind the Econo Lodge tonight at half past two. *Green Pea* and *Butternut Squash* will meet you and escort you to our discreet nearby meeting point. Wear only black."

The *legendary* Green Pea AND recently introduced Butternut Squash? I imagine I'm honored.

And the Econo Lodge, our towns most infamous . . . *Room Rental Arena*. A horny, crack-user's comfortable wet dream. Meeting BEHIND an already unsavory location? Escorted to an increasingly secret area? Yup, pretty sure I'm going to be murdered tonight.

I disobey her instruction of silence and turn her oration into a conversation, "Arina, this DEFINITELY sounds super sketchy, like some sort of cult or something."

She wastes no time.

"FIRST of all, I SAID not to say a word. Like, dude, I said **pleeaase.** Secondly, we remain unnamed until the *Ambassador* chooses your title. There is no Arina; I'm called Humble Tigress moving forward."

That's at least marginally better than *Butternuts* or *Butterballs* or *Buttered Biscuits*.

"Lastly, and most importantly, you big fucking baby, *it's nothing like a cult.*"

37

I arrive at the Econo Lodge parking lot at 2:32am. I'm wearing black work boots, a pair of slightly worn black dockers, and a black sweatshirt with the hood covering where my headphones would be. I look around for Green Pea and Butternut Squash, whatever that means. I see a shadow flash on my left side in the already black night. As I turn my head, I feel a warmth creeping behind me. In an outwardly cowardly fashion, I simultaneously jump into the air while turning all the way around.

"Our Ambassador kindly appreciates your punctuality in the future." The person condescendingly scolding me is a petite Asian in her late twenties. In the center of her throat where a man's Adam's Apple would be is a tattoo of a flaming frog with X's where its eyes should be. She has a Monroe piercing on the right side of her face, as well as a thin bar through her left eyebrow. She's very hot and very terrifying.

"I presume you're the yet unnamed then. . . ." she continues before turning her head about 30 degrees to spit on the ground inches from my feet.

I look around although I'm not really looking for anything, "Yeah, uhm, I suppose, I mean, I do have a name, though, it's—"

"Enough words without meaning, unnamed little boy," she interrupts. "I'm called Toasted Green Pea, and this is Butternut Squash."

Next to her stands a giant. Admittedly, she's very small, so it's not tough to tower over her. This man, though, seriously may have giant's blood. Half-man, half-god, or however you might create a monstrous, modern-day mega-human.

You can see he shaves his already mostly bald head, but his hair is starting to grow back a bit on the sides. He's got droopy woodgrain eyes and I imagine the strength of ten men. He doesn't look *gym strong*, but he looks *strong strong*, like his strength was gained chopping down trees and moving massive stones out of necessity.

Mr. Squash, looking down from way above, nods his head slightly. I reciprocate the gesture. There's no small talk, or medium or big talk either, they just begin moving, slowly, at first.

At the end of the cheap hotel parking-lot exists a small barrier about waist high . . . or knee high or shoulder high, depending on which of the three of us you ask. I follow while they climb over and shimmy down the steep grassy hill. They're suddenly track stars or ninjas or Olympians.

They're SPRINTING. What are they running from? I'm trying to keep up but I'm gasping, they're gaining distance. This wasn't supposed to be a race, or I wasn't informed of such at least.

Why is it that I even *want* to keep up instead of turning

the fuck around? Arina? Answers to the questions about my brain and my dreams and the universe? A break from the *boredom*, maybe?

Probably Arina.

It feels like my marijuana-lined lungs are going to pull my back and chest together for a smooch. I can't even see them in front of me. I'm slowing down but still managing to move forward. My quadriceps are on fire and my eyes are squinted, trying to see in fron—

"Aahhgghh! Shit!" The fucking branch-monster got me. I'm tumbling down a hill I can't even see, completely unable to brace myself for the series of bumps, thuds, cracks, and smacks that occur. When I'm finished bodysurfing down the rock terrain, I feel like I've been shattered into pieces.

Face down, I slowly make sure all the essential parts of my body are still in working order. I press my palms into the wet dirt, and no longer in any rush, begin to look forward and lift myself up.

¡FLASH! There's a faint orange light ahead: it's a candle.

¡FLASH FLASH FLICK FLICKER! ¡FLASH FLASH FLICKER FLASH! It's then that I'm actually able to see the dozen or so accompanying candles surrounding me, held by people dressed in all black, in the middle of the woods during generally agreed upon sleeping hours. Wonderful, and pretty much what I expected. Oops.

Scared enough to honestly piss in my pants, I say nothing. A few seconds pass before there's movement coming towards me from the right. It's Arina, thank god.

"Jesus, Rin, what the fuck is all o—" ¡CRACK! My dearest's closed fist against the southern end of my face.

Maybe I should have raised my hand?

Arina looks at me in a way she never has. Not an endearing way, if I had to guess. "I'm called Humble Tigress."

Fucking ouch, I think she's wearing a ring.

"No more words without meaning, not until you're named. Or, like, we'll never get anywhere."

Or rings, plural.

"Please take a seated position for now." Miss no-longer sweet or kind secretary crush insists. Maybe she was never sweet or kind at all. I mean, lots of people are sweet and kind when they *need* something, and everyone occasionally needs *something.*

I don't know if I should obey her command. Their command. I briefly debate running. As I look around, a raspy, almost grinding yet high-pitched new male voice echoes from behind me.

"I know you're thinking of running, new friend. I wouldn't do it. My *Travelers* know these woods quite well, and based on the blood exuding from your chin, I'd wager you don't."

I didn't realize I was bleeding. I bring my hand to where my beard would be if I could grow one, and I instantly feel the house red falling down onto my neck and sweatshirt.

"No need to sit down though, friend. It's time for you to become named! That way you can speak and such!"

I don't know what I've gotten myself into. I certainly don't want to be renamed anything, let alone one of these absurd names. Lobster Raisins or Origami Hippo. Does NOT appear that I have a choice though.

"Ok . . . yeah, sounds . . . good?" I reluctantly reply.

IT STARTS WHEN YOU STOP

Our newest speaker is slowly and menacingly circling around me while all of these NON-cult members silently stare.

"OH!" He seems to have genuinely surprised himself. "My oh my, where are my manners, new friend? I haven't introduced myself. I'm the *Ambassador* of our group of Travelers. I'm called *Goat Feathers*."

I'm truly not surprised at this point. Goat Feathers sounds about right.

"As for you, it's imperative for someone of your status to be named promptly."

My status? I notice that the Travelers are unsure what this means as well. There's suddenly darting eyes and neck movement all amongst them.

"Let's see, let's see," Mr. G. Feathers continues, "Hmm . . . you **were** tardy for initial screening **aan**nnd unable to remain without words, as if profoundly incapable of following directions. You also showed very minimal athleticism in the woods, mediocre at best. No offense, of course, friend. Hmm, wha**tt** shoul**dd** i**tt** be**ee**? . . . AH!"

His eyes light up almost literally. "From this point onward, you shall be called . . . *Deaf Turtle*."

Deaf Turtle? That's like the most Horrible Hip-Hop alias ever. I'm not thrilled. I hear the rest of the Travelers snicker as if their names are any better.

The Ambassador hears the muffled laughter and his demeanor instantly switches gears. He looks around slowly at his loyal comrades, "My beloved Travelers, this is no laughing matter. . . . I believe our fate may be in the hands of this Deaf Turtle."

38

In what feels like the preparatory phase of me being human-sacrificed by a man called Goat Feathers and his coterie of associates, I think of why. Why I'd allow myself into a situation like this at all. I go to a place in my headspace before she'd call me Deaf Turtle, before she'd break skin with her finger jewelry.

"Hey there. This is Arina calling from the office of Dr. Fox Viqar. I'm leaving this message for my good pal, Hiro Takafuji, to remind you of your appointment tomorrow, April 8th at 5:00pm." Her soft and sweet voice is an honest pleasure to my ears. I've already listened to this voicemail, I'm actually on my way to said rendezvous, currently just a few moments worth of forward momentum away.

The recording continues, "We look forward to seei—" PP PP FF FF PP, there's an assortment of taps and fingers and muffled words against the phone's speaker, until another familiar, but less pleasurable voice steals the

IT STARTS WHEN YOU STOP

phone spotlight.

"Hirosabi . . . can't wait to hang mañana, amigo. I've got some especially special goods for us." He sounds like a combination of drunk and zipped up and far gone from sanity. Marked in phone history at 2:29pm on a Tuesday.

The waiting room is incredibly chilly compared to the comfortable weather outside. Goosebumps appear on my bare forearms. I signed in; there were no other names written on the sheet, just a drawing of a porcupine done by the doctor himself. Unsurprising.

Arina returns to the scene with a mug of steaming coffee held in both hands. She's dressed appropriately for the office-tundra, with an oversized black knit sweater. "Oh hey, Hiro!" She carefully hustles over to her desk and sets down her hot beverage.

"How are you**uuuu**? Uhm . . ." She looks around briskly before continuing, and without waiting for my response, "Dr. Fox actually stepped out, but he should be back, like, any moment."

She's so pleasant and perfect to be around. I wish I had the courage alphas have to just start talking and not stop talking and not nervously just look at my hands. At this point, we've already become close enough that you'd think I would actually feel worthy of speaking to her.

"No worries," I reply. She probably smiled back after my awkward smile in her direction, that's just her kind nature. I keep looking at my phone, full of blatant nothing at all. If she looked observantly for even a few seconds, she'd notice my desperate attempt to save face. Instead I give my eyes an extended tour of the office I never pay enough attention to.

As I sit and wait, I start to notice several little intricacies about the room I haven't caught before. I've never had to avoid staring at a woman's never-ending eyelashes for so long. Every unique item seems to be in deliberation about which of two opposite realms to live in. An expensive, Alex Cooper rug with several noticeable cigarette burns. The Seletti sofa I'm sitting in currently, a lavish prize, covered with cum stains and alcoholic spills and sorted secrets.

I wait. I wait and I wait and I wait. Thank goodness Blaire didn't accompany me today. She would have, I'm sure, if she didn't have to go be a nanny for some spoiled rich kids for the duration of the day. Poor girl would have been devastated not to see the star of her daydreams.

Eventually, Arina's voice awakens me from my woken slumber of a space out.

"Hey . . . Hiro . . . HelllIOOooo . . . like, where are ya?" Back to real life, like I was smacked away from my tunnel vision of anxiety.

"Oh, sorry, I was thinking about . . . uhm . . . sorry, is Dr. Viqar back?" Even reciting these words in a journalistic fashion is painful. How much less smooth could an individual be with a female. I'm a cringeworthy television character come to life.

I expect to see a look personifying her discomfort with my lack of social skills, but instead I lift my head up to find a sympathetic look resting on her symmetrical face. Just a soft smile showing her adorable dimples. Genuine kindness radiates from her, almost something you can feel.

"Sooo, I called and texted him 16 minutes ago when you got here."

IT STARTS WHEN YOU STOP

Holy shit. 16 minutes? I legitimately zoned out for **16 minutes** to avoid speaking to or making eye contact with a female I'm interested in. Yikes.

"No response yet, I think **maayyb**bee he took off for the day. You were his last appointment, no surprise there."

I'm filled with annoyance. Truly, I'm already high and I didn't feel like speaking with him, or anyone for that matter, but my time . . . the valuable time I would have likely spent doing nothing, gone. I squeeze the wooden arm rest like I want to destroy it and fill my hand with glossy splinters. Another small nothing that I allow my mind to turn into a detrimentally serious something.

Why the excited voicemail yesterday if you're not going to show? You didn't HAVE to barge into MC Arina's beautiful, yet mostly scripted, voice message, I'm thinking. Frustration flowing and building and erupting. Pulsing with each heartbeat.

"HIRRROOO, ya there, sweetie?"

How many fucking times will I be woken up while already awake? Sweetie, that's something at least. Again, though, I feel soothed by her tone or verbiage or intonation. I don't answer, not with real words at least. I figure why start being a coherent human being at this point? I just sort of giggle in a way which admits my embarrassment.

"I'm hungry . . . " she says, smiling back at my goofiness. "And bo**oorr**red. Like, if he's done for the day, I think maybe that means I can go as well. Wanna accompany me for some food, Mr. Hiro?" I'm caught so off guard, but I feel like I haven't spoken an actual word in multiple forevers.

"Yeah I love food, for sure. . . . I just don't drive an—" It's like I try my hardest to say the worst thing, I couldn't ask for a better moment to be cut off.

"Hey, you . . . relax for a sec, okay? I know easier said than done but, like . . . try, for me." Try I shall, although *trying* to relax is like an albino trying to find melanin on the beach.

"I've got my Mom's car, and I know you have that $30 copay, at least. I fly you buy? Like, you come with me of course, and I mean . . . I do have money. Ugh, HA!" She's definitely a little goofy too and that makes me feel so sincerely comfortable around someone so objectively out of my league. Staring at my frozen, basically broken face, she continues, "C'mon, I just wanna order way too much drive-through without seeing their shame eyes when they realize it's just for one person."

I imagine she just felt bad, watching me drift away into my thoughts and agitation for what would have been a third of my session. She's basically the prom queen sitting with the nerdy new introvert at the empty lunch table. A candidly character-defining moment for Arina in my personal story.

I clear my throat the tiniest bit and give my best effort at direct eye contact. She has flawless skin like a porcelain doll, accompanied by just a few hardly noticeable freckles around her nose. The hairs right in front of her ears curl adorably and they make me smile. "Yeah, don't threaten me with a good time," I say as I decide I'm not too proud for pity company, not from her.

I try to slowly stand up from my chair, as opposed to leaping out of my seat in excitement which is what I'm more likely doing. She shuts off a series of lights and screens and fans as she walks around from the other side of the desk divider. When she finally reaches the side of the commoners here with me, she tilts her head slightly and opens her big brown eyes wide.

"Alrighty. You ready to do this thang?" She asks in an even sillier manner than seconds prior.

"I am." I decide to go out on a limb a little bit, "So, you wanna smoke some special appetizers on the way?"

She turns her head towards me while we keep moving forward through the parking lot towards what I've learned is her mother's vehicle. "Oh ok, Hiro, I see ya." She giggles. "The bowl is already packed for us in the center console."

She looks genuinely happy. I'm simply unprepared for this. I'm shocked I was even able to formulate the proposition, let alone her say yes. Leave it to me to turn a golden opportunity into a present, and plain rude, source of anxiety.

Several steps further, I notice I've gotten to the car door without tripping or stuttering or dropping a container of Flintstones vitamins. 'I know I should be thrilled, this is what I want. Stop overthinking.' Not the first time I've felt this manifesting self-sabotage. It's almost comfortable, honestly. It's not like I don't know what I'm **supposed** to think, it's just not **those** wheels turning.

'What if I take too gargantuan of a rip and cough and spit up like a toddler?' Unlikely situation, sure, but that's the usual film strip genre playing in my head. 'What if she doesn't think my weed is good? I mean, it is, but what if hers is a lot better? Even worse, what if it's the same weed from the same handsome source?' All are thoughts my unhealthy mind chooses to focus on. These brooding hypothetical situations are better than some of the others, at least. 'What if there are other sneakers in her car? Like, another dude's sneakers but 3.5 sizes larger.' Might just be a friend's or relative's or twosome she found hanging from a power line, but how could I know? How could I not wonder? How could I not worry?

I'm just a cute little puppy to her. A plaything. A furry friend to rely on when in need, but left alone to piss and shit on the floor when she's occupied with something more worthwhile. A pet. A pet that she'd never, or should never, consider a source of sexual stimulation.

I manage to grasp and pull the car door handle towards me. As I sit myself down and feel the hot leather on the skin jacketing my bony elbows, I try to stay focused, despite the foreign voices and my own inner voices and the cheesy radio voices to foreseeably come. I look at her, she smiles again, and all of those voices are washed away.

39

"Our fate is in the hands of the Deaf Turtle," the Ambassador says.

Do turtles have hands exactly, is my first thought. All of the surrounding Travelers look shocked, and at least several look appalled as well. I don't blame them; I still don't know anything about what's going on here, deep in the woods surrounded by mostly strangers in ninja attire.

The Ambassador realizes this I think and continues, "Let me back up a little. You've been well acquainted with our most Humble Feline, and you've been escorted here by Toastiest Green Pea and Butternut Squash. Allow me to introduce you to *Caffeinated Sloth, Small Yellow Boar, Salmon Wings, Fluffy Russian Hat, Hairless Wig,* and *Crystal Bunny Man.* We are a group called The Travelers. . . ."

Those sure do seem easy enough to remember.

". . . We've come together through more than *exceptional* circumstances. Each of your unique experiences, abilities, or knowledge represents pieces in our grander puzzle of truth. You don't know it yet, but we all share a bond deeper than any horoscopes would match up or online dating algorithm could compute. We're all something like soulmates and blood brothers and enemies and old lovers, because we've all seen it or heard it or felt it, the *presence*. I KNOW you have. I know a lot about you, in fact. The coma, the vivid dreams that have been lingering afterwards and always, and I especially know about the voices you've been hearing. . . ."

I feel violated yet intrigued.

". . . You see, Deaf Turtle, I was also *supposed* to die, but here I am. This *change of plans* occasionally causes . . . malfunctions of sorts. For whatever reason, my malfunctioning has given me special sight into the minds of others suffering. That's how I was able to begin assembling our group."

"Malfunctions?" I ask. He grins a little and nods his head back and forth the tiniest bit.

"We're just science projects, MR. TURTLE, but I already know that you already know that."

40

So how many alcoholics prior to AA know they have a problem? Some, not many. I imagine it usually comes to some emotional intervention or serious screaming match or sexually unprotected all-time low. Not to be confused with a sexually unprotected all time *bottom*.

No one *really* binge drinks, it's just social. The several drinks per night, several nights per week, type of social. And alcohol is a drug, apparently,

SO...

Any one or two or three time a week cocaine user is NOT an addict. Seriously. And *how dare you* assume something like that! It's just occasional.

The victims in domestic abuse cases usually had it coming, in their eyes. They just pushed a little too hard. It's just personal, impossible to understand from the outside.

Point being the person with the problem, in a variety of cases, is often times the only one that isn't aware of the situation. I understand schizophrenia is similar. I had figured I should read up on the subject, just in case. I suppose you don't see people waiting patiently with their IDs and insurance cards to politely inquire about their delusions of grandeur or their overall Diagnostic Statistical Manual chart either.

Usually everyone figures things out when someone is dead or arrested or riding cross-country on a stolen bicycle. *I'm certain I'm not imagining things* says the schizophrenic says the drunk says the addict. I mean, I'm pretty sure, but how many times have I said I feel disorganized?

Paranoid.

Delusional.

If I WAS to tell anyone about the current going-ons in my life, I can't imagine they'd believe me easily. Let's see, there are the post-coma, apparently non-human voices I hear, which of course give valuable information to a mysterious group of strangers in black named after items found primarily at Whole Foods. We can't forget about the all-knowing, all-powerful supermodel of a supervillain, Dr Viqar, my psychiatrist. Then the finale, our plan, our responsibility, to *get rid of him* and save mankind. That part's my favorite.

Swallowing all of that information is easy, just like swallowing a big red brick is easy.

Do I even believe me? It's tough to say honestly. On one hand, there's seriously **NO** part of what I just said that **doesn't** sound like a schizophrenia forum. I may as well start wearing a tin foil hat to go along with all of my other stereotypical behavior. Wait, actually, would that . . . no. See? I could definitely be losing it.

On the other hand, **FUCK THAT**. I *know* the voices

are real, they have to be. Plus, the Travelers . . . we can't ALL be nuts. A shared psychotic disorder? A Folie à Deux, if you may. I know this term because the internet knows all the diseases you may ever acquire throughout several degenerates' lifetimes.

Or the Ambassador could be some master manipulator? I've heard about people like that on TV and movies and horrifying old newspaper articles acquired quietly from the public library, but I've always figured, 'Psh, no one could be that good,' Which I still think . . . I think.

I mean, could he be **that** good? Unlikely. He couldn't have just pieced everything together, said all of the right things. No, he *knew* things.

What if I created all of them in my unwell mind? All of their faces and bodies and voices. All of their attitudes and sex appeal and first impressions.

Would it be better or worse, given the circumstances, if I were just sick and all of this has been in my head?

Seriously.

I don't even know.

It's either I'm completely, all the way insane or there's some alien fax machine located behind my eyelids. An old, broken satellite that everyone thought didn't work anymore. That only I understand and only Mr. Ambassador Man knows for sure that I can hear. So he says.

He says a lot.

Most people usually say a lot.

41

The *Ambassador,* Goat Feathers, leads me into a discreet cabin in the middle of the woods. It's probably a murder cabin. His group of silly named accomplices follows closely behind us. Probably silly named murderers.

They all begin lighting candles and lanterns, some with Bics and some with Zippos and some with matches. All equally fire-inducing.

Once the partially furnished room we're in is adequately illuminated, Mr. Feathers whips his whole neck sort of ridiculously in order to look at me—it seems painful. Then he begins to slowly walk towards me.

"I'll need to do a full reading," he says.

Goat stands about five feet and five inches and is probably about 70, 71 if you ask a Korean, but looks to be in good shape. His full head of hair is a mixture of mostly white and grey with dark patches next to each ear. His eyes are dark brown but have grayish blue rings that surround the darkness. One more loop of mystery.

IT STARTS WHEN YOU STOP

Just a footstep's distance away from me and still looking straight into my eyes, he presses his right palm into my chest while making a fist with his left. It's calming at first, but then I *feel* his acquired power. His malfunction. And I mean, quite literally, I feel it.

It's a few deep breaths followed by the static electrical shock you get sometimes when you touch a doorknob, except it's lasting second after second while I'm stuck in the wave of current. It's Blanka or Raiden or Pikachu at full blast, until it's done, and it's like there was never any pain at all.

I watch his expression turn from happy-go-lucky and confident to distraught and overwhelmed in an instant. He looks back up, towards the whole room.

"Oh, dear friends, it's what I've feared most. . . ." Ambassador Goat Feathers hardly manages to say. The whole room tenses up and gives their visual attention fully towards the Ambassador's words to come. I'd love to just ask outright what he means but I figure the chances of me getting slapped or punched or kicked by one of these Traveler goons is high, so I just wait.

Before any of these eager beavers oh-so-curiously inquires what the bad news is, Mr. Feathers continues, "It sounds like we're just the beginning of this grand horrible experiment." He looks truly speechless. Defeated and older than just a second ago.

I decide to take my chances and ask, "I'm sorry to interrupt, and for your unfortunate news, but you know **this** from touching my chest?"

At this point, as long as a lie he tells me makes some amount of sense, I'll be satisfied.

"Well, for starters . . ." He replies, "This isn't **MY**

unfortunate news, it's **OUR** unfortunate news, and that includes you, Mr. Turtle."

The group of Travelers standing and sitting around us gives me a collective '*DUH*' look.

Feathers continues, "And yes, I essentially just read every word of every sentence of every page of your brains lifetime diary. Everything you've ever seen, heard, or experienced has just been transferred into my endless inner filing cabinet of Traveler information, with a lot of the nonsense filtered out, of course. Oh, and fairly important to mention, because knowing specifics seems quite important to you . . ."

I wouldn't exactly say I'm focused on *specifics*, but sure.

". . . this sometimes includes things you don't recall. Dreams, subconscious or repressed memories, even your own births! Ol' Butternut over there was a big one."

Mr. Squash grins sincerely like the lovable simpleton he likely is. Green Pea rolls her eyes as if they've gone through this on more than one occasion.

"Don't worry, the unfortunate situation didn't occur during your birth, and it certainly had nothing to do with Blaire because she seemed to have healed up *just fi—*"

"Sir!" Arina, sorry, I mean Humble Tigress, politely yet assertively interrupts to save me from developing irreparable mommy-issues.

"OH! Apologies, kind friends. . . ."

Wow.

"There was a conversation that took place during your long slumber . . ." My heart suddenly begins to race, I'm not sure why. ". . . I regret to inform all of you, lovely Travelers, that this conversation took place between some higher up controllers or conductors or conduits to our own demise, and our person of interest, Dr. Fox Viqar." Something that actually isn't TOO much of a surprise, at least given Tigress's prior investigative-style diner questioning and my muddled mind.

My right heel is tapping against the floor at twice the pace of my heart. The whole group of *us* looks at our self-proclaimed Ambassador waiting for what comes next, our heads nodding slightly while our eyes say *Please, do tell.*

Well, except for Butternut, he's legitimately looking at his hands. Is he tripping on something fun or is he truly mentally challenged or just fully disinterested in this conversation?

"You see, Turtle, the Travelers and I have known for some time that Fox has been playing an integral part in our lives. All signs point to him, we just couldn't make our move, or any move, really, until we had all the pieces. Now that we do . . ."

He sort of just drifts off into his own thoughts or plans or desperate prayers. I see the whole gang of us scurry back and forth at each other with our eyes. Honestly, for an Ambassador of some freakin' chosen group, *gifted* with communication with gods or spirits or talking grapes, this guy is kind of a bozo. Suddenly, I feel like I'm fogging in and out a bit.

"YES. I know," He continues, "I feel your eyes, I'm still here, friends. I am! Just tough for me to find the words. . . ."

-¡**KEEEEEEEEEEE**!-

Pieces begin to form in my head.

Migraines with pictures.

Headache movies.

"Itt'z juts thot he'ss wantz twoo axetends—"

Sharp pains pierce throughout my head and my heart as the lights flicker and I close my eyes and collapse to the floor. I re-dream and remember and re-live some conversation from another lifetime. There's real conversation happening around me. Ambassador Gropefingers flaps his jaw at my fellow cult loyalists but there's only sharp pain flowing through me, so I fall down and just remember. Against my will . . . I remember.

42

I'm here a little bit, but mostly I'm not. It feels like I've returned to my coma. Visually there's just amusement park mist . . . but there are voices, three voices. One of those voices belongs to our dear and familiar Fox; the other two voices are not English or French or Chinese or Gibberish or sign language. It's the aforementioned grunts and Chili-Wednesday bathroom stall noises that make sense in my head. The way a little mumbling, drooling, hardly lingual in the first place toddler human is understood by his or her birth-givers.

For some undivulged reason, my unconscious mind sends word to refer to our new headphone heroes as *RawzGulup* and *Banshee*. For now, though, I'm electing to note them as *Sizzlebiscuits* and *Dirty Pants*. There's nothing at first, just the intersecting paths of warm and cool air to create fog.

Suddenly there's a ¡**SCREECH!** followed by mumbles. Cloudy distant mumbles that seem like they're slowly getting closer until they start to sound like fragments of words. They eventually work together with one another.

"Thank you for your time, I truly appreciate you making time for this meeting."

That was our something-tagonist speaking. The medical doctor who shares recreational drugs which I love with me extremely frequently. I'd want to say protagonist based on just that; Blaire and any other woman without visual or truth-telling impairment would surely agree based on their limited knowledge. But he's definitely not that. Not that at all. But how antagonistic exactly? Not enough pieces presently.

He waits for a second voice to chime in. He doesn't wait long.

"Not a problem, FFOGH HHAUXVQUAR." An accurate pronunciation of the Fox's name, I imagine. Our current speaker, Sizzlebiscuits, continues to answer. "We appreciate all of the hard work you've put in during your extensive term in human form. You must be using all of those silly appendages with ease and grace by now!"

Sizzle Bee blurts out some sort of grunt. I think it was a laugh. It sounds like when Donkey Kong jumps on a lizard monster's head. Maybe that's actually what's happening. Lizard monsters make as much sense as anything else.

The third voice, Dirty Pants, enters the conversation and immediately sounds more stern than his preceding peer.

"*Yes, Fox*, **QUITE** some time you've been lingering on that odd and sad planet, almost as if you've grown fond of them. You do know your interspecies sexual misconduct policies, don't you?"

Sizzler Baskets interrupts his nowhere near overly

polite business associate and does his best to keep the situation calm. "What I think my colleague means is that although we appreciate your contribution to the *SCIENCE CORPS*, asking for this many repeat terms on one planet is no doubt . . . rare."

Dirty Pants reinserts himself into the conversation,

"What I MEAN is what I said. What the fuck is in it for you? There is a plethora of higher paying local jobs available. Other more advanced relocation opportunities as well. It's not logical, it's borderline . . . *human!*"

"Gentlemen, gentlemen," begins our always, ever-so-charming and most familiar voice. "I *assure you* it's logical, at least once you understand fully. You see, I don't want to just extend my stay on this silly blue planet. I want to expand the project into something far greater than it's ever been."

There's a brief couple seconds of silence during which I imagine the three of these people-creatures having a serious exchanging of facial expressions, skeptical glances, and judgements.

"While your initiative is certainly most appreciated, I'm not su—" Sizzlebiscuits begins to say until being cut off by his big jerk of an associate.

"This is an experiment, Fox. We are in the **MIDDLE** of an experiment, we're not changing it and starting over and losing all of our data because **YOU** are having some whatever time of your life crisis."

If I know 'Fox,' which I'm truly unsure about, actually, he's not giving up just yet.

"I'm afraid your request is deemed illogical. The experiment has long commenced," Sizzlebiscuits adds.

I bet he's so excited he finally got an uninterrupted

word in. Back to our antihero, though.

"Please, gentlemen. Allow me to further explain! I don't want to *change* anything necessarily, just widen the scale. Ponder, ruminate, reflect. What do we **really** utilize the *control humans* for? To compare, right? **BUT**, we already have a basically infinite database of numbers and figures on their species at this point.

"We have the resources, we're fully staffed, and I am doing my very best to do something in between begging and insisting to remain in my direct supervisory position. What better way to truly understand the weak and inferior feelings of these dummies than to *infect* all of them and see what transpires. Every last fucking one of them.

"The Chinese, mass super-depression. Indians, 100% level 9 Bipolar. Hungarians with Borderline Personality disorder. All of em! HA! A wave of Philippino grandmothers becoming SO obsessive compulsive out of what seems like *nowhere*. Canadian high school students' teenage angst will continue to increase at full blast until their brains burst into bite-sized pieces.

"It will be so beautiful. Every light-eyed Lithuanian and sun-tanned Arab could have super fun Alzheimers.

"Fuck them.

"It shall be glorious. The entirety of Morocco will be inflicted with Anorexia. Hundreds of millions of pounds lost collectively.

"FUCK THEM.

"Please, you handsome devils.

"**FUCK THEM**, for science."

43

My eyes snap open like rubber bands being flung from a child's fingers. I'm still in the same damp room with the Travelers. Goat Feathers is telling them all what I just re-experienced. My thoughts echo out of his lips. I feel his words. All through my body, I feel their sensation shimmying down my extremities.

I've got the chills all of a sudden. Goosebumps. I look at the Travelers' reactions. I see them thinking what I'm thinking. Digesting that information. EVERYONE in the world will be mentally unwell.

I mean, sure, is anyone truly *well* mentally ALL of the time? But we're talking grander scale here. Suicides and crime and unemployment will skyrocket. Drug addictions and alcoholism and no-call no-shows. A problem that experts will be too lethargic or lost in delusion to deal with.

Even the drug dealers and beer distributors that should prosper in such impoverished times will lack the motivation needed to make sales altogether, or else need to sell only odd numbers of bags standing on one foot to make the bats stop flying through the store. One big giant shit-show full of tears and death and body odor.

I see *Salmon Wings*; he looks deep in thought. I watch as his face becomes more and more appalled, second after second, as thoughts compound in his shaved bald head. He's presumably in his mid 30s, with a pirate flag tattoo on the left side of his hairy neck, and a full and fierce beard that hangs around nipple length.

He's attractive in a petrifying way. I suddenly imagine he and the Toasted Green Smokeshow getting married and having beautifully intimidating Gerber babies. He starts breathing heavier and opens his sapphire blue eyes wide, waiting to figure out what he should say or do.

I turn my gaze to *Small Yellow Boar* and *Hairless Wig*, sitting tightly together on the gaudy, 70's style orange and brown love seat. They're hanging on to the Ambassador's words and holding on to each other's hands. Both of them are petite females, young, probably in their early 20s. One is brunette, the other blonde, definitely neither is hairless. I definitely don't recall which is which yet.

The brunette boar or wig or whatever has a full bottom lip that is hanging open as she sinks into the *reality* of Goat's words. My previous dream's retelling. The room's collective expression is dismal and deep in thought, as it should be.

"I'll kill Dr. Viqar," are the words which exit my mouth. "I'll do it." I surprise myself by saying this. Am I capable of killing someone, or some*thing*? Even if that pseudo-person is basically the Anti-Christ. Is this even a 'plan' worth suggesting? I definitely just volunteered myself, so I better hope so.

Everyone in the room seems equally as surprised as I

am. Their eyes are hopscotching around from one to another. Quiet mumbles to each other create an audible hum in this cabin in the woods. Anticipated-murder-OF-me cabin to planning-a-murder-BY-me cabin.

"Quite brave of you, Turtle, but it will surely take all of us. Would his plan continue even if he was dead?" asks our Humble Tigress softly, but to the whole room. I look to the Ambassador, as if to get his 'permission' prior to speaking.

"I don't think we can be sure, but the other two voices did offer a lot of hesitation," I say. No one is arguing with me. "If Viqar is out of the picture, then perhaps things will at least remain at our current homeostasis. We're aware, we can work from there."

Salmon Wings makes his voice heard for the first time in my presence.

"What other choices are left? We know we can't *reason* with him. We have no way to reach his superiors and plead for our lives. We can't hit what we can't see. In other words, we can't fight THEM, but we can fight HIM. I say we take Viqar out and hope to at least keep things maintained as they are. Ambassador?"

Mr. Feathers doesn't look thrilled that homicide was such an immediate option. Or maybe he's upset his genius leader self has no better solution. After a moment of contemplation, he looks around the damp, dingy room and feels everyone's moods before responding.

"At this particular moment, friends, although he's probably of much more informational use **alive**, this seems to be the action in our best interest. Although we never WANT to kill any living being, we've also known that we may end up having to terminate the doctor for a while now, him being the Supreme Evil One and all. Anyone opposed to the execution of Dr. Fox Viqar?"

Silence. An empty hush. Not a single face indicates opposition. Some seem more excited than others, but all are either on board or are too scared to be the brave one willing to interject. No hands raised. No voices heard. Nothing . . . silence. I think we all hoped someone had something better, but we don't.

"Well then, it's decided."

44

There's been so much nonstop stimuli occurring around me the last couple days. Essentially no ceasefire. It's been inconspicuously easy to steer clear temporarily of the ants, the automatic negative thoughts, trying to create the worst possible situations in my head. Arina even found a moment to discreetly and guiltily apologize for hitting me, which also helps. It almost feels like I've been living the life meant for me. Not so much thinking, just acting. Ant and snake gym.

I think of how I've surely disappointed one of the scarce people in my life not worth disappointing. My impromptu and unannounced departure from regular life may feel something like a vacation to me, a freeing experience, but it could never feel that way to an uninformed and likely unhinged Blaire. I didn't mean to be such a no-call-no-show, not to her, it's just that everything in my life seemed to be escalating so quickly. Seems to still be escalating so quickly.

With my established and acknowledged track record of

mama's boy, there's no chance she thinks I'm just away, safe and sound. Rebellious but remaining fastidious about my in-home routines, I'm beyond doubt that the instant her initial feelings of fear and worry arose, there have been no moments of improvement. I'm rarely able to unravel my own tangled psyche, but I know her.

She's unquestionably hung several thousand missing-person flyers next to various roommate wanted ads and minimum wage career opportunities and a poster searching for missing Maximo Montalvo, the 8-year-old big-eared giant English lop rabbit. At least it's better than the countless hours unavoidably horrifying herself on the internet. Facts and statistics can be tough to stomach sometimes. Real horrors are the most terrifying. A shiver flows familiarly from head to floor.

I begin treading in dangerous mental water. What if the search parties and the prayers and the borderline-threatening voicemails to the worthless or at least ineffective detectives all fail? Total yield of zero results. No heroes finding Hiros. What might she do next? Who could she desperately seek for any shred of last-gasp collaborative aid?

Oh no. What if she went to Viqar? Fuck. It's not inconceivable to think she may have run out of other options and gone to him in hopes he'd seen or heard or received carrier pigeon of me. **Fuck**. I knew I was acting inconsiderately, but it was for the greater good. Her greater good. Our greater good.

I know that between all of the several negative-thought-wheels turning, there's got to be **some** sense of rationality left inside of my busybody buttinsky brain. It tells me this is only a slim likelihood, an automatic negative thought taking control. I know this already. There's just . . . something else . . . a feeling. A strange sensation that this is some sort of cerebral truth being sent over from Goat Feathers inadvertently. I'm caught inside of a bad thought's shadow. An inexplicably villainous object passes but its oversized shadow lingers.

Along with the yet unwarranted feeling of mental privacy invasion, there's a much meaner thought loitering on its side. A negativity pulsing through my bloodstream. One hardworking heartbeat at a time, I know it's a shared feeling of impending downfall.

Not something we can see. Not something that our tiny or perfectly proportional or cartoonishly embarrassing ears could hear. Just a bodily sensation, at first, until the smell. The smell, it tickles my nostrils, excites them. Entices them. That familiar odor tugging on my nose hairs is similar to that of the charcoal mist which occasionally waves over from unfamiliar houses on nice days. One minute too long on the grill or powdered sugar propane or just another negative thought come to fruition.

The smell becomes all too prevalent. Heavy. Real. The visual flashing of Traveler movement around me stirs me back into the surrounding world. I inquire internally if I may be having a stroke. I've heard of metallic or chemical smells being related, and it does smell like burnt toast. But no, my entourage is fire drilling for a reason. The smoke from above, on the first floor, has begun seeping down heavily, nowhere else to go.

I run with the rest of them the best I can, but every step up feels like a hundred full bong rips of ash launched into my chest. One seven-inch rise at a time, I struggle and fight and gasp, feeling the whole time like I'm drowning. Like I'm under the ice. 'I need to get there,' I keep thinking through the stairwell and engulfed first floor. Aesthetically glorious and physically painful and mentally empowering. 'I need to get there,' I keep thinking. Not for me, but for the Travelers around me and the passengers on the flight.

My body happily and instantly collapses upon making it outside. I doggedly dig up the strength to lift myself up. I notice we're all still here. She's still here. As I footstep backward, we all gaze at the wicked flames tearing apart our travel-housing-unit just a couple splinters at a time, coughing up carbon monoxide collectively.

I notice something on a grey and white and black birch tree a hundred or so paces away. The static from ear to ear, the ground crackling apart beneath me. It looks at first like your average adolescent public notice of love, a heart with his and her initials carved inside of it. Something lets me know there's more; somehow, I need to inspect further. I can't help but move forward, I have no choice, I'm just going.

The dust from the tree's new carving is fresh. You can still see it dissipating into the air like a lemon twist's zest above a scotch on the rocks. There's an intricate bulletin made up of calligraphy residing between the defined lines of a cartoonish heart.

'Silly fucking dreamers. Hopeful morons with the clearest of death wishes,' it says. Another dusty pace forward. 'You could never end up a step ahead, you should know this. You **do** know this,' I read. Oh no.

Everyone behind me continues stumbling forward, one by one as they catch their breath. 'I found myself an unparalleled souvenir to ensure we don't wait too long to have a nice little get-together.'

I want to just close my eyes and go anywhere else. I already feel who, not what, his souvenir is. I shake my head and clench every developing muscle in my body, all without intention. I can sense the footsteps behind me halting abruptly one pair at a time. I force myself to continue scanning the life-altering landscape alterations. The wooden-canvas hieroglyphics seem to be on every tree in sight, like Fox had a group of delinquent art students on an odd field trip. Needless to say, not in the approved budget.

'Fox and Blaire.' It's the middle of the night but the message is as clear as day, in between the delicately yet intently drawn lines, with blustering orange and yellow and red behind me. Everybody wishes they were a psychic until it's just all of your worst dreams coming to fruition.

Next tree over. 'HA HA, HA, HA HA.' Sick goddamn motherfucker. Next tree over. 'Fox and Blaire.' NO NO NO NO NO NO. Next tree over. 'You're simply outmatched.'

45

I'm enthusiastically sinking into a curiously exotic couch in a new but fairly neighboring setting. We left the Lincoln log cabin and piled into black matching SUVs. My feathers were pretty ruffled to notice for sure, but I believe two jet-black Nissan Rogue SL editions. The car ride seemed to last several Earth's orbits.

We still seem to be in the middle of nowhere, just at a top of a beautiful mountain kind of nowhere and less like a creepy axe and body storage cellar. We're staying in what essentially is a wilderness mountain resort. We came, at least partly, with the intention of making our grand world-saving homicide plan, but in the time spent so far there's been minimal headway. Ambassador Goat Feathers disappeared off the face of the Earth, it seems like. I have learned a great deal about my fellow Travelers, though. *My fellow* Travelers.

Our almost real-life pirate, *Salmon Wings,* for example, is an artist. Not like a regular thirty-something year old millennial or millennium ago artist, working at a gallery but still waiting tables at Olive Garden, or maybe literally picking olives from a garden. He's a particularly peculiar artist; that's why he's a part of this damaged goods hero squadron, in fact.

Apparently, some years ago, he broke into a drug dealer's home with what he referred to as his 'militia.' He paints us a vivid picture.

"Yah that guy Sunny was a real dirtball, ya know what I mean? Selling to little kids, messing with local businesses, and not even being discreet about the wild-ass hooker ring being run from his basement. Dead ass, his basement. I know well enough people need their drugs and broads, trust me, I know, but be an adult about it, no need to be all up in everyone's face about it every second, ya know what I mean?

"So anyway," he feverishly continues, "Our plan was to run in when we knew he had the *least* number of goons patrolling. We had a guy on the inside, *Rock*. Besides Rock, we were willing to smoke any fool in our way."

Salmon Wings makes me wish I could be a savage when I grow up.

"We're not animals, though. We were gonna sell everything we got responsibly, out of our elementary schools and into the bar district and local colleges where they belong. Take our share of the money but then give back to the community, ya know? The Youth Center, Tom's Coffee that does open mics on Wednesdays, OUR Parks Department. Hell, we talked about renting a spot for those *working girls* to share. Stuff that **helps people**, not just Sunny's friggin shine, ya know?"

He's steaming. Something like a hardened hipster Robin Hood. Also something like a man with a sword who'd raid your boat and take your goods and rape your women.

"Anyone we took out would have been inconsiderate lowlife scum, so fuck it, break a couple eggs. Things are going smoothly, we get in, we get the stuff, and we only have to silently take out one piece of garbage in the process. On the way out, though, one of those motherfuckers came out of a closet or something swingin' a baseball bat. Old school lookin' wooden one."

Pretty sure he doesn't mean coming out of the closet metaphorically. That'd be a whole weird thing.

"Shit was seriously crazy. My guy *Cali* took him out REAL quick, but . . . son of a bitch caught me nice in the temple before Cali's bullet flew between his eyes."

Hm, I'm thinking maybe we let this wild Salmon lead the Fox murderin', given he's a legitimately experienced madman and all.

"I don't remember, obviously, but these dudes told me it was like a fountain of blood leaking from my temple. They thought I was cooked for sure, but they grabbed me anyway. They might seem, and often act, like degenerates, but they're good, loyal degenerates. They were **stumped** when I opened my eyes in the getaway car. Chato told me I better get the stains out of his whip. Psh, piece of shit old Civic."

He laughs; he's been laughing most of this story.

"Anyway, after that, I started having these NUTS dreams and when I woke up, I *HAD* to recreate them: the people or scenes or events or whatever. I used to do tattoos for a living, but I never did anything like this. Obsessive style, ya know? Watercolor, chalk, crayons, didn't matter. Doesn't matter. More detailed than anything I've ever done before."

He looks at me really seriously out of nowhere. I look behind me to make sure I'm not standing in the path of someone more relevant. He starts nodding his head and looking down at his pocket, then me, then his pocket, then me again.

"Shit, well, here . . . this should give you the idea."

He reaches into the chest pocket of his frayed, sleeveless flannel shirt and takes out two crumpled up pieces of paper, of *trash*, and tosses them onto the distinctive triangular glass-top coffee table sitting between us. I pick them up. One actually is trash—a receipt from *Pita Planet*.

"Oops, sorry about that." He chuckles. Too naturally lighthearted, it seems, to ever possess malintent at his core.

As I uncrumple the other piece of thermal receipt paper, he adds, "Oh, yah, keep in mind I drew that a few nights ago at this falafel building, before I met you."

. . . A falafel building.

The picture that Salmon Wings vomited through his fingertips is only about the size of a 3x5 notecard, the ones the smart girls used to study for social studies in middle school. It's **incredibly** detailed, though, and equally disturbing.

It's done in red pen with a cross-hatching pattern used to create the background. It's three familiar characters in our story thus far. In the distance, amidst all of those miniature red x's, is Dr. Fucks Viqar, standing with his arms folded and a grin that shows his toothpaste commercial-quality choppers.

Next up is yours truly. I'm on my knees in agony,

probably screaming or begging or *praying* for vengeance against the Fox, because the third figure is someone well known to me. She's someone that hasn't stopped trying her best, despite how horrible I've been. Despite how horrible I still am sometimes. Despite how horrible I may become.

In this drawing given to me by Salmon Wings, done prior to ever seeing my face, or hers, there she is on the ground. Only half of her face is visible but it's still easy enough to identify even on this tiny, horrible masterpiece. It looks like there's some sort of explosion coming from my direction. She's attempting to allow the flames and fumes and smolder to pass over, but I fear they'll engulf her.

I feel the way I look in this Traveler's dream doodle. Furious and bitter and pathetic, reaching towards this wonderful person. This person whom I could always tolerate most in our frustrating world. The family matriarch. Mother Dearest. My Beloved Caregiver, Blaire.

NO . . . Nope . . . Nope. Absolutely fucking not. This will **NOT** be **FUCKING** happening. I **won't** stand for this.

"Sorry man, who's the chick? I was hoping it was just, like, an old babysitter or somethin," says my accidentally anger-eliciting illustrator.

I hardly hear his words. I'm drowning in my own feelings, overwhelmed all of a sudden. My chest feels clammy . . . tight . . . heavy. My limbs are tingling just enough to notice it's happening. I manage to re-crumple the photo in my hand and let it fall onto the beautiful, brand-new mahogany floor. I'm the one steaming now, shaking with fear and rage and disbelief.

"This picture isn't right," I struggle to say like a shy

child with a speech impediment. Salmon or someone else says something but my head is too filled with fury to hear anything.

"I won't let this become true! I **WON'T LET IT!**" I scream while someone else is speaking. I've lost control.

It's then that I hear a brief, high-pitch shriek, and everything seems to flood over me. My throat is swollen like I was bitten by a Tiger Snake or a King Cobra or a Brazilian Wandering Spider. It's as if I can't speak or breathe or swallow. The familiar panic feeling where you're CERTAIN you're going to die. You're supposed to know you actually won't, but inside, you never do *actually* know.

I sit, or more like fall, onto the Italian leather couch to try to get myself together. I feel motion on this luxury sofa beside me. It's Arina, I mean Fierce Jungle Kitten? She reaches towards my face and, given the prior face slappage which took place, I can't help but to just close my eyes. She puts her hand on the back of my neck gently, and it's instant. Everything is gone, it's . . . incredible. Unbelievable, almost as if . . .

"Everything is fine now . . . like, I know." My beautiful Arina whispers softly and sweetly. It's as if I've heard it before, "That's the gift I received when *my* brain malfunctioned."

4b

"You could NEVER bother Fox during his meditation time. . . ." Arina tells our group of Travelers during one memorable Viqar brainstorm in the discreet preparation mansion. Even during full conversations dedicated to murdering our nemesis, I can still hear how she swoons for him a bit.

". . . You'd never know what was actually going on in that office Tuesdays and Thursdays between 10:30 and 11:30 AM. Not at first, at least." My guesses would be naps or porn or extraneous drug use.

With all attention on her, I look at all the eyes watching her paint her word picture, all those new eyes connected by new faces to all those new ears listening intently for any valuable information they don't already know or haven't already experienced. Fluffy Russian Hat literally has a 5"x7" ringed notebook ready to jot notes, as if when his secret weakness is revealed it'd be something you would forget. Could forget, even.

She continues, "I had come to expect just about

anything walking into that room. Refusing to respond to regular knocks or polite requests had become a precedent, so when there weren't patients, which was usually the case, I'd learned to just walk in. I'd enter somewhat carelessly up until the first time I saw him shooting his bow and arrow indoors with an almost empty handle of tequila hardly hanging on to his fingers.

Weeks later, I walked in, more cautiously, to find him fully clothed, smacking an exceptionally large Asian woman's naked ass with a splintery wooden paddle. Among other questions, I wondered mostly about how she got in without me seeing."

Butternut Squash's bozo eyes, sleepy and simple, still focused on our speaker's story.

"Then there was the time, well, one of the times, that he, like, **really** scared me. I heard a shout followed by a laugh and, what can I say, I'm curious, so I slowly opened the door and peaked my head in."

Salmon Wings' pellucid blue eyes, intent on relating this story to his own scattered sketches.

Green Pea's dark, mysterious eyes, ready to uncover the keystone which cracks the case.

"The room was dark except for an adjustable desk lamp and some out of season Christmas lights near the blinded window. Once one shoulder passed through the doorway, I felt his strong hands grab me by my waist and pull me inside, shutting the door behind him."

My irrefutably sad, jealous brown eyes, focusing on the wrong fragment of the story.

"He carried me like I was weightless to the dimly lit desk and dropped me, almost threw me, really!"

Bunny Man's heavenly blue but sorrowfully aged eyes

invested in her verbiage. Just soaking up wisdom like one of those things Blaire bought from some maniac on late night television was supposed to soak up liquid spills.

"I looked up to see a white table, so I thought . . . false! Same old beautiful brown circular Heritage coffee table as always, just covered in cocaine. Like, drenched in it, seriously."

Attention is so incredibly valuable; I can't believe how unmoving all of these pairs of eyes are. Just stuck on her. Everyone living in the moment, focused on the words entering the atmosphere now.

Not before.

Not after.

"I looked up at him and realized for the first time that he's wearing what I believe is referred to as a banana hammock . . . and it's, like, leopard print."

It WOULD be leopard print.

Douchebag.

"His face looked like shit, well, relative for him at least. His eyes looked like he hadn't slept, like, ever. There was a combination of both fresh and dried up coke and all varieties of accompanying snot surrounding his nose and upper lip. His bottom lip was chapped and bleeding and he had the creepiest smile I had ever seen him wear. I didn't know what was going to happen."

We know she makes it out alive, so there's already less suspense than an average episode of *Game of Thrones*.

"It seriously looked like he had gone swimming in blow, you guys. The white powder was all over his chiseled chest and photoshopped abdominal muscles. UGH, his body was almost frustrating to look at."

Russian Hat's observant hazel eyes noticing my

perturbed brown eyes all green with envy.

"I thought I may actually be in a very real amount of danger, and then he just asked me, 'Want to do a couple lines with the ol' jefe?' I scrambled. I asked him to let me run and grab my purse quickly, and then I sprinted out of the room and out of the building for the remainder of the day."

That last part of her story seems like it may contain some untruths. Scratch that, it **for sure** seems like an oddly placed, bold-faced lie. Something about her intonation or demeanor or some indescribable feature changed. Or, then again, maybe just my brain being a jerk again.

Plus, I could have sworn she was momentarily fearful of being molested or murdered, yet when she found out he just wanted to share drugs, and **THAT'S** when she wanted to bolt out of there. Oyster house levels of fishiness. Didn't she basically just orgasm talking about his sculpted body? She probably would have licked all of the white residue off of his torso.

"ANYWAY, the point is, all of those times, never once was the door locked. Not once! I would have bet **aaan**ything on an open door back then. Yet, I came to find out that there **were,** in fact, actually some certain off limit times. Those Tuesday and Thursday slots were truly non-negotiables. I learned simply through performing my basic job duties . . . trying to transfer calls during 'business' hours, clean, bring him coffee or alcoholic day beverages."

I wish my brain didn't always jump to the places it does. Instant worst case scenarios, usually involving lies and deceit. But it does, and has, and all I can think of is a trembling Arina following around Dr. Fucksandwich Jafar like a goddamn puppy. An adorable puppy, except horny. My jealousy levels and self-loathing ratings must be turned up sky high. Lots of juicy data for our mystery scientists up wherever they are.

"So like, at that point I just sorta **haaa**ad to know, ya know? I decided to try using one of those babysitter cams where the fuzzy little stuffed bear watches everything that goes down in your living room and ensures the safety of your children or whatever. I figured anything too cutesy would have been thrown away or turned into a bong somehow, which admittedly would've been, like, so cool. But I managed to find some super weird five-foot-tall giraffe with a video recorder in between his tiny eyeballs. It cost me $119.95 plus tax and shipping, but I thought it was the most up his alley."

It's sweet that you know so much about him, is what I'm thinking. Of course I don't vocalize that, but Ms. Hat still looks inquisitively at me while eight other focuses remain on our drop dead gorgeous speaker.

"Luckily, I'm pretty sure he was tripping on acid or mushrooms on the Monday morning I decided to present him with this odd, unwarranted figurine of a gift. He looked at it as if it were *real*. A live baby giraffe gifted to him in the office. He stared and petted and talked to it for like, several moments. 'Hello, animal friend of Earth. I will not eat you like these illogical **true** beasts of Earth. You are not the one who should fear my kind.' Knowing what we all know now, these silly sentences make more sense. At the time, though, it felt impossible to determine whether it was anything more than LSD speaking. And like, plus, a lot of Indians are vegetarian!"

Pretty certain that's at least mildly racist, but possibly

some validity, I suppose. Certainly a bit naive to ignore those or any other ramblings, though, I'm thinking.

"So anyway**yyss**s, it did in fact work like a charm!"

She does her picture perfect, borderline ditsy smile that I so thoroughly enjoy. Everyone else hunches forward an additional inch. We've finally gotten to the good part, after all.

"Well, the bulk of those private office hours was seriously just him sitting Indian-Style on his cleared off desk, not covered with a sheet of snow at those allotted times. His arms shooting straight out in opposite directions, eyes closed, stuck for the whole *session* without his chest even moving slightly to signify he was still breathing.

"So, nothing Fox could do would be surprising at this point. The weird part came from the recordings themselves, like, plural. The same odd coincidence that made it not a coincidence. As I watched him reach towards opposite walls with opposite hands, clearly straining his body yet appearing calm in the face...."

The face that's his and not his. The face they designed or stole or made in some sort of create-a-player, video-game-style, body-choosing-machine.

"... There were ... sounds, in all of them, not just one. The first and the second and the third and I couldn't watch to see how many more, not at the time. Like one and two and three conversations in a frog-person language."

Frog people doesn't even sound farfetched at this point. Maybe all of our problems can be blamed on the goddamn frog people.

"It went back and forth and the video would go all haywire too. Like, the waves of air you see hovering above flames, or shimmering refractions near asphalt on hot days, except only surrounding Fox, and only while that foreign amphibian-like voice was present. It was almost as if..."

¡SLAM!

Everyone, myself not excluded, jumps a little bit, some more than others. That Toasted Green Superfood may act like the hardest out but that fit Asian martial artist almost literally jumped out of her skin. I mean, not literally.

Gross.

"I KNEW IT!" The source of the previous slam comes from the hands of our interrupting speaker crashing down against the coffee table, knocking over Butternut's orange juice and Boar's hot tea. My black coffee stays intact, actually. Perhaps truly it is just a coffee table?

"Well, I suspected it at least! Seriously, friends!" a still very amped up Goat Feathers shouts, trying to convince everyone, or probably just convince himself, that he already knew whatever it is he definitely thinks he knows now.

"Suspected WHAT, exactly??" Everyone thinks but Sloth says, or more accurately slurs.

G. Feathersburg slams his same right palm as before flat onto the table once again. He's shaking his head and smiling and looking up into the air. "My goodness, of course," he continues, "it was the only prospect that made any sense!" He's shouting and tossing his arms around like an Italian inflatable tube man in a manner that makes it tough to know whether he's thrilled or pissed or something different altogether.

"There was just no way for me, uhm... US to be sure, but now..."

IT STARTS WHEN YOU STOP

He is a truly peculiar man.

Bunny Man has had enough foreplay, "Damnit, old man! Sure about WHAT!?" He is definitely younger than Mr. Feathers but is by no means some youngster in his prime.

"You're all so impatient," Feathers replies. "When we've already been waiting for so long, my anxious friends. Really, our lives collectively have all just been strategy games of *patience* and position against our controllers . . . against Viqar."

Cult speech.

"Please tell us, Mr. Goat!" our beloved short bus passenger, Butternut Squash, whines. A man so monstrous, so big and scary, yet so innocent, like a scared little boy. Now everyone's eyes are no longer focused with interest, but with frustration. Annoy the rest of us? Sure. But you don't upset somebody's *special* younger or older brother, no matter how physically intimidating they may be. Our Ambassador's face is also a portrait of dismay, but his grouchy mug is simply due to the fact that as soon as simple Squash gets involved, he MUST abide.

"UGGHH, OK, you needy ladies and gentlemen. What I've suspected, and what it seems to be, is a practice referred to as Interplanetary Communicative Meditative Telepathy."

I feel as if whatever that is may only be referred to as such by Goat Feathers. Truly odd and wondrously brilliant and very feasibly a cult leader guiding us to our deaths.

"Not making it a whole hell of a lot clearer, baby," Hat comments in her Caribbean dialect.

"Apologies once again then, friends. I.C.M.T. is essentially a mental cellphone, a way for two brains to connect and converse from any distance . . . I **knew** it," Goat begins to explain.

It seems like maybe my brain is an accidental receiver in this super bizarre intergalactic data plan.

"The phones at the supposed 'therapy office' have been tapped since Tigress's second week working with Viqar, his home even before that. Not much of a task, really, considering he leaves his stately mansion unattended, front door open, with mounds of assorted methamphetamines on various tables and accompanied by dozens of full acid sheets. Be assured without any doubt, he is a mad man."

My whole life recently has seemed like I tripped and fell and swallowed one of those delicate sheets containing 100 individual hits of awe-inspiring LSD. Nothing seems more possible or more make believe than anything else.

"Needless to say, I suppose, but mail and email and each and every social media and dating platform were closely monitored as well. Trackers on all of his luxury automobiles. His Dodge Tomahawk V10 Superbike, a $500,000 motorcycle, was definitely being tracked while it flew at over 100 miles per hour in residential areas. Everything I could think of, including the most desirable and willing Miss Humble Meowmeow, our beautiful female data-extractor." Willing. My stomach churns and I know my face is crying jealous disgust. Arina, under normal circumstances, might blush and smile or maybe do the complete opposite based on that series of compliments or judgements. But this time, she's much too curious.

"But Ambassador, I reported this to you immediately after it took place. Why didn't you—"

"**BECAUSE**," he interrupts again. "It just wasn't . . .

enough before. UGH. You couldn't get it, my lovely friend. Not all the pieces were there yet. And you simply cannot solve a puzzle without all the pieces."

47

We're in the basement of Goat's Palace, most of us. Its interior is fit to host an extravagantly elegant ball, although I'm not certain if it's Ball Season. There's a surplus of snack food, tons of fatty salty goodness covered with cheese or filled with cheese, many of which end in -ITO. There are cookies and brownies and chocolate-covered pretzels.

More awesome things covered in awesome things, I remember that Tootsie Roll given to me in Fox's office. Given to me before I knew he was the enemy, and then providing that same information to me in an ironic fashion.

Most of us have either enjoyed some amount of aforementioned refreshments or consumed them simply for pragmatic sustenance. Not our new pal, Caffeinated Sloth, though. He's palpably full from all the pills.

Our host is off once again putting together the pieces of life's grand puzzle or drifting from one Traveler's brain to another or jerking off into a sock like a teenager.

IT STARTS WHEN YOU STOP

Salmon Wings is out back teaching Fluffy Russian Hat some introductory yoga positions. Their loss—we have Jenga.

Maybe Salmon is looking to swim into the pants of Miss Hat, at least 20 years his elder. If anything, though, I'd say it seemed the other way around. Regardless, we have a legitimate *Space Invaders* machine in here.

I'm comfortably seated in some giant leather chair. It's coffee brown, and its back extends at least 18 inches higher than my tallest dark hair. Green Pea walks past me, continuing to survey the area, and I watch her as she heads towards the dusty closet door tucked away in the corner of the room. She slowly and curiously opens it, and inside of this garage-sized space in the wall are dozens of classic board games I probably would have played previously in life if I had a real father or any sort of fake father that hadn't sucked so seriously hard. I wonder if he would rather play board games or be dead, because he is way dead at this point.

Green visually scans the vast options of both luck and skill in front of her as I faintly hear Fluffy and Salmon return across the room. She blows some of the dust off and surely regrets it, as it immediately erupts back in thick cloud form and she begins a 10-20 second coughing spree. The sound of her struggling lungs grabs the attention of Crystal Bunny Man.

He and Caffeinated Sloth had been playing a Heads-Up Texas Hold-Em Tournament for cigarettes, because we're in prison, apparently. It looks like Sloth was living up to his name and just mentally drifting into some tropical forest, so I imagine he isn't too distraught when Bunny Man throws down his two cards on the table and **sprints** over to see what *trouble* Green is getting into. I can't say for sure he even noticed. Half asleep on his branch, slowly chowing down on twigs and leaves and fruits if they happen to be born next to his bed.

"FUCK! Is everyone OK?!" bellows Bunny Man.

He's in an uncomfortable panic, alert and aware of some unseen danger but unable to prevent our harm.

"Oh god, you gotta get down!" Bunny yells as he *lovingly* tackles Green full force to the ground. All eyes in the room are watching and most of their respective bodies are darting over to make sure everything ends up kosher.

It only takes one stern but patient smack in the face from Green for Bunny Man to look up with confusion and slight embarrassment and surely some facial sting.

"Aw man, shit, sorry about that," he says in between rapid, shallow breaths, "PTSD must have kicked in a bit I guess, smoke coming from a closet takes me back to somewhere I don't like to remember. Seriously, I'm . . . I'm really sorry."

Green hops to her feet without using her hands. "All good," she nonchalantly replies. Wig and Boar both kneel down to pick up the board and single game piece that escaped from the accompanying box which landed near their four tiny feet. The piece isn't a little wiener-shaped one like from *Sorry*. It's not a tiny Parcheesi poker piece either. It's big and ancient and shaped like a heart.

I still couldn't tell you which of them is which and the more time that passes, the more I'm committing to never asking. The skinnier hot one picks up the old wooden heart with both hands while the skinny hotter one flips the board over to its intended position. On it there are no properties to purchase or triple word scores or plastic hippos full of appetite. Just letters and numbers, a Yes and a No, and a Goodbye without a Hello.

"Oh, cool! A Ouija board!" yells one of them or both of them or perhaps just one of their phone apps.

Fluffy Russian Hat steps towards them and looks at the almost definitely hand-made square and its alphabet written in faded black cursive script, "Actually, it doesn't say Ouija on it, so this is a spirit board, and I recommend you stay away from that thing. It's evil."

Wig, I think, the one with the blonde highlights in her brown hair, not the other way around, looks to her more sun-kissed friend or lover or who knows and makes a face denoting, 'Ew whatever . . . who cares, lady?'

"I'm serious," Fluffy continues, "We've got enough on our plate already without trying to talk to spirits, don't we?"

I don't necessarily disagree about staying away from it, but only because it's the only thing here that isn't an actual game. I mean, there's Mouse Trap. That's probably like six full minutes of rodent-hunting recreation. Or we could even play that game, Cee-Lo, the one high-school kids and high school-kids play outside of the 711 on Market Street. I'm not exactly certain about the rules but I'm sure it's played with dice . . . which we have, just saying.

Fluffy Russian Hat is a roughly 47.81-year-old woman who has aged quite well, if I had to guess. I'm not an expert in Jamaican anthropology or history or language so the best I could say based on the few sentences we've exchanged is that she probably hails from Black River, found in the St. Elizabeth Parish. Just a random shot in the dark though, really. Well she ¡**storms**! out while managing to fit in a warning stare for each of us in the room presently, everyone except Goat Feathers. We all need an absent father figure, right?

The blonder of the **W**ig **B**oar **S**uper **B**est **F**riend **F**orever **C**lub insouciantly says, "Yikes, um, what a bummer. But like, they sell them in stores, so like, how bad could they be? There'd be like, lawsuits and stuff."

My love, Arina, might have a slight problem with excessive use of the word *like*, but nothing like this stereotypical, blonde, bozo beauty queen.

Brunette Boar, we'll go with that for now, she says, "So yeah, guys! Let's see what the 'boogie spirits' have to enlighten us with?" She does jazz-fingers which would rightfully infuriate Hat. "If anything, we already have Hiro's brain-phone or Salmon's artwork full of *sight*, and also a lot of super pretty watercolor flowers." Her face and body language perfectly mimic her partner's.

Butternut Squash comes from nowhere with an empty coffee table as if he had been concealing it in his wallet. He has the unorthodox strength of a centaur.

"Not to mention the dreams we share, and used to share with her, and maybe still do share with, our bestest friend in the entire universe, the third point of our triangle . . ." Brown Boar says as the opposite colored Wig places the board on the table and shushes her with her right pointer finger pressed against her Persian Plum colored lip-stick mouth.

Dream sharing. I wonder if the triangle mentioned was a love triangle; even for *bestest friends* they cuddle a lot. Maybe they're 'Intense Friends,' those beautifully inappropriate and complicated friendships.

"I'm gonna go get some air, guys," Bunny Man interjects. "Have fun, lemme know if you find anything noteworthy." He still seems a bit shaken.

"Psh, bummer, he's kinda hot," Boar says as he walks upstairs.

"Ew, babe. . . . He's like 100," Wig replies.

He is not in fact 100.

The most beautiful amongst this group of beauties, at least in my opinion, makes her presence more known than it's been in quite some time, "Everyone else down to see whether this board is cursed or blessed or nothing at all?" She asks the group.

Cursed or blessed or nothing at all, that sounds like the about me section of my nonexistent dating profile.

There are 8 of us in here I think, and we all nod our heads or mutter different versions of the word yes. Well, except for Butternut. He claps his hands together up by his chest making his elbows look silly, if that's a thing. Green rubs his back and smiles at him the way a new mother smiles at her first perfect little miracle sleeping soundly. I'm itching to understand their dynamic.

We all huddle around the table that Butternut easily tossed here for us, the dense Beech wood table that you'd never believe was picked up by only one man. There's a lot less action and a lot more looking around to see who's actually used one of these before. Just as everyone is about to admit our collective inexperience, Caffeinated Sloth slightly awakens from his zombie-dopehead-like state.

"Uhm, yeah, we all put two fingers on the magic heart and start on the G, then we move it around in slow circles to uhm, warm it up, ya know? Uhm, while we decide what we want to ask it."

Way to own that one, Sloth, we all are probably thinking but not saying. I am at least. What DO we want to ask? Several options come to mind instantly, as do multiple out loud questions from different Traveler's mouths.

"Where is Viqar from? Is there any way to stop his plan?" one of the female voices asks.

I'm more wondering whether Wig and Boar do sexy time together, and what kinda of *shared dreams* they were talking and shushing and not talking about.

"We all gonna end up dead?" Sloth mumbles. It's a fair inquiry. He continues, "If so, uhm . . ." He giggles, "might as well say fuck this noise, right? Let's score some fire and party until the end of days, right?"

I'd rather know how this junkie's power works exactly, something about being a finder of people like us. People like cult members or secret heroes or delusional morons.

"Ever since I got hit by that car leaving my plug's crib, uhm, the only thing that lets my body overpower my brain is hard drugs . . . top quality and lots of em. Otherwise I just start walking or running or whatever, I get all tired and shit, and I have legit NO idea where I'm going, right . . . except it's like I do because once I see the right random person I've never met before I just stop dead. . . ."

He shakes his head and makes a crooked mouthed face, "Maann, that whip shoulda just taken me out, right? Because deadass, I'm not trying to just go around finding people like some damn radar machine and then just have the world end anyway. We all gonna end up dead? Uhm, yeah yo, ask that."

As soon as his informative urban soliloquy ends, his face goes back to being a droopy cartoon dog. Sloth's wasn't the worst question in the world but it's pretty grim and not necessarily helpful, that's what our shared expressions indicate at least. At that moment, Butternut's elbow-pad-sized right elbow, full of hair and dirt and dried ashy skin, knocks some small item off of a tan and ebony credenza standing between us. I'm not even sure what it was, a set of keys or a phone or a miniature golden crown, doesn't really matter.

I begin kneeling down to pick up aforementioned mystery item but my attempt at common courtesy does not go as planned. My knees buckle in pain, a reminder of my flight down the hill on my way to meet my current star-studded cast. Perhaps a proactive act of hostility by our Ouija spirits warnings against this whole ordeal.

To prevent myself from collapsing pathetically onto the floor like a sympathy-invoking elderly woman, I use my non-rugged, non-blistered, delicate Asian right hand to gently catch the area just next to Butternut's said elbow armor. I may as well have given him wet willys in both ears, extra wet, because his body strikes a more-than-startled pose. It looks like his brain is going to burst like a Gusher candy through his nose when he picks me up above his head from underneath my armpits. Now's his big moment to begin spewing the first real tangible words I've heard come from his never-quite-closed mouth.

"Generalized anxiety level 8.812! Sexually specific anxiety level 9.131!" He's looking down and away with tears filling his eyes. "Bipolar tendencies 8.186! Self-efficacy 2.311!" It's me that should have tears in my eyes, with his zucchini fingers crushing my ribs. His vocal debut will surely be painfully memorable for me.

"Professor!" Green Pea yells to the giant Squash in the nick of time, probably just seconds before my potentially gruesome death. He looks to her as if that was their S &

M safe word and drops my already bruised and worn-thin frame on the hardwood floor.

Professor? New question for the spirit board. He keeps vomiting terms from the Diagnostic and Statistical Manual of Mental Disorders, paired with precise numbers attached, presumably about yours truly, but quietly now and into his hands.

"Schizophrenic tendencies unavailable, coping abilities 3.116, borderline personality disorder ratio 7.889..."

He keeps going and going, more and more quietly with each exhausted utterance. T. Pea rubs his back as silent tears run down this sensitive, confused giant's face. She turns to the rest of us onlookers with a kind resolve, "So, for real, how about we see what this magic board is made of?"

48

The human brain is a work of art. I'd tell you to *think about it*, for instance, but good luck doing that with a broken encephalon. We're all aware of what a super-computer lives in our heads, in charge of literally everything we do, capable of growth and change and incredible creativity. So, I won't list every task or problem-solving opportunity that we encounter from ambitious morning erection to bedtime night-cap, just a few particularly interesting points.

Your physical health and your mental health may seem like two distinct personalities, but actually they're bunk-mates and they're super clingy and they essentially share feelings. It makes total sense that depression is so often correlated to higher risk of heart attack, weakened immune system, trouble with memory or decision-making, fatigue, and a Spaghetti Eddy libido. Brain sad, body sad.

So, this almighty jerk of a brain basically does whatever it wants, but what's interesting is that it's actually even busier while we're asleep. You may not remember your dreams, but there's more activity going on behind those eyes of yours when they're in the closed position. The issue, though, is that the most frequent feelings manifested in our sleep-films are anxiety and anger and sadness.

Or maybe you battle bad dreams and know how to nix nightmares by practicing the art of lucid dreaming. There's a whole subculture of people attempting to control every detailed second of what happens while they beauty-snooze. Flying through the clouds and firing their bosses and fucking whoever they damn well please. Every imaginable pleasure.

Naturally, once you've mastered this real-feels sleep videogame, it makes 100% sense you'd just want to dive on in, maximize your pleasures asleep and minimize your struggles while awake. Ugh, being awake, what a drag. Well there's a drug for that, pal.

Throw back a few Dimethyltryptamine before nighty night and you'll just sleep and sleep and sleep. Dream and dream and dream. An infinite cycle of REM bliss where you live like a fucking god.

Now if our brains are powerful enough to make us go from sick to well and they are lifting more brain weights while we're asleep, then why is it so farfetched to imagine the tangibility of *precognitive dreams,* the magical future-telling gypsy dreams. We've all had them, some odd dream-event turned odd waking-state deja vu event in the middle of the day. Maybe some of us have them a lot more than others.

Maybe some of us are more naturally gifted or doomed. Cursed or blessed or nothing at all. Abraham

IT STARTS WHEN YOU STOP

Lincoln had a premonition dream about his own assassination. Too bad that kind of thing wasn't scientific and still isn't—he may have done more than just mention it to one other human being. Shoulda, coulda, woulda.

Going along with this theme of super interesting pseudo-science is the idea of the collective unconsciousness, a concept coined by Swiss psychologist, Carl Jung. An easy example is when you think of an old friend you haven't spoken with in ages and then they inconceivably give your phone a buzz just hours later. Putting your thoughts into the universe and hoping for the best.

Voodoo Bokor.

Magical thinker.

Gullible cult-following idiot.

Science experiment.

Complete hallucination.

What if those ideas of the collective unconscious and precognitive foreshadowing and lucid dreaming are not so far apart, but actually intertwined? Everything is connected, after all. You and me and he and she and Dr. Seuss and a bag of potato chips. Everything.

There have definitely been cases of individuals having shared dreams, down to every descriptive detail. But it's not every day that strangers stroll down the sidewalk asking about others' dreams, so generally there are only a few instances we'll ever find out about. Spouses and siblings, particularly twins, are fairly common but still almost always assumed to be **at least** an exaggeration, if not complete horse shit. Really, the only empirically accepted examples, no surprise, are those dreams shared between therapist and client.

Why would that, why **could** that, take place? A damaged person sharing an identical experience with their healer. Their lives may be direct opposites the vast majority of the day but for the few moments while that defining dream took place, they were without difference. They were kindred spirits or soulmates or sock-puppets for some alien society.

Maybe the sad sap seeking help just *wished* desperately enough for their therapist, the person whom he or she has been spilling their guts out to, to actually be able to understand. **Really** understand.

Or it could just be a bunch of fancy scientific terms simplified to mean they were in the exact same *Brain State,* assuming that being at said brain frequency would result in completely identical brain content. It's like some type of algorithm mankind hasn't discovered yet. Or again, maybe they're all just make-believe dogshit lies.

49

"Well damn, looks like we all learned your mental neurosis baseball-card statistics just now. Like, pretty rough scores . . ." Arina says to me just after I've been released from Butternut's animal-like clenches, in a harmless way, of course. My imagination tells me she's starting to sound like me at times.

". . . even more intense than most of us here. Well, a lot of the categories at least, things must have been really tough at times."

We're all circled around the table our Butternut Monster so kindly hurled here for us to call upon some spirit or alien charlatan spirit or pseudo-science non-spirit.

"Yeah, that was . . . something," I reply. She smiles at me and my body feels warm and nothing else matters at the moment.

Brunette Boar, or was it Brown-Haired Wig, shit . . . I thought I had it. Well the talkative of the two takes control of the textured brown, chipped, heart-shaped game piece.

I believe Sloth's closed mouth had mumbled that it's called a *planchette*, and there's a clear glass circle in the middle so that you can read the letters on the board or die of a fatal atrial septal defect or feel true heartbreak.

She holds the planchette with both hands in front of her perky chest where her real heart and presumably real breasts live.

"I don't mean to, like, be Miss Bossy Pants or anything . . ."

I see Caffeinated Sloth actually look to her pants as if he should find some indication of her bossiness on her tight black denim jeans. He seems disappointed when no such flashing sign is found. 'That body tight, though,' his face conveys after a second's glance.

"It's just that . . . well, like, Paulina and I . . . **I MEAN** Hairless Wig! Hairless Wig and I . . . our duo used to be a trio. The dreams we experience together used to have a third brain involved. . . ."

Either the hottest or weirdest three-way ever is what I can't help but instantly think.

"We need to ask her why." She consciously stares at nothing, her eyes beginning to swell with wet signals of sadness. "That needs to be our first question."

At that moment we all instinctively know it's time to move our index and middle fingers to the shared planchette. Fourteen fingers together is a bit cramped, and thank goodness, because Arina and I are basically holding hands intimately. I mean, I'm also sharing skin-space with Butternut and I'm incredibly worried he's going to smack me against the wall like a handball and tell everyone my suicidal probability rate or something of that nature, but I'll still take it.

IT STARTS WHEN YOU STOP

Everyone is quiet, silence all around us for the first time since silence was invented probably, or at least since I was surrounded that introductory time in the woods. Bad Boar Beauty breaks the silence.

"Tasha, you there? Can you hear me?" She asks her friend or sister or lover whom I assume is extra dead. If anything, I think we should be asking 'You there, Devil or Zombie Jesus or Alien Pop Star?' But that's just my opinion so no big deal.

We're collectively moving this supposedly mystical or possibly evil planchette in slow circles counterclockwise. No one would argue our participation in the movement up until this point.

It's the bombshell blonde, Hairless Wig, who speaks up now, "Tasha baby, sweetie, my love, are you ther—"

SHHWWIHH, the planchette slides directly, no layovers, to YES. Oh shit, I'm wondering if we actually . . . did we . . . **no**.

Wig, whose name for certain has recently been exposed as Paulina, continues, "Why baby? I know you were sad, ok? Just like us. Just like ALL of us, alright? But . . . but what are we supposed to do now?!"

She's full-force sobbing, tears falling from her blue, probably Eastern European eyes. More snot running to her lip than seems possible from her tiny nose. We wait for something to happen. We're breathing deep, all of us holding gently but firmly, ready to move or be moved, exchanging quick glances at one another in between staring, ferociously awaiting any hint of ghost message.

I begin to think the YES was a fluke, I'm pretty certain we're all in discreet agreement, ready to give up but humoring Blah Blah Boar and Paulina Wig Wog for a moment mo— SHHWWIHH, our fingers are thrown somehow to the letter I. SHHWWEWW, we all move together to the letter M. SHHWWIHH, SHHWWEWW, SHHWUHHW, SHHWWIHH. This magical or unreal or possessed planchette is flying almost too fast to read S-O-R-R, it's happening so quickly none of us have a chance to even question whether this is really happening, Y-L-O-V-E-Y-O-U.

Our fingers SHHWWIHH nimbly and SHHWWEWW boldly together. Most of us are in awe, attentively absorbing our first experience with the supernatural, well, MY first experience at least, can't speak for anyone else. Wig and Boar weep in uncontrollable disbelief, not knowing exactly what they're supposed to feel. P-L-E-A.

Anger that she's gone without proper enough explanation? SHHWWAHH. Happiness and appreciation for the fact they get to *hear* a friend say she loves them one more time? SHHWWIHH. SHHWWEWW. SHHWWIHH. S-E-S-T-O.

Motivation to fucking **ruin** whoever decided to be the final straw in her *heavy* life. Desire to fucking DESTROY the *person* who's going to be thrilled to perform the same dirty deed to as many young women, and I assume men, as possible. A *NEED* to REMOVE FROM EXISTENCE the motherfucker with plans for oh-so-much more. SHHWWIHH, SHHWWEWW, SHHWWAHH. P-F-O-X-K-N-O.

My eyes are too busy watching what I'm pretty sure my hands are not controlling to notice if everyone else's eyes and hands are doing and not doing the same. They've got to be. SHHWWAHH, SHHWWEWW, SHHWWIHH. W-S-2-L-A-T-E.

IT STARTS WHEN YOU STOP

Miss Psychic Ghost continues for just a touch longer, one more series of inexplicable SHHWWIHHs and SHHWWEWWs. B-Y-E-L-O-V-E-R-S-N-B-I-G-B-R-O.

Wig and Hat take a brief intermission from their tearful late goodbyes, hopefully filled with unorthodox feelings of closure, to look at each other with determined inquisition. Before they could both even think the words 'Big Bro,' a voice from near the doorway utters, "Tasha?"

The sad, shaky voice belongs to Crystal Bunny Man, who's just walked back in with Fluffy Russian Hat to retrieve some forgotten mystery item, possibly one knocked over by the Squash.

"Damn, so you really are gone."

Shock and confusion and overwhelming sadness fill the room even further.

"I didn't even know any of you guys knew her . . . shit . . ."

Silence. I guess nothing should be surprising at this point. I'm dumbfounded, we all are, it's a dumbfoundation, in fact.

"Everyone said you were dead when you disappeared but I just thought . . . I don't know . . . **fuck!**"

Standing next to a distraught and generally unstable Bunny Man as he paces to and fro, Fluffy hesitantly takes one step forward. "I realize this is less than ideal timing, to say the least, but Miss Wig . . . Miss Boar . . . we need to talk about your dreams. . . ."

We all give her looks which express, 'Dude, couldn't this wait?' Our *new friend* Crystal Bunny Man is grieving over his sister, gone at about half of his own age, presumably. Plus, his PTSD has recently been proven to be the bona fide article, after all.

"All of those sad peoples' dreams that happened long ago or haven't happened yet. Programs and machines and waking up drenched in sweat, you're still sharing these dreams, but it's with me now, my girls . . ."

Holy soap-opera *small-world* occurrences, Batman! Really though, what the fuck, I'm thinking. Is someone messing with anyone? Is everyone messing with me?

". . . I've always had them, strange dreams, but ever since . . ." Between her beginning to blubber hysterically just a second ago along with her already thick Jamaican accent, it's becoming challenging to make out her words all full of feelings.

". . . Ever since my beautiful son, Steven, well . . ." She sniffles and wipes away some of her tears and nose tears and she has our full attention whether she wanted it or not, ". . . Once he *left* us, it's felt like my dreams have some inexplicable damn connection to something I can't reach. . . ."

Wig and Boar, all four of their light blue or hazel eyes are surrounded by long dark eyelashes and are filled with tears. They're nodding their heads, showing her some sort of unique understanding, some special bond like only twins or triplets or experimental error-induced dream triplets could ever REALLY understand.

"It's you two, I can FEEL that now, please help me understand more," she continues. She pleads. Hardly a dry eye in the room, she walks hastily into a serious group hug with her new wonder-girls.

Our magic healer and my personal fantasy, the Tigress, slowly creeps into their warm embrace. An outsider might assume she's being rude and intrusive, but then he or she would see multiple tears begin to evaporate into the air and almost everyone's tear-ducts begin to dry. Not hers, though, they become red and puffy and yuck.

Those observers, they'd see some sort of feeling almost like acceptance coming from Hat and Wig and Boar. Not from our handsy uninvited hugger, though. Nuh- Uh. Her face looks like she just threw back several Polish-wedding-sized shots of vodka on a hot day thinking it was water. Instant green face.

The healing experience that IS their embrace comes to an end and there's some sort of closure in the air. I mean, not so much for our more humble than ever Tigress. Closure in this situation meets her in the sense of a finale of her current consciousness. She takes one step, and then another step, and then in what seems like slow motion, she buckles to her knees and falls to the floor. Goodnight and thank you, my martyr princess.

50

It's been a whole morning, daytime, evening, and a few hours of nighttime now since we've seen our Ambassador for more than a flash. Our group of mental artists and spirit healers and inter-dimensional dreamers that have spoken so generally highly of him, bonding over billiards and 90s video games. Human GPS systems and victims of lightning strikes or falling animated anvils all jumping out of their seats during life-changing games of Street Fighter II Turbo. A formerly groundbreaking scientist and his most brilliant student playing Mario Kart 64 against a *gifted* writer whose mental illness led him to homelessness after his military service.

Who's who is time-consuming and unnecessary and admittedly a bit lazy at the moment, but we'll specify as it becomes pertinent, or maybe we won't. The point is we're all here, and a good deal of the tension has cleared from the air in this luxurious greenwood getaway after becoming acquainted with one another. Acquainted seems like something of an understatement.

Then, right in the middle of my big darts comeback, the front door flies open riotously and immediately draws everyone's full attention. Our very presence is graced by the return of the king!

He comes into the room at a quicker speed than the door itself. He's the same familiar body with a new energy.

Red Bull energy.

Coke binge energy.

Manic end of bipolar energy.

He's holding something.

"I think I've figured it out!" Feathers shouts, as he paces back and forth like a person unwell.

After enough seconds go by, it's *Fluffy Russian Hat*, our motherly island woman, who asks, "Figured out the specifications of our assassination plan, Ambassador?"

The Ambassador is talking but not facing anyone directly. He's still pacing. We're all listening in case he's actually answering Fluffy's question, but instead he's mumbling just above the mute setting. MUMBLE MUMBLE. All I can make out is something about patterns and comparisons. MUMBLE MUMBLE. He's seemed so together with his lunacy until now. Dementia episode?

F.R. Hat, probably pointlessly, continues, "Or perhaps an alternate plan to stop Fox?"

The Ambassador ¡**SNAPS!** back to reality, both literally and figuratively. He almost jumps so that his body and full attention are faced at Hat. Somewhat sounding like himself again, he finally blesses us with a response.

"It's . . . **that**, it's, it's **both**, my friends. The language, their language. We can understand their words based on your collective dreams and transmissions and such, but comparing Hiro's translations versus the audio has given me . . . **enough**. *Remembering* what he hardly remembers . . . it was different than reading the rest of your journals somehow. More complete. More clear. Just more. My friends, my family, my fellow Travelers, we're going to send a message, we're going to communicate. Hell, sweet peers, we may even pow wow."

What does he mean by that? What could he mean by that? None of us have the chance to inquire before his toddler sugar-high returns and he scrambles and scurries into the basement. We hear the locks, plural, **CLINK, CLANK, CLACK** behind him.

"What in the FUCK was that?" Salmon says to the whole group.

"Duuhahuuhahaha," laughs Butternut; he really is simple that one.

With the affirmation of Goat Feather's continued uselessness, it's now time for our daylong bonding session to cease, and for business to commence.

PART FOUR

OUR FIGHT'S FRUITION

51

We've arrived. It's time. *We* being the Travelers, led by Ambassador Goat Feathers, or maybe we're leading him at this point, it's tough to tell. He's here, at least. *The time* being the moment we planned and prepared for at our log cabin mansion, the trendsetting new friend getaway. When we do what we have to do to save an entire planet from severe depression or schizophrenia or clinically thinking you're a duck. To save our whole species. To save Blaire.

We found our location thanks to our human GPS, Caffeinated Sloth. We know now he's an especially interesting man, a substance-abuser, but with some real substance. Witty except about ten seconds after the appropriate timing. Awkward and the only one unaware of it. Noticeably and objectively very smart but just can't *perform* because of the drugs.

A songbird with stage fright.

A stud with ED.

A Lamborghini Countach with no engine.

His smart, dumb idiot self is also covered ear to ankle in tattoos. We look like a gang. We are, so that's good.

Sloth's ink isn't interesting and imaginative like the artistic collection that creates Salmon Wings. You take a look at Salmon W. and, after the initial fear induced by the skull and crossbones flag on his neck, you realize every picture on his body is an honest to Ganesha work of art. Art that could be sold. It could tell a story. It probably does.

C. Sloth might have hundreds of tattoos or he might just have one full body fish-net tattoo. It's a collection of pot leaves and clouds of blunt smoke and words like loyalty and family and honor.

At this point, I have no reason to believe he is not, in fact, honorable. Despite whatever he's not-so-subtly doing every twenty minutes for twenty minutes in any bathroom available, private or public, he has gotten *us* here.

He.

I.

We.

Us.

Where is here? 'Here' is several twists and turns from where any of us resides, hours away from any of our pillows. We're outside of a mansion surrounded by nothing. The finale in *Scarface* when dozens of militia surround Tony Montana's luxurious drug den. But we're the antagonist in that comparison. I'm hoping this story has a similar end result with less drama in the process. It's tough to feel that way, though.

We're around the border of what seems like our twentieth middle-of-the-woods stately manor, but instead of a spa weekend resort where we plan our kill mission, we're **here.** Ready, armed with swords and bats and tasers. There's a gun or two or several dozen, despite some of us usually holding European views on gun law.

Small Yellow Boar's right hand is still clenched with Hairless Wig's left, I think. They're so in love they are practically one. They have matching machetes, though, which is undeniably badass as well as adorable.

Fluffy Russian Hat, the materfamilias of our group of monsters, holds a staff with both ends sharpened enough to glide right through your narrator with ease. Any Ouija related anxieties have far passed. She stands steadfast and with purpose.

Salmon W and C Sloth, our inked-up muscle, carry an intense array of weaponry between them. There are a pair of nunchucks and a pair of sais because they've been dying to become Ninja Turtles, obviously. Neither would dare show up to such an event without a fancy blade, a Gentak Makara or a Honyaki or something else awesomely anime-sounding. One of them has a license to carry and the other has a lack of concern for the Ruger SR on his waist. Once again, which is which is irrelevant.

Our sweet Butternut Moron is probably smiling and probably drooling but definitely carrying around an axe. It's an axe made for a giant, but it looks miniature in Squash's catchers-mitt-sized hand.

We're armed like this because we *know* that we have to be. The artistic messages from the brain and fingers of Salmon Wings, pictures drawn of Fox the way grade schoolers draw Spiderman or the Hulk or Jesus. Always triumphant. Strong. Standing over the defeated opposition.

Apparently, it's only when you start drawing everyone else's heroes, Aquaman or the Little Mermaid or King

Neptune, lying in puddles of their own blood with X X eyes, that it's a problem. Then all of a sudden it's time for specialists. I wonder what their shared analysis would be of our situation.

52

We're together yet scattered, the Travelers and I. All of us trying our best to be seen by each other yet remain invisible to the rest of the world. An odd and familiar feeling. Creeping around the perimeter of Fox's army base of a property, we're all mentally preparing ourselves for whatever might happen. Striving to remain brave while heading towards his hostile homestead, an honestly astounding abode.

It's tough to think we have any type of chance at all, like imminent doom is in our future. My future and the Travelers' future and your future, if you're in fact a human person.

New curiosity arises from a very recent Salmon Wings original, done with ketchup and mustard packets on a concrete canvas outside of a drug store and drive-through pharmacy. Again, a shockingly detailed depiction of our not-from-these-parts nemesis. This time it's a full body view. He's standing at the sink shaving with just a pair of boxer-briefs on. Mustard briefs. Tigress and Fluffy and

Wig and Boar are all obliviously swooning over a ketchup sketch that I could ruin with my soft drink.

I probably should, attempt to get their minds right. I don't want our murder/capture mission turning into a MFFFF orgy after S. Wings and G. Feathers and C. Sloth and I have been oh-so-creatively killed by the beautiful alien monster man. I don't, though, because there's something different about this illustration from the dozens of others he's drawn of a *man* he's never met or even seen an actual photo of.

In this particular expressionist piece made of condiments, Viqar is missing a toe on his left foot. Not only a major imperfection to his perfectly created fake human form, but an imperfection that he hasn't naturally fixed. No Wolverine auto-heal or lizard tail limb-regrowth or cranial sacral super-session. At least we can potentially axe or saw or machete his limbs off if he blackswan jujitsus at us. That's something. We're still hoping bullets work as well but you know what happens when you assume—an alien destroys your entire species. Bunny Man has a few Molotov cocktails ready as well, maybe fire is his weakness? Crystal-Eyed Bunny Man is our real soldier. Former marine, former military instructor, formerly able to speak to his little sister in person. Currently seeking vengeance against the quack shitbag 'doctor' whose malpractice was **at least** partially to blame for her suicide. No one knows complete details of how her sessions went, patient records and reports and honesty were all always quite scarce with him. But there were 39 outgoing calls from her to 'Dr. Fox 🔔 ♡'.

His military background has given our group of strange or special or chosen no ones some sort of direction. Additional ambition. We all know what needs to be done, and we all have our own personal drives, but hearing a man like Bunny's heart rebreak telling stories he's probably told too many times, or maybe allowed him to tell for the first time in a long time, it gives you that extra emotional push into the **feels zone**. The murder zone. Right into the zone we need to be.

His story connects us, bonds us with his pain and Wig's pain and Boar's pain and all of our pain. A bunch of empathetic sad-sacks. Our group of special individuals are all one at this moment, as we prepare to destroy an evil alien higher-up in human form who's planning to paint the world black with oil-covered tears.

We're doing what we must, risking our lives for the greater good, but instead of receiving medals, we'll have to destroy the evidence, because what was just described is unquestionably a murderous cult basing their evidence on dreams and gypsy mind-readers and drawings done in sandwich spreads.

A cult of lunatics. Or a selfless, something like religious act to save mankind. And fishkind and birdkind and insectkind. All of us. **Us**.

Just because the masses say the few are wrong, or crazy, or weak, doesn't mean they are. A group of maniacs saving the sane. That is what we are.

53

Primed for Fox's arrival to one of his supplemental party villas, one we're confident he thinks we're unaware of, we're still hyped up on adrenaline and feelings and fear. Salmon Wings and Caffeinated Sloth may also be slightly or not so slightly energized from Sloth's bag of drugs we, I mean, they used to go last minute skiing just moments ago. We didn't, I mean, THEY didn't ask the others, they imagined there'd be judgment. You never know though, everyone likes a good time.

It's a Sunday night. For some people, Sunday is a holy day filled with church and prayers and family brunches afterwards. Whether you actually believe in said holiness or not is irrelevant; there are crepes and omelettes and mimosas.

During football season, millions of Americans become die-hard fans dedicated to destroying their trash-talking friends in their fantasy leagues. For them and so many of their spouses and friends and relatives, Sundays revolve around the game. Sundays are full of traditions.

IT STARTS WHEN YOU STOP

For Fox Turds, Sunday was a day free of responsibility and full of dangerous drug combinations and brothel frequents. He usually spends the entirety of Monday sleeping it off, part of his surprisingly reasonable attendance on most Tuesdays. Apparently even intergalactic superstars feel hungover.

These Sunday Fundays were similar to most of his days but turned to maximum intensity. We hope that when he becomes the drunken sailor, we'll have our best chance. Hopefully one of the lines he sniffs through hundred dollar bills, or blue dolphin Molly pills he washes down with Wild Turkey shots, will impair him enough for one of us to chop off an arm or tase him repeatedly until the battery runs out or fill his head with jacketed lead bullets again and again until there's not any head left.

We've discussed whether capture would be necessary . . . or in any way possible, but Goat Feathers is quite certain he'll be able to impersonate him via I.C.M.T. At least enough to **abort mission**. It seemed simple once he broke it down, kind of. So long as Viqar is gone, we're good. Goat's odd behavior as of late has worried us all a bit, but we have no choice now but to be collected. Time to waste is not something we're in possession of.

We're in position when we finally see two headlights shine faintly in the distance. They're slowly growing brighter and brighter. Two yellow beady little animal eyes opening wider or getting angrier or catching sight of you for the first time.

My chest feels clammy like when the beings used to turn my anxiety levels to 8+ and I wasn't aware. When I thought it was just physical insecurities or genetics or upbringing or . . . I don't know, Vaccinations? Ignorance is bliss. Turns out it's some creature at a screen probably hating his job like you hate your job as a Paralegal Assistant or Target Assistant Store Manager or Keno dealer.

Bunny Man looks ready, eager even, to pounce from the bush he's hiding behind across the street.

Just as the car creature's eyes are waking up, driving steadily towards us, Humble Tigrina grabs my arm just above my elbow, "Whatever happens, Hiro, I'm glad you're here with me."

As if my heart wasn't already beating fast enough. In this moment I'm invincible, I move my lips towards her and give my best attempt at a possibly poorly placed passionate embrace with my dreamperson. My first real kiss, better late than never. Better right before possible death than right after. It's only a second or two after I reluctantly remove my hand from Arina's perfectly sized lower back and look towards the oncoming vehicle that I know our plan is starting out less than ideally. Tasha **did** warn us. . . .

The car creature's eyes swell at a much angrier rate than they're supposed to, really angry! Really Fast! But then Mr. or Mrs. Car Villain's eyes just shut off as the FOXMOBILE continues to fly in our direction, ricocheting from left shoulder to right shoulder the whole time.

Whig and Bunny and Boar fastidiously prepped the 150 yards or so between Fox's onrushing hotrod and our group. The earthy asphalt road is littered evenly with nails and screws and glass but we'll be relying largely on sound at this point, his headlights out or his car animal's eyes closed, to know when those tires make contact with our 'Home Alone' style deterrent. But that's not what we hear.

IT STARTS WHEN YOU STOP

Instead, we hear the sound of the FOX-ROD in off-road mode, bouncing up and down and left and right and all over but still heading right towards us. Arina grabs my hand and squeezes, **hard**. I squeeze back and pull the petite, perfect person she is out of the danger zone. Mighty heroic of me, but it doesn't even end up being necessary.

At the last second, before I either would have saved both of our lives or landed us both under the tires of Viqar's Bugatti Veyron or Koenigsegg CCXR or whatever beautiful piece of machinery he's whipping around this week, his vehicle takes a sharp right and **¡CRASHES!** into the light post.

Our limited source of artificial sunlight has transferred from the 30ft posts every 80 feet or so to the blazing fiery explosion that is or was a $3,000,000 sports car. As much as we'd all love to wish he just hit some bad bump or frustrating banana peel he couldn't control and did our work for us, we know it'd never be that easy.

In either case, this was certainly not the expected commencement. The flames and smoke emitting from the FORMERMOBILE are momentarily entrancing until I see the light attached to Crystal Eyed Bunny Man's cap turn on. It's oddly bright for something so small, it's most definitely military quality. His face is visible, his eyes truly are crystal balls filled with miniature oceans at this snapshot of time. Not like a New Jersey ocean, either. I mean, a good one.

Bunny man has a real name, although we're not supposed to know it. It's Eugene, he openly announced moments ago, perhaps to remind us all that we are homosapiens and not ducks or kangaroos or lampshades. Well just as Eugene the Bunny, our *new friend* and *military commander*, begins lifting his arms to give a command, I see what looks to be an exhaust pipe glide right though his throat, beginning at his giant Adams apple and ending a foot behind the back of his neck. His lips continue to wiggle like two little worms trying to make words.

If I make it through this, I'll surely be traumatized. Well, more traumatized, I mean. Instead of his struggling, agonizing, floundering body falling to the ground as it should, our newly deceased or currently *deceasing* cult superhero teammate and fellow human person is held up in the air by none other than Dr. Fox Viqar. There's blood dripping down the metal cylinder onto his hand and Swiss-made MontBlanc Timewalker, but you can see him smiling.

That heartless motherfucking monster.

Our bloody Bunny Man Eugene's eyes are still open, and still crystal balls, but now they're filled with red nothing. Nothing except the reflection of Fox's smiling murderer mouth full of movie star incisors and bicuspids and premolars. I haven't been sure of a whole lot recently, what's real and what's not, but what I'm looking at is definitely real or at least definitely horrifying.

Some part of me was maybe hoping that all of the voices and strangely named characters I've met along this crooked silly path were never real in the first place. That I'd spend my days playing checkers and wearing shoes with no laces so that I can't use them to hang myself in some looney bin, with regulated meals and meds and minds. That's somehow less scary than what's *actually happening*, although I would've never thought that was possible.

IT STARTS WHEN YOU STOP

Fox *really* just obliterated his car on purpose because he knew we were here, and then butchered our military coordinator with a piece of his flaming, real life, action figure transforming vehicle.

This . . .
This is real.

54

A sudden coma memory resurfacing.

The screech of an electric guitar erupting from an arena-ready amplifier. Loud and shrieking and horrible but beautiful in the right context. I hear it but can't tell whether it's right or not. Are there background percussions and an accompanying bass? Maybe some funkasaurus playing keyboard way too emphatically? Or are you just begging '*your god*' to let you fall asleep?

When you're truly and seriously depressed, you just wish any bad dream will be your last, here or anywhere. People not *infected* with these seemingly silly pseudo-suicidal thoughts don't get it.

No use explaining, they won't get it.

No use trying, they can't get it.

Right now, I don't hear any other instruments playing along. No mental anguish, either. No devastating emotional hardships or cymbals or audio engineers or wishing for demise. Just the fifth fret of the E-string on level septillion boost and overdrive and distortion.

It should make me furious. It should make me insane, perhaps a bit late for that, but it should.

At any extreme point during these emotional episodes, I'm pretty certain Blaire is usually heavily involved. I may be dozens of levels ahead of my student peers in any field of academia, but life skills can bring some seriously frustrating issues which I admittedly struggle with.

New people.

Phone calls with strangers.

Phone calls with non-strangers.

Faking respect for idiot teachers and moron authoritative figures in general.

This is where I pathetically begin acting my age, a boy who needs his mother, the angel she is. But her location is a panic-inducing mystery. And . . . where am I? Where Where Where Where Where. Blaire is or was always there but she's not now. She's in the furthest thing from good hands.

The buzzing sound of that vibrating string amplified through its speaker pierces my eardrums differently now. It still rings but it's unplugged. Natural. Not acoustic. Animalistic. It's more of a hiss than anything else.

It's then that I *feel* some sort of sight again. Seeing or fake-seeing or see-sawing, I don't know. But instead of a neutral white or tan or black nothing, there are . . . snakes. Wonderful!

The snakes look like tadpoles at first, just little green and black lines that could hardly be living creatures at all but are. It's like they're growing or combining or expanding or exploding. Whatever it is, they're bigger and angrier and more prevalent. They swirl together like a kaleidoscope, dangerous and mesmerizing. Deadly, just like most beautiful creatures. I don't see any snake mouths begin to move uncharacteristically, but I do start to hear voices.

"We've programmed the maximum security level self-destruct feature in all of the requested subjects, and we've ordered for all future assignments to include at least level 3 alpha software, which will still deactivate the humans brain with ease. This way we can choose whether we save the corpse for dissection study or destroy everything around it for at least 6 mauvgow."

The snakes surrounding me no longer look like friendly gummy worms with eyes. They've gained definition, they've been hitting the snake gym, whatever we imagine that might look like. They *look* real now.

They *feel* real, slithering and sliding on all sides of my catatonic body.

At least I feel something, truly anything is better than nothing. Emptiness is the worst.

"Thank you, Rawzgulup, your work is of grave importance. Our ability to make high risk test subjects inoperative is imperative."

Adrenaline junkies jump out of airplanes or off bridges to feel as alive as possible. The severely depressed just want to feel alive enough to actually live.

The foreign voice with authority, Banshee, continues, "So all it takes for us to turn these dummies off is to put in our passcode, huh? That's wonderful. I assume the manual switch you guys generally assemble won't be accidentally accessible by the subject?"

There's not much awareness of my own thoughts, hardly even of those homeless voices talking about passwords or lock combinations or math problems at this moment.

Snakes.

Just snakes.

Hissing at me, in my face, I'm reminded of what dog kisses feel like, as forked tongues hit my cheek and chin, on and off, so fast they feel like they're sliding. Almost like a slobbery tattoo gun. Electromagnetic cobras and Copperheads and Eastern Hognoses. Their sheddable skin has developed texture and patterns that dance around my face hypnotically like figures made of shadowy iridescence during an acid trip.

"Great question, sir! But no worries, we've got you covered there."

Rawzgulup sounds like quite the sycophant suck-up Suzy. He continues, "We've designed it like a missing puzzle piece inside the *chin,* found in the southern-most point of the mandible region of the skull. Knowing its location, we simply use a key similar to that of the lav-ron but falling straight down. Any other blow to the area will affect the subject in normal, stupid human ways. Broken bones or blood or bladder irregularity."

I'm staring at some type of deep-blue and pink Rhino Viper directly in its rude, beady, little green eyes, its skinny purplish black tongue flaring all over the place. If I could in fact locate the sensations of *my* normal stupid human bladder, I'd most definitely be wetting myself in irregular fashion.

Suzy Boot-Licker keeps explaining to his jefe, "The human tooth is quite similar to our entrance inducer tools, only smaller, as you may already kn—"

"OF COURSE I know that! What is your point!?" Alien

Boss Man exclaims in a manner which would assure anyone that he did not in fact know that at all.

"My point, Sir, is that technically the subject COULD use his or her own top two front teeth as a conduit to their own life's expiry, but the physical pain would be horribly excruciating."

I know at one point I was the proud owner of a pair of feet and legs and balls, but whether or not they all still exist is beyond me.

Just snakes.

"Hmm, sounds questionable, Rawz. How excruciating are we talking?"

Snakes.

Just aesthetically wonderful, venomous killers.

Bull snakes actually hiss-screaming at me from all directions. Showing the black insides of their mouths, their natural inner darkness.

Just snakes.

"Past the physical pain threshold maximum of any human subject tested thus far, sir. They'd have to remove their bottom teeth by pushing them straight out, away from their face. Quite the doozey already, huh sir?"

Even in whatever strange language they're speaking, Suzy Kiss-Ass totally sounds like a spaz. Spaz on, sir.

"AFTER the bottom teeth are removed, the human would have to specifically use **their own** top teeth to bite down through their excruciating fresh wound hard enough to completely dig those choppers 100 percent into their gums. *GUMS*, really a silly thing they have surrounding their teeth, right? And that name! *Gums*, HA! Am I right?"

Spaz.

IT STARTS WHEN YOU STOP

Hiss.

Snakes.

I'm completely drowning in them at this point. The multicolor typhoon of snakes, that is.

HI*SS*. Hi*ss*.

My newest black, red, and yellow *friend* continues its song in front of my face, as *he* or *she* moves in for the smooch. I wonder if it'll be my final smooch. I don't know how snakes reproduce, admittedly. Not at all. Even if I could move, I truly don't know if I would.

The snake bites down, and I . . .

I let go.

55

It sounds like multiple cars backfiring while the whole neighborhood simultaneously enjoys some high-caliber firework explosions. Instead, though, it's Salmon Wings and Caffeinated Sloth standing about twenty feet aside of one another, both firing round after round of lead round noses or semi-jacketed hollow points directly at Viqar.

It's a filthy sight, really, an amazing display of misfortune. Fox is using Bunny Man's fresh cadaver as a shield from both directions while incorporating Olympian-quality mat work and unrealistic leaps as if he were an NBA player . . . or a cat.

He's a horrible hell monster in a human costume looking to cause an earth-sized suicide party but you almost want to root for him just because of how sheerly impressive he his. He's like the away team smashing up your favorite group of athletes in their own stadium so badly yet so beautifully you change into an opposing jersey.

Dozens of bullets soar through the air and strike our

new, yet *late,* friend, Bunny. Some go right through his body and narrowly miss our handsome devil while he weaves and wobbles and seems to enjoy himself by the fire.

I'm on top of Humble Tigress. When our inked-up gentlemen started spraying slugs from their automatic weapons, I had instinctively jumped to cover her. I'm pressed partially against her, my beautiful Mediterranean Queen, and even amidst all that's happening, I have to struggle to not let her *feel* any of my other instinctive manly drives.

By the time Crystal Eyed Bunny Man's body is just a sundry of unrecognizably ruined pieces, Viqar has ballet danced his way behind the unsalvageable, giant car-shaped lantern. Salmon Wings takes the lead and gives the signal to follow, a Glock 19 machine pistol in his left hand, an all-black sai in his right.

He, Fluffy Russian Hat, Small Yellow Boar, and Hairless Wig begin moving stealthily from their various locations on the opposing side of the street. On our side, Green Pea, Butternut Squash, and Caffeinated Sloth begin doing the same. I suppose that means it's time to reluctantly remove myself from beside, or technically on top of, an angel whom I'm desperately in love with to go probably die a gruesome death instead.

As we jump up from the damp grass and begin ninja jogging towards the battlefield, my heart's puppet master looks at me in a way that I could really get used to. Lovingly. Lustfully.

Onward we go. All of us, except our Ambassador, who's just decided to either completely lose himself or lose his sanity or cease to exist altogether. Who knows, but suddenly he's not here. Where the **fuck** are you, Goat Feathers?

Another shitty father figure to replace my absent or dead or imagined prime father figure. No time to think about that or anything else; we're slowly moving with intention to the vehicle.

Wig and Hat unsurprisingly have adorably dangerous miniature cross-bows ready to rumble along with their close range weaponry. Arina and I have matching Walther P99's and Green has a Benelli M2 shotgun, but I can't help but wonder if they'll matter at all. Maybe that's *them* lowering my self-efficacy levels deep down to one or two— I'm sure they'd do much worse if they were paying closer attention.

Why aren't they paying attention? Wait . . . are they paying attention?

56

We swarm every angle of the flaming wreckage that Fox drove here. Guns ready. Crossbows and arrows ready. Swords and axes and bats and laser-guns and hate and vengeance. All of it ready. Whether any of US could really be ready for this is another matter entirely.

We're all looking for our clear headshot when we see a person-sized piece of car fly into the air and we all instinctively look up. While our stupid human eyes can't help but look away from the target, we become the targets. Sometimes instincts can be a real sonofabitch, ya know?

Just footsteps away, it sounds like a metal baseball bat just ¡**CRACKED!** a home run out of the fucking park. I hate baseball, but I do wish it was that sound. Instead, it's a scalding hot remnant of bumper meeting the skull of our humble giant. Our sweet man baby. I've joked about him not being able to get any uglier but I realize now that I was so very incorrect there.

"NOOO!!" Green shrieks.

Our poor lovable ogre.

"SQUASHHH!!" She screams and shudders simultaneously.

The first hit takes him down to his knees. "Ahhwwnngg!" He grunts in apologetic agony. He looks up with his dumb confused eyes towards Green, and before she even has time to take a step forward or shed a tear or whisper goodbye, **¡CRACK!**

And once again, before Butternut's massive, lifeless body is even affected by gravity, Dr. Hoax Viqar is using one of our own as his human shield while also being a real dancing queen. A Swayze, a Travolta, a something or someone horribly sensational.

While maneuvering his way AROUND bullets, he twists his torso and thrusts his arms away from each other, managing to catch not one, but TWO arrows coming from different directions. One is immediately and effortlessly returned dart-style into the throat of our still too stunned Green Pea. Quicker than a flick of an eyelash, right into the frog tattoo I inexplicably felt connected to that first time she scared the shit out of me in the Econo Lodge parking lot. She gurgles horrible, inaudible cries as blood spews from her wound.

I'm tirelessly trying to get a shot at him, any shot. As I'm about to let off another round, the other arrow comes my direction via a wicked behind-the-back-style fling. I know I'm not fast enough to move out of the way. I just close my eyes and prepare, but instead of a sharp piercing pain in my chest or stomach or face, I just feel a body rush me followed by the **¡SMACK!** of concrete against my cheek. I open my eyes to see Salmon Wings with an arrow, my arrow, stuck in his side. Smiling, he does his quick fake chuckle.

IT STARTS WHEN YOU STOP

"Fuck it, brother. Let's rock," this savage hero says. Rock we fucking shall, my friend.

Viqar is using both bodies together as a malleable shield now, the same two bodies that I chased through the woods, that I chased to the rest of the Travelers, that I chased into this moment. As he shields himself from the bullets coming from Tigress and Whig and Boar and Sloth, his intricate tap dance brings him up close enough to my current position on the road that an opportunity arises for me. A lightbulb appearing and flashing above my head. My handgun has been knocked out of reach, but my Japanese Tanto blade hasn't.

I try with everything I have to slice his nearer leg right in half, and I nearly succeed. My blade gets stuck about three quarters of the way through his leg made of who knows what. He doesn't flinch or yell or acknowledge it, he just prepares to kick my teeth in when I see a black metal ninja star land dead center into Viqar's right eye.

"¡**AAGGHH!** ¡**MOTHER FUCKER!**" Fox finally screams at stadium volume. I look behind me to find out that for the second time in thirty seconds, it's Salmon Wings saving my life, this time using a move from the ninja superstar playbook.

Viqar launches Humble Green Pea's tiny mangled body into Humble Hunter Cat's similarly tiny, but still perfect, body hard enough to make a not at all tiny impact. Her gun drops from her hand and finds its way into the *wrong* hand before it has a chance to hit the ground. His newly imperfect leg collapses under all of Butternut's dead weight, pun clearly not intended. Too soon.

Another black star flies by but this one is blocked by one of Squashes limp, giant octopus hands. And then it's just target practice for our injured, one-eyed, and now armed superhuman nemesis.

¡BANG! Right in between Sloth's no longer caffeinated eyes. I see his opiate-soaked brains fly from the back of his head as he *jumps* backwards. No more painful and confusing treasure hunt for sad people you've never met.

¡BANG! ¡BANG! The two lovebirds leaping opposite directions doesn't work out for either of them. Headshots, two for two. Not the modeling headshots I imagine they're used to getting compensated for. Their lives were both filled with interior pain and exterior beauty. They've finally traded those incredible faces for freedom from suffering.

Fluffy Hat, out of nowhere, arrives just in time with some serious axe contact. Unfortunately, it's mostly contact with our beloved and ruined remaining corpse. She does, however, manage to clip his infirm right leg a bit, just centimeters from where I did, even as he somersaults away. As she continues to charge towards him, and the gunfire has calmed momentarily, I make my way as well, equipped with just my dagger and my adrenaline.

"You are FINISHED!" She passionately roars in her thick island accent, her axe held viciously above her head. Striking position.

Only a few yards away from Hat's vigorous swinging, I hear Salmon's footsteps behind me. His tight fitting black and tan Hawaiian shirt is completely drenched with blood from his gnarly arrow wound, his eyes are nothing but pupil and firetruck red, but he's still as fast as I am. Faster. Again he smiles.

"We got this. **You** got this, brother. The world is

counting on you," he mumbles through his awe-inspiring beard, filled with dirt and blood and sweat and probably regret and possibly still hope.

"On m—" Hat only starts to say as Fox jumps a few imaginary hurdles and grabs both sides of her shouting jaw. ¡**CRUCK**! Says her neck as her hatchet lands and *clinks* on the ground next to what was once Butternut Squash, right before Fluffy Russian Hat's strong Caribbean body falls beside it.

Our entire group of Travelers, our missing papa and myself included, was so filled with hope that we've begun to burst into one big, horribly bloody mess. Filled to the brim with hope for answers or world betterment or at least a continued world to live in. Many of us already taken out and flicked aside. Pawns two-thirds of the way through a match.

Fox hops onto his one functional leg, the left, just as Salmon Wings starts throwing the best punches and kicks and stabs and grabs and everything he's got. I don't know where his strength is coming from or how long it will last. Things are seeming tougher than we are as I move as quickly as I can to Salmon's aid.

Fox is mostly forearm-blocking everything but we've got him moving backwards, hobbling backwards, really.

HOP SWING BLOCK HOP SWING BLOCK.

HOP HOP SWING SWING BLOCK BLOCK.

SWING. BLOCK. SWING.

I somehow manage to dig my Tanto dagger into the front of Fox's right shoulder. I twist the blade, yearning for him to suddenly feel pain. Wish not granted. Instead, he launches off of his still intact leg. His leap takes him at least 36 inches in the air while spinning clockwise and away from us for a beautifully crippled flying roundhouse.

Fox's just barely bloody lower right leg, which is just hanging on by a delicate thread below the knee at this point, cracks me in my right ear hard enough that the threadlike body tissue is finally torn. Fox's entire knee to stylish Italian shoe smacks against the hot concrete covered by flaming pieces of wreckage just as I do.

Trying to take advantage of Dr. Viqar's completely one-legged current situation, our MVP so far, or mine at least, Salmon Wings, sprints directly at our monopodular enemy. I see Arina on the ground not more than a few feet away from me. She must have hit her head when she was knocked down by the bloody cannonball that Toasted Pea became.

There's a small puddle of blood under Arina's perfect face. It's personal pizza-sized, the blood, not her face. Salmon Wings charges shoulder first into Viqar's one standing leg. The thud when Salmon forcefully delivers Fox's body, along with his own, onto the concrete battlefield is audible. Loud, actually.

I see Salmon pull his last-resort ice pick from his side, and aiming for our final boss's remaining eye, STAB! STAB! STAB! Three out of three, CLINK! CLINK! CLINK! into the road as Fox whips his head around wildly to dodge the strong, but exhausted, attempts.

I look again at my most beautiful Tiger, "I hope there's more," I say aloud, to her and to myself, before turning away again and running with my exhausted body towards Wings and Fox.

Before I'm even halfway, I see my *real friend* Salmon's ice pick dig into the surely perfectly pigmented skin above Viqar's shoulder, inches from his neck. I naturally feel a

IT STARTS WHEN YOU STOP

glimmer of hope, I keep running as hard as I can but before I'm close enough to make a difference, Viqar grabs Salmon Wings magazine-quality beard and pulls it closer and closer until his chin and then nose and then forehead and then eyes are all grinding back and forth against the same black ninja star he threw into Fox's eye in the first place. Back . . . and forth . . .

"AAAAAHH, you dirty alien PRICK! GGGGRRAAAHH!" He yells and yells as I run and run and struggle to not get caught in my tracks. Back and forth. Just before I leap onto Fox and try to finish this, ¡THWOOP! I feel a jolt in my neck, it doesn't hurt but I drop my beautiful Japanese babe. Jap and cheese blade. Hmumm I'm dizzy.

THWOOP. THWOOP. THWOOP. THWOOP. THWOOP. Five feathery white and orange darts in the face, neck, and *heart* of our nemesis. One more THWOOP. Followed by an "Eep." A relatively wonderful Eep, considering the circumstances, because it means *she's still alive*.

As everything is getting fuzzy and even darker, I see him. His shining, feathery white hair glowing like a Care Bear's nightlight: it's our Ambassador, Goat Feathers. If that's even his real pretend name.

PART FIVE

LONG DISTANCE YOGA SCIENCE

57

I feel like you feel directly after getting your wisdom teeth out. Much more physical grogginess than your run-of-the-mill LSD trip, not quite as confused as when I was in my comfy hospital gown immediately post-coma. It's hard to open my eyes, it's so bright in here, wherever **I am**.

"Mm . . . Bb . . . Gg . . . Rr . . . " There's muffled whimpering. Wherever **we are.**

I'm beginning to see that we're in some type of empty office building or abandoned warehouse or giant operating room. Wouldn't be the first doctorless doctor's office I've been to recently. Continuing to flutter my eyes, I begin to see the secretary I've dreamt about spending my life with since hours after meeting her. There's dried blood covering the whole left side of her faultless face, all throughout her voluptuous dark brown hair. She's awake and looking at me with eyes that look like they've run out of tears.

"Bb . . . Rr . . . Mm . . . Mm . . . " Those muffled baby

noises are coming from behind the strip of duct tape covering her always alluring lips and orthodontist brochure smile. She's on an old rusted metal fold-up chair with her legs and arms bound to the chair's legs and arms with cable ties. All I want to do is rescue her.

I'm coming, I won't let anything else happen to you is what I TRY to say, but what is more accurately heard is "Mm . . . Mmgg . . . MmMmUh . . . Uhmu . . . Rr . . . " It appears my mouth is also taped shut.

Also, upon further inspection, my limited limb-mobility situation is identical to hers. I'm screaming to her on the inside, though. In my head, from my heart. Every muscle in my unfamiliarly drugged body is clenched, trying to break free and save my princess, secure her love forever, or at least her safety, or at least her comfort. Wipe her tears, clear away her crusty cardinal-colored mask.

¡THUD! A faint but explicit sound behind me manages to pull my attention away from my damsel in distress. I turn my head, but really my drowsy voodoo-damaged brain just sort of falls down until my chin meets my chest and rolls heavily to the left.

¡THUD! When I manage to refocus my gaze, I see something *good* about this. Hopefully. I think. Maybe. There stands the invincible Dr. Fox Viqar, imprisoned in some sort of bullet-proof, monster-proof square holding-cell. It must be made of composite-plastic or metallic glass or magic marshmallow building blocks.

He's definitely screaming but his room must be completely soundproof as well, no stifled cries for help or various swear-word combinations or confessions of love like us commoners. He's standing on his one leg as if that's how he was born and raised, not an ounce of tremble in him. His facial expressions seem to be bouncing back and forth between the hysterical laughter of a lunatic to a devil-person ready to literally rip your head off with his bare hands and devour it.

He takes ten or fifteen small hops backwards and breathes in a way you can see clearly, as if he was a real human with weed-stained lungs, then one medium-length hop forward to LAUNCH him the remainder of the way to the colorless force field. As he seems to hover merrily through the air, he stretches his neck so he's chest first, but his head is touching his back. He looks like a fucking dolphin. Inches away from contact, centimeters actually, maybe even less, he whips his face, not head, full force into the rigid cell wall.

¡THUD! Each collision drives that intricately crafted, 6-sided ninja star further into where once lived a cornea and a retina and a pupil. Whatever it takes I suppose. I feel like it must be way into his cerebral cortex by now, but Viqar's body, human form and otherwise, is still quite the mystery. At least our presumably late pirate friend, Salmon Wings, would be happy to know Dr. Fox needs a peg leg and an eye patch.

TCHJEEK TCHJEEK TCHJEEK, the soft jingling of keys immediately draws mine and Arina's attention. We hear the CLACK of the deadbolt followed by the sliding KREET sound of the key entering and turning and opening the door which separates me, my dream girl, and our collective nightmare from who knows what else. More personalized prisons? Torture equipment storage unit? Regulation-size NBA basketball court equipped with a spa? One thing at a time.

One thing at a time even though I have so many questions about so many problems that really I'd just like to scream it all out SO loud. Difficult given the sticky grey tape with all the little wispy threads coming off everywhere.

RRRAAEEHHWWW.

That wasn't a cat, although it meowed similarly. It's really the door being shoved just hard enough to open. I see that stupid white hair like a bright shining light floating through the door. A shining light floating above the dirty piece of walking shit that we now know is Traveler Ambassador Goat Feathers. We, now only being me and Arina and the enemy we COULD'VE FUCKING HAD!

FUCK . . . FUCK . . . FUCK!

My heart wants to hate him more with every step he takes, but the TTX or the 蠱 or the pixie dust makes me forget feelings. An enlightening experience when there's not anything. No stress or regret, just oatmeal brains and comfortable places to sit.

He looks so goddamn pleased with himself, like everything went exactly according to plan. Every last detail. I'm eager to know what aforementioned plan IS, and given we're not dead and he's walking towards us, I'd wager we find out now-ish.

"Well hello there, old friends and new." His gaze fans slowly from Arina to me to Dr. Fuckface Viqar who ¡THUD! is clearly not done trying.

"I suppose you probably have some questions, like, where are you? Why have you been double crossed?"

¡THUD! "Why is HE still alive? . . . You look angry, friends, and while I recognize why, I'm hoping to all work together amiably, SO, allow me to begin explaining things further."

¡THUD! He's dressed in a creepy black robe, like he's become Judge Feathers all of a sudden. It's as dark as a shadow, coated with calculated golden iridescence forming a symbol I've only seen so many moons prior during a story from Blaire. Goat, or *Your Honor,* walks a few footsteps closer to Viqar amidst his next . . .

¡THUD! I survey the otherworldly artwork or ideogram or random shape assortment made of first place remnants on the back of the black cloth drowning his body.

He just stares at the raging, hopping monster man like he's a giant turtle in an aquarium. A baby monkey or an adorable sea otter at the zoo. Isn't that probably what we'd do with space aliens anyway? Put them on display for money? I mean, if they weren't intelligent enough to try to kill us all or ruin our brains to the point of worldwide suicide or anything like that of course.

"OH, sorry, my friends," Feathers seems startled momentarily before regaining his focus. "Where were we? Right! So, for starters, you're both very welcome for being kept alive and chosen to participate in this once in a lifetime opportunity. Once in a billion lifetimes, really."

It seems like the voodoo poison in my body might be wearing off, or the alien poison in my head is turning up the rage meter to dangerous levels. Probably both.

"I believe we've briefly touched on ICMT, basically Fox's process of mind-texting his higher-ups wherever in space they may be."

"Bb . . . Gg . . . Rrr . . . Rhmm . . . "

Beads of sweat are trickling down my face as I exert

100 percent of my strength, of myself, into removing this chair from the surface it's bolted to.

"It's a wonderfully interesting process. So, in order for me to get a proper meditative signal, I need to be proximal enough to your brains, and they both need to be functional, ie. **alive.**"

¡THUD! My eyes can't help but focus on my dearest Arina, still so beautiful yet so afraid. She closes her eyes and stabilizes her breathing. It looks like she's half successful at trying to remain strong even though she must be thinking, 'So what about ME? Everyone else is dead, and I have no mental data-plan to help you. What sick role do you have for me!?'

Or maybe she's just wishing she could get laid once more before death. How would I know? Either way.

Goat Feathers walks towards me and continues, "Congratulations, Deaf Turtle; you're an integral part of the process, my dear friend."

He removes the grey duct tape from my mouth. Slowly. Painfully.

"You're a worthless delusional fucking creep!" I shout, with tears of anger filling my eyes.

"It'll be great, friend," Goat continues. "You'll be assisting me, assisting **us**, rather, in venturing off with our brilliant foreign scientist overlords into space. After so much planning, it's finally time for the Travelers to begin traveling."

58

Arina is no longer out of tears. I know this because even though I'm focused on the words of this scramble-screen-haired LIAR, I see a small water droplet fall from her cheek and explode on the old white and black tile floor. I look back at the blue rings hugging his almost black irises and spew every painful thought I can.

"SPACE! How would that . . . how could that even work, you lunatic!? Just gonna show up in your silly new outfit and start shaking hands and introducing yourself to your *new friends*? Let's see how that goes for ya, bud."

I just want a response from him, any response. Like a little boy jumping up and down for Dad's attention but never being quite as important as the lukewarm beer in his hand. Goat is some sort of zoned out schmuck, looking at Viqar in the terrarium again.

"YO!" I shout, "What the **fuck**, old man?! So . . . we're going to space? SO FUCKING WHAT!? What about Salmon Wings?! What about Butternut Squash? Green.

Wig. Hat. Boar. Sloth. Bunny. All of them. You just let

them DIE!"

It's then he finally gives me his attention again.

"No, DEAF Turtle. I didn't let them die, I let them play their roles. Their roles in *everything* led them to that battlefield, to that graveyard now, I suppose."

He chuckles and Arina vibrates in her chair with rage.

"Gg . . . Gg . . . Rr . . . Rr . . . " she says under her still duct-taped mouth. I'm sure I agree with her muffled sentiment. Goat Feathers continues his never-ending monologue.

"They were important, until they weren't. Then they became important to dispose of, just the sad truth of things. They *knew* too much, even when they didn't know what they knew. You know, dear friend?"

I hate his fucking voice, always calm when it shouldn't be. Serene almost. Bob Ross's voice coming out of Jack Nicholson's calculated kisser.

He moves his gaze to our racially ambiguous princess. Her facial expression is altering from utter desperation to murderous rage a little more with each relaxed footstep he takes towards her. By the time he's standing in front of her, she's staring him intensely right in between those sea-colored rings enclosing his dark eyes, no sign of blinking whatsoever.

Staring contest.

Korean Eye fight.

Bruce Lee style super alpha-male intimidation.

I'm surprised she hasn't bitten through her sticky grey mouthguard and attacked like a rabid dog or spit fire like a dragon in the face of the old, ashy-colored Goat.

¡THUD!

His stubby, dry, cracked hand reaches to the piece of

duct tape covering her perfect pouty lips. Once again, he begins to enjoy ever so slowly removing the narrow strip of binding material, seeing the skin being pulled centimeter by centimeter. Fucking sadist.

BUT, I can assure you he got less pleasure this time than the trial run with me. The poorly raised pit bull presently residing inside of my raging angel does in fact make its existence known.

¡**TAK**! It sounds like two drumsticks **crac**king together, but is actually Arina's top and bottom teeth meeting each other, or perhaps meeting the series of bones and tendons and ligaments that create the shape of G. Feather's thumb. Tough to tell which.

"AAIIH! You animal!" he cries as our foaming-from-the-mouth babe spits out three quarters of his right thumb. It hits his all black, ankle-high, slip-resistant sneakers before arriving on the checkered tile floor. She's laughing uncontrollably while blood and skin and cracked cuticles still exit her mouth. She may have lost it, and I can't tell if I'm disgusted or aroused. Somewhere in the middle, most likely.

As Goat uses his fresh new, oh-so fashionable, glinting black voodoo alien robe to apply pressure to his blood spewing appendage, he's still screaming, "You're just delaying things, not stopping anything!" He's momentarily overwhelmed. "I can't believe this mess, you goddamn RAT!"

I can **certainly** believe the mess, given the artsy fountain of blood.

I can **certainly** believe the aggressive and beautiful and animalistic act, given the deaths and double-crosses and poisoning and kidnapping and uncertainty of what's to come.

Arina can't seem to choose between the unnervingly sinister laughter and burning rage and deep depression inside of her, but at this precise moment she just looks exhausted.

Still not breaking eye contact with our captor, "What is it you want from **me?** You just watched as all of the people **you** brought together, all of **your** *soldiers,* **your** *friends,* died one by one in front of you. In front of us. You probably loved it, you sick fucking liar. Yet here I am tied up in this creepy, giant distributing warehouse with the TWO important pieces of your interplanetary yoga phone call, except I don't see my place in your silly fucking plan. So again, what sick purpose do you have for me?!"

Goat Feathers opens his eyes and mouth simultaneously, looking truly shocked by Arina's words. He shakes his head and holds his hands behind his back. All nine fingers, still covered in vermillion and applying necessary pressure, remaining annoyingly calm.

"You speak of me in such an unflattering manner. Justified I suppose, but if you'd just *see* this for what it is, you'd realize I'm *blessing* you. This is a GIFT!"

His tone becomes more aggressive. He looks at me briefly then back to Arina, returning her samurai stare this time.

"What **are** you here? What **is** your life? Really. An existence with minimal enjoyment or emotional freedom due to our *clear superiors'* science project. Who's to say for sure that eliminating that monster would have stopped his horrible plan from coming to fruition? If our foreign geniuses, our hopefully soon to be newest friends, accept us for helping first-hand, that's our only true option. Even more importantly, we're learning all the secrets of the universe! Invaluable knowledge! I hope you'll soon learn to thank me for this glorious opportunity I'm presenting you. In fact, you're welcome again in advance." Arina's face looks truly blown away, no longer overwhelmed with rage or sadness, just shocked that that was really Goat Feathers reaction. THAT was his statement.

That traitor to our group.

That traitor to our species.

She looks at me in a *this fucking guy* fashion. I don't know why, but even amidst this unbelievably absurd moment we're in, my instant reaction upon seeing her unrivaled face is to nervously look down and away. I guess battling a kung-fu space alien and saving the world's wellbeing hasn't given me a newfound sense of confidence. Not yet at least.

I see the formerly ultimate Dr. Fox Viqar standing behind the soundproof wall bubble on his remaining foot. He appears to be laughing. He's missing an eye and most of a leg, but he certainly hasn't lost *his* confidence. He's beating on his chest now, big king gorilla on campus. Arina begins speaking again and my gaze leaps from the Silverback pack leader to the flawless tigress on my right. She starts to growl and then roar out some adjectives and nouns and profanities.

"HA! Oh thank you, oh great thumbless slimebag. Is that what you want? Thank you SO MUCH, you spineless bucket of shrimp shit, for ruining everything and killing everyone. That certainly includes the three of us, because you have no way of knowing this plan is any more likely of success than our previous plan, you brainless moron. AND you still haven't told me what I'M doing here, you sackless puppy dick!"

I am so incredibly impressed with her bizarre series of insults towards our imprisoner. Horrible beautiful language.

Poetic word vomit.

"WOW. Just . . . WOW. And I thought you spoke poorly of me before. Yikes," Goat Feathers says. His heart looks broken. On top of everything, he's a grey-haired little baby. He turns away and closes eyes, his eight fingers and lone thumb rise to meet his temples, like he's deep in thought. Million-dollar question, no lifelines left.

"Well!?" Our stunning new aggressor continues. It seems to visibly sting him. "WELL!?" ¡sting! The feeling of true anxiety, being all the way overwhelmed. "WELL!?" ¡STING!

"ENOUGH!" Baby Feathers cries. Seriously like a toddler I should add. Shrill. "It's because you're *special* to me, OKAY?"

Holy throw-up line. Sharp Teeth is not impressed either.

"How touching, I'm *special* to you, how annoyingly cliché. Let me guess, I'm like a daughter to you? Or I remind you of someone you used to deeply care for?"

She keeps poking the bear but is interrupted by the loudest goat noise I've ever heard.

"STOP! STOP! **STOP!** I will **NOT** answer those questions or ANY other related questions, **OKAY!?** You are just special to me, Arina. As are you, Hiro."

My beloved and I look at each other with wide inquisitive eyes. Special? Arina and Hiro.

Together and Special.

59

Tie dye clouds flood the void that is my brain. Happily drowning in euphoria. I feel asleep but I know I'm not because my eyes are forced open. I can see Goat Feathers reaching record levels of lunacy, peak mania, but I presently own no opinion about it. It feels like I'm peeing myself. Maybe I'm peeing myself.

I've never done heroin, but I imagine it's somewhat similar to what I'm experiencing right now. Here but not. I can't move my lips, let alone contribute to any conversation, but I can see Viqar, unable to move with a plethora of wires and cables and switches and clamps connected to his head. He looks defeated for the first time.

Weak.

Mortal.

He's tied with metal-wire ropes reaching into the floor and then to who knows where. Then there are barbed wire restraints. And then there's live copper electrical wire half an inch away from every inch of his underwear-model body. I'm sure all of that and more will be necessary at some point in the near future, but at this moment he looks happy and helpless, tied up a million and one times.

His one good eye looks at me, a brilliant red gloss surrounding the green iris all over. He's no longer screaming or chest pounding or head butting. He's just floating, high as a kite like me.

I'm unsure if we've been drugged with actual drugs or with poison drugs or with fermented Zambian poopoo drugs, but whichever way I'm sure it would sell like crazy. I don't know where Arina is and I'm certain I SHOULD be distressed about that, but nope, still just bliss. Am I melting? I'm almost definitely melting.

While I am probably becoming a puddle, I move my gaze back to our second present villain, Ambassador Goat Fucker. He looks something like a conductor the way he's orchestrating his plugs and monitors. Eventually he reaches behind a spot in my view still covered by one of the few flashing tie dye spots. He pulls out something unexpected: an ordinary grey yoga mat. The mat has an attached grey pillow that says *chill* in pink. Some sale item likely found in the check-out isle of a department store, somewhat anti-climactic.

Oh well, I'm still on a cloud right now. I mean that probably figuratively but we really never did get the address for this place. Maybe it's on a cloud? A cloud where I'm melting. A cloud where I'm melting and peeing and becoming acid rain. Probably not, though.

I do my best version of turning my head to look once more for Arina but all I find are more bursting blotches of flashing red and yellow and orange paint, and a lot of the same creepy laboratory scenery as before. An unfortunately familiar scene. When I eventually get my point of view back towards Goat, he's sitting cross-legged on his brand-new exercise mat. You can tell it's unused by how enthusiastically both ends are flaring towards the ceiling's center from being rolled up for so long.

He doesn't appear to be breathing in an ordinary yoga fashion. Not the usual in through the nose out through the mouth, focused meditative breathing. Not yet at least. He's inhaling and exhaling rapidly with his lips puckered a bit, like he's ready to whistle or smooch or blow a poison dart. I think he's actually just incredibly nervous about whatever it is he's about to do. At this point, I couldn't even guess whether he's going to blow up the Earth or do his first downward dog. Either could be pretty intimidating I suppose.

Slowly, G. Feathers begins to steady his breath until eventually he's completely still. Statuesque. He breaks his monk-like pose only slightly with both hands at the same instant. He moves them slowly away from their previous location atop his knees and places them on two small dials located on either side of his seated position on the mat.

"RRROARRGHH! AAUUU! FUCKKINGZHH BAHHHH!" Viqar manages to yelp before he "COUGH! OOHWAHHGGG!" And coughs up a copious amount of blood on to his already stained cherry undershirt. Goat Feathers just smiles lightly with his lips pressed mostly together, allowing only enough space for the air of his exhales.

So seriously outer-space high right now. Hehe, *outer-space high*. No pun intended, but that irony is out of this world. *Out of this world*. Once again, accident. Goat certainly spared no expense in terms of drug strength.

Goat Feathers' right hand is his first to firmly grasp one of the black circular dials. The same right hand highlighting his mangled and unsanitized thumb. The hum of some sort of machine becomes increasingly audible as his fingers turn slightly. I can't see where said machine is exactly but it's definitely somewhere and it's definitely doing **some**thing. It's not loud, really, but the buzz is growing, and everything is vibrating the tiniest bit.

Before I even have a chance to become remotely inquisitive, our second animal-named nemesis begins to utilize the opposite dial with the fingers on his respective hand. As soon as it clicks past its very first notch, I realize what it's for. Goat's slightest clockwise left-handed movement could likely induce my overdose at any second. In an instant, the red and yellow and orange spots divide. Multiply.

Ohly shits. This feells nise.

Viqar shimmys a littble bit, like an old man dance thAt sucks but dousn't becaws it makes everiwone smile. Goat Feathers' left hand mmoves a few inchas in the sam direction and begured playing whitch anothre knobb.

Okie doke, there I go a little bit. Whew. He must have turned it down a bit because my thoughts seem somewhat intact. He remains completely stationary the entire time. His same thumb and pointer and middle finger move one superdrug-adjusting dial to the right and crank it enough for me to instantly know complete sobriety isn't happening any time soon.

It's like my brain is still turned on but the hum from before has grown to a staticky buzz. My vision is more blur than not. A bunch of fuzz, some of which creates an almost expressionistic painting of flashing colors, showing

IT STARTS WHEN YOU STOP

me a level 10 acid trip view of my surroundings. Amongst the fuzz and blur and buzz and static there are the first *words* I recall hearing in what feels like ages.

"CheskBRrUhhhLL . . ." our meditating Benedict Arnold says in an all too familiar tongue, a language I know but never studied. A language unique and immediately recognizable because of its kinky burp noises.

A language I wish he hadn't learned.

Learned through me.

"CheskBRrUhhhLL," the Ambassador says again. "CheskBRrUhhhLL, GgghHawwfbrllh!"

His dry heave vomit noises actually mean, "Greetings, from a *friend*." He waits a moment before trying again, "Greetings, from a friend." I know he hasn't moved because the popping balloons of color haven't danced away from the outline of his straightened-back seated position.

My body is completely useless. Rapid onset, hopefully temporary, quadriplegia. I would warrior pose the crap out of this old yoga jerk if I were physically able.

This is when other sounds begin to emerge. First there's additional static, breaking like a radio station just out of range, in and out. In and out. Silence strikes momentarily before a bass-filled new, but maybe not new, voice answers the Ambassador's call. In and out.

"Wildly illogical human. Where is Fox?"

I wish there was any hope that this voice came from somewhere in this room. Maybe that'd be just as bad, but it wouldn't be broadcasted or hallucinated in my head at least.

We're one of those super retro rotary telephones from the early 1900's that you need two hands to use. I'm held by one of Goat's hands to his ear while Viqar is held near his mouth.

"Don't worry about your associate, my friend." Goat Feathers replies. "He's safe, just oddly intoxicated, even for a drug user of his caliber."

"UhrpGRaphRrr!!" Our long-distance phone call recipient grumbles at a timbre near impossible for any human to make, like an electric bass speaking out of the hole from a former smoker's throat. I don't automatically know this exact word like most others. I assume it means MOTHERFUCKER or DIRTY SHITBURGER or ORGANIC CUNT SAUSAGE.

You never know, though.

"Typical, flawed Fox. Losing sight of mission goals in just a Pyleon's lifetime. Worthless weakling."

Well shit. If Fox is what they'd consider a *weakling*, well then, yeah, **shit**. Our alien executive continues to speak in his frankly disgusting dialect while I continue to wish I could budge an inch.

"Congratulations, Earth Person. Understanding our seemingly anti-scientific method of communication is difficult enough for a human, let alone recreating it, and to find a way to arrive on OUR meditative frequency. Truly impressive work, human man. Really. Almost unfortunate that you'll surely have to be exterminated immediately. Spending your life pursuing truth only to find it and be brought to an end before having the chance to share it with anyone. Before you actually have a chance to make your existence mean something. I believe this is an example of what your species refers to as irony."

There are some belch-like gurgles that once again aren't automatically interpreted in my inferior frontal gyrus. I'm unable to tell if it's some sort of giggling or more static or some unprovoked alien beat boxing. It doesn't matter anyway, the same series of blurry flashing lights that represent Goat Feathers responds, "What wonderful news, newest friend! I was hoping all along you'd say something just like that. EEEH!"

Holy feminine feathers.

He continues, "Apologies, it's clearly challenging to withhold my excitement. You see, if Fox is unable or unwilling to complete said execution of yours truly, then I know you or some other trusted official will be sent here to take care of the job. I just know it!"

Goat is speaking in a care-free manner unfit for the situation, and even somewhat uncharacteristic for him in general. His stone posture is unchanging, at least I think. I mean not that my brain is in top-notch thinking condition at the moment, but the blurry sequence of hazy colors I see remains constant.

"Your tone . . . that's what intrigues me, objectively inferior creature. Continue your silly death wish," our foreign overlord says through Viqar through me to the Ambassador.

"If you feel you must end me, then so be it, *my king*, but I can do so much more for you alive than deceased," Goat Feathers, the cringey doormat, replies.

He seems certain, but given our limited knowledge of the afterlife, I don't think he can accurately estimate their use for him once he ceases to live.

"Mr. Milky Way Man, it strikes me as quite unlikely that you could offer me much of value. You speak with a very limited amount of reasoning. So much word dancing you do."

I don't know if those are his chosen words exactly or if it's just how my brain is opting to interpret them.

His words? Her words? Its words? My words?

Is it my brain interpreting? Or is it **their** brain really interpreting their own words. I've never actually taken a look inside of my own head, the ol' thinking cap; maybe there's a little sticker with **PROPERTY OF SOME FUCKING SCIENCE LAB #475** or **PROJECT PERSON** or whatever. I mean, they had always been controlling or tinkering or laughing at my severe depression and such. Sure, it lives in my head, but I wasn't in any amount of control for such a long time, whose brain is it really?

A Russian spy living in America, acting American, speaking their carefully crafted English, and shoveling down McDonald's, well he's still under Red Control so he's not an American, follow me? My brain has been that Russian alien spy until an accident gave away its identity. We're all spies and we don't know it. We've always been.

"Allow me to explain, sir," Goat Feathers begins to bullshit, "As a fellow man of science, I can offer you **firsthand** reports, case studies, interviews, whatever you could possibly need, I've got it. I can help!" You can hear the grunt-like fake laughter from our fate's decider while Feathers continues.

"I've already gathered up and eliminated several *damaged* individuals dangerous to your experiment here on Earth. I've learned **YOUR language**. I've reached out to you via a communication process thought impossible by my entire species and highly improbable by yours. And, of course, I DO have your soldier here with me, alive and . . . maybe not *well,* but alive! These are all objective truths. My king, my friend, my savior, surely I must be worthy . .

."

The Ambassador's judge on the other end of our brain-powered walkie talkie waits only a singular second before responding, "Worthy? As a traitor to your own kind, you're unworthy of even an honorable death."

Thanks, Alien Guy or Gal, my sentiments exactly.

"Reaching us is undoubtably impressive, and we WOULD prefer to deal with our letdown of a science cadet internally. Unfortunately, however, this is not nearly enough to—"

"WAIT!" An even more insistent than usual Goat Feathers interrupts, "Please, don't finish your ruling, sir. There's one more thing."

"GgguhRR!" Just an angry groan from far away. "Speak, human . . . NOW."

Even if I wasn't physically fastened to my present location, I'd probably be stuck simply due to suspense. Goat Feathers, even in his deep meditative state, finally begins to reveal his nerves. "We've got a baby on the way, you and I. Wow, oh my, no, sorry. The two of our species is what I mean. A half-breed."

Even in my drug-induced pseudo coma, I can feel my heart begin to beat faster. Instantly thinking the worst.

"The seed of your soldier. A son or daughter soon too special to be accepted. Soon to be considered half-built by satan, by most citizens of Earth."

Instantly knowing the worst.

There's just deep breathing full of bass in the background. He must turn another dial or flick a different switch or tickle his nose a particular way because a door a few feet from me opens seemingly on its own. And then I see her again. She's full of tears. So completely full of tears.

"I have next to me the happy couple." NO NO NO NO NO NO **NO** NO **NO NO** NO NO. "Dr. Fox Viqar and the surely soon to be Mrs. Arina Viqar, full of joy and love and a seriously mixed-race baby!"

I thought I was too high to feel sadness, too sedated to feel anything, really, but it's like I can almost literally feel my heart bursting into 1000 pieces.

"OK, interesting human man. You remain for now. Expect to be seeing us soon."

PART SIX

WHERE OUR ROADS MEET

FINALE OF SNAKES

60

You ever have one of those moments where all the dots connect all of a sudden? Everything clicks. You could be struggling with a work problem or math equation or foreign language and then ¡BAM! You realize exactly what your mental roadblock was, and . . . no more struggle.

It's impossible to plan a glorious moment like this. It'd be nice to say, 'Yeah, later on today I'll figure out I've been using the wrong verb conjugation or value of y or data analyzing tool,' but that's not how it works. They just **happen.**

I'm hobo-drifting from one train of thought or dream or fantasy hallucination to another. They're all the same or they're the furthest thing from it. Being an apprehensive teen, my first stop on the brain tour is the female crippling my fragile heart. It's like I'd trade back every ounce of joy and excitement and over-infatuation that ever was or could have been to not feel this horrible grinding emptiness inside of me.

The best weather is the absence of weather. The best love is the absence of love.

The next train station my mind sneakily hops off at is the thought of the Travelers, not traveling to space or to the deepest depths of the human spirit or to Myrtle Beach. Only traveling to Heaven or Hell if that's still something to believe in. The masses believe it, so it must be true.

Train crash. I'm dropped off in the woods. I'm used to picking myself up surrounded by this sort of wooded scenery by now. As I stand up and begin slowly trekking the terrain, I see movement. I hear movement. The chatter of a pygmy rattlesnake accompanied by a gentle vibration of everything in my line of sight. I feel movement. The faintest earthquake humming below my bare feet.

Behind what looks like a giant Baobab tree, one of those thick African ones, comes a dark shadowy figure. The figure is my height and my build and, upon closer inspection, my complexion, bone structure, and general demeanor. I stare in a fully frightened fashion at this augmented version of myself and I'm frozen in place.

The seasons are changing rapidly around us, 180x fast-forward pace. The green bushy atmosphere we generally ignore turns cranberry and apple cider and pumpkin pie. Those colors have their moment and they die and we stay the same.

Christmas-cold and brittle branches breaking now, they snap and they **¡CRACK!** and they snap and they *¡HISS!* I break my gaze with other-dimension me but he's quicker than a reflex, his shadow-hand grips my jaw like you grip the ball in your dog's mouth while playing fetch.

"Look at **me**, boy," Demon-me practically says to me,

his inferior. My own inferior.

The swarming den of black and brown branch-snakes pile on top of one another in a less than arbitrary manner while I remain immobile. They far surpass the abilities of any reptile I've ever seen on Animal Planet. No prior mention of slithering, savage, little team-players tornado-ing together on any of the *Most Dangerous Creatures* shows I've seen.

They're creating some new sort of giant monster using a textbook Mega-Zord method. Every tree is every branch is every snake is every part of this towering new beast. These legless predators have ironically created a bad-ass new brute fully equipped with functional legs. The engineering here is truly noteworthy.

I catch myself drifting and becoming entranced with this beautiful terror of a sight occurring all around me, and by that, I mean that Shadow Me grabs my jaw again, **harder**, more rigidly this time.

"Shh," I hear from maybe-myself.

The horrifying snake congregation stands as tall as any roller coaster I've ever digitally created and saved and destroyed.

"Do not be afraid. It's your larger purpose," I hear from my subconscious or my dark mirror version or God.

I feel the wind attacking the back of my neck and arms and legs, almost scooping me off of whatever earth-like surface my feet are stuck into and right towards the constantly shifting nightmare. My peripherals inform me somewhat of what's happening around me but my focus is only straight ahead, staring into the eyes of this odd funhouse version of myself, it's the only place I'm allowed to look. I'm not sure what *I'm* capable of, after all.

Otherworldly Me removes his dark right hand from **my** face, slowly bringing it to firmly clench his own chin. His equally creepy left hand eerily rises to meet its counterpart. He and I are on super-slow-motion while the seasons and snake community and horrifying coil-creation are living out full and fulfilling lifetimes. Lifetimes of Galapagos giant tortoises or koi fish or cats, all nine of them.

He begins to pull down the lower portion of his jaw with a grievously forceful momentum about him. As he does, I suddenly hear what I can only describe as a terrifying... pressure. Like you leaned right through the 17"x 11" window on your flight to Tampa and now you're struggling with every bit of strength and endurance you could ever hope for to not be thrown out of this Airbus A330.

He keeps pulling and I keep wishing for the perfect yawn or swallow or piece of gum to thwart the agony occurring in my eardrums. I've never been in a situation where I wanted to collapse to my knees but truly couldn't, not until now. I wonder if I'm dreaming, I wonder if anyone else is sharing this petrifying experience. For their sake I hope not.

"Embrace your destiny," continues the voice of Buddha or Mufasa or my occipital lobe's primary visual cortex, '**Our irony** is the best entertainment. Let go and embrace destiny.'

I'm filled with enough fear and confusion to faint upright. Snakeosaurus has begun taking minivan size steps towards us, hundreds of scaled venomous assholes striking the Earth simultaneously. I can't hear anything besides what I'd guess is my brain being vacuumed out,

IT STARTS WHEN YOU STOP

but I can feel those footless footsteps. ¡BRRRRT! ¡BRRRRT! Underneath my paralyzed limbs.

He pulls down on his chin, full force now, as if it's supposed to pop off or expand or dispense a giant shadowy pez candy. ¡BRRRRT! ¡BRRRRT! I'm feeling certain I'll never hear properly again. ¡BRRRRT! ¡BRRRRT! The pressure has my eyes on the verge of popping out. ¡BRRRRT! The 1800 snake-piece devil-puzzle is one or two footsteps away from sealing our fate. ¡BRRRRT!

Other Me must have reached his pain threshold or desired jaw location or maybe he just slipped, because all of a sudden, ¡**SNAP**! His top and bottom rows of teeth collide into each other in an incredible cringe-worthy fashion. It happens so f—

—-FLSSHH—-

I peel open my eyelids and I feel the sting—Devil-Hero-Hiro must have had mother-fucking dynamite teeth. My eyes would be open wide in disbelief if the shining sky above me, now a smoldering orange, would allow it. The seasons are no longer changing, there's no nature left to evolve into carnivorous creatures lacking eyelids, and certainly no oversized Spirit-Monster wreaking havoc.

I make an effort to move my left foot forward, and to my surprise, I'm able to do so quite easily. Then another step and then another. Everything I can see is in ruins, either still mildly on fire or previously on fire and then stomped on by hundreds of pairs of black and red and yellow firefighter boots. Another step and another. Everything is cigarette ash or dust or dissipating particles.

Another step and then just one more before I see the steaming pile of Other Me in puddle form in front of me. It or He or I look like a pile of shining black tar with a pinch of aubergine-colored blood oozing out. This stranger or twin brother I assume I'm hallucinating sacrificed himself, didn't he? But why? Maybe . . . maybe there didn't need to be a reason.

61

The drug setting must have been turned up high for a while. Real high. Or it could have been more ancient Chinese mega-scorpion poison? Whatever it was, I feel like I just woke up from something remarkably intense. There's no more haze surrounding my thoughts, just the sharp, sudden, painful realization that what happened prior to my most recent slumber actually happened.

Everything unbelievably perfect that happens in a dream always just ends up being that, a dream. None of my dozens of . . . what we'll call, *intimately* realistic dreams with a less-than-fully clothed Arina have ended up with me waking up beside her. But seeing my teary-eyed beauty, looking at me with fear and shame and conceivable regret, of course there's no chance that one was only a nightmare. Nope. Just shining saltwater on her cheeks to match her new natural glow.

FUCK. Don't think about it don't think it don't think abou—

My brain is so used to having *Automatic Negative*

Thought Levels set so sky-high that even with my recent supplemental control of my mind, it's still not always a picnic.

I'm in a new setting. It's almost pitch black, which isn't particularly ideal when trying to stay out of one's own head and focus on surroundings. Wherever I may be, it feels damp. My butt is planted in what I'd wager is a plastic patio chair, and my hands are pressed against the scattered wet spots remaining on the armrests.

I'm not tied up anymore. I'M FREE. I frantically jump up before remembering I can't quite see anything. With my feet planted firmly on what seems to be hard taut dirt or something similar, I take slow, deep yoga breaths in and out, trying to get my bearings straight. Before I can decide whether to sit back down or remain st—

¡FLASH!¡FLASH!

•

Two ferociously bright lights appear at my 10 and 2 o'clock. It's like they're erupting. Blinded by darkness, then too bright to see. They're seriously like two miniature suns, both with the sole purpose of giving me permanent retinal damage.

I stretch my eyes as open as possible, then close them as if I'm trying to seal them shut forever. Open wide once again, and close tightly. My eyes are performing a sun salutation, and as they finally adjust to the mysterious lights surrounding me, a *new* voice startles yours truly with a simple greeting.

"Hello, Hiro." It's a deep and classically manly voice filled with vibrato and accompanied by some sort of

IT STARTS WHEN YOU STOP

African accent.

"Or should I call you *Deaf Turtle?* Our *'new friend'* Ambassador Goat Feathers seemed to be inclined that that name suits you more favorably." Tanzania or Kenya or Burundi, a country where Swahili is the native tongue.

"Or we could always stick to your case number, Project Person, Earth-Viqar Division #11352, but that surely seems less fun." My eyes have finally become near fully accustomed to the light.

"Who the fuck are you?" I ask the seemingly giant man slowly walking towards me. He says nothing yet. I look to my left and quickly to the right, and both ways again as if I'm Frogger preparing to make my way across the screen. I'm not sure who I'm hoping to see, my group of deceased Traveler friends? The remaining two, Ambassador traitorous bastard and my dearest scalawag Rina? The police who'd most likely toss me into a straitjacket? Or maybe Blaire, the person I'd probably like to speak to most and am desperately worried about but am also desperately wishing unfastened herself out of this whole disaster situation somehow.

"Where are we?" I ask as I continue to take slow, baby footsteps backwards. The man looking right into my soul is tall, really tall, 6'7 or 6'8 maybe. He's also big, so big, probably around 500lbs. He's fat, definitely, but below those 200 excess pounds is a muscular 300-pound beast. This ebony giant, dressed crisply in a tan Givenchy suit, slowly forms a smile. It shows the top row of his perfect set of pearly white choppers. It honestly looks kinder and more genuine than any smile I've seen from Goat Feathers or Viqar or Todd or any other fake father figure I've had the privilege of having.

"Do not worry, young Hiro, all is well."

His voice is familiar. Hauntingly beautiful. Intoxicating almost.

"You're safe and, I know more importantly to you, Blaire is unscathed as well."

He sounds so much like he should be narrating a nature documentary that it takes me a second to soak up what he just said.

"Where is she?!" I try to scream but really just whimper.

I was fearless when only my life was on the line.

On the plane with turbulence again. Now, all of a sudden, another human life, a life I value so much more than my own, is along in that shaky plane and that gives me a case of the goddamns.

"She's nearby, young man of Earth, I assure you. No harm has been done to her, and none will, so long as nothing wildly farcical takes place on your end."

I'm hanging on to every word of some strange man I've never met before. A stranger here with me in an unknown location, a stranger who knows my name, and more importantly, her name.

"Tell me who you are." I pat my pockets, right and left and back-right and back-left searching for any sort of instrument that could be used as a weapon to defend myself, but no dice, nothing.

"Seriously . . . WHO ARE YOU?!" I say with anger in my voice and fear in my heart and tears in my eyes. I must have let out enough steam to startle him because his face suddenly changes from a seemingly sincere happiness to a profound sorrow and shock.

"Mr. Hiro, I'll forgive your hostility this once as a token

of good faith, and because I understand you humans so often think illogically. Some more than others, of course. Simply imprudent human biology. Your *friend* Goat, for example, a brilliant subject, yes, but a truly silly and mind-poisoned being."

I don't know whether I should attack or run or sit and hear him out. I do love the idea of anyone speaking poorly of Goat Feathers so I elect to continue pacing on rewind while our unnamed associate takes antelope strides towards me and speaks *at* me. It'd be *to* me if he'd answer a goddamn question I've asked.

"Please," he says sternly yet politely as he pushes the palm of his right hand towards me, signaling we've walked far enough. "Our destination is on the verge of readiness, it is quite nearby, and we are simply to speak. Remember, you are *no longer* in danger. I believe this qualifies as a germane opportunity for a pinky promise."

Another person telling me it's ok now. Another person trying to be the answer to the last person who said the same words and became the problem.

"Allow me to introduce myself. The closest pronunciation of my most true name is Dr. Banshee. What you are seeing, as you've been seeing with Viqar for some time now, is a unique human body which I have engineered. While he chose one of our most objectively handsome models, I decided to go with this massive African body. Don't you love it?"

He does a little spin with his hands above chest level and jazz fingers spread wide. Unexpected. I just nod as he continues to speak and surprise.

"Seriously, aren't I HUUGGEE!? You should see my *front tail!*" He grabs his crotch with both hands and looks straight at me with his most photo ready smile, showing off all of his quadruple chiclet-sized teeth.

"KIDDING! I know it's just hilariously big human genitalia used for both procreation purposes as well as waste disposal. HAHA, WHAT!? What an absurd appendage, seriously."

I stare at this silly foreign giant in disbelief as he thoroughly amuses himself. I've given up asking my seemingly straightforward questions to this humongous man-baby.

"Once again, my apologies, it's my first time here. I've only ever driven these human beauties in the simulation module back home; this though, this is the *real deal*."

He straightens his posture and adjusts himself, brushing off his shoulders and maneuvering his tie clip to the perfect position. He'd probably be content talking for a several-day span, but I try to politely nudge things along.

"Please, Dr. Banshee . . . my 'unscathed' mother, she's *innocent* in all of this. I just need to **know** she's alright. Please. Where is she? May I see her?"

Banshee's face appears to show consideration and maybe even understanding. I wouldn't quite say concern, though. No.

"Yes, of course," he answers as he tinkers with the already perfect knot of his pink and grey diagonally striped necktie.

"Please, Mr. Hiro, we need to augment our body placement just slightly; follow me right this way."

There are no roads or paths or trees in sight, just the formerly blinding lights which have now dimmed to being only faintly there at all. Without a phone or a flashlight or a star in the sky, Banshee knows exactly where we're going despite being brand new in his body. He seems to be sensing or smelling or hearing where our exit coordinates are.

"You see, I've been in charge of this entire project for a long time, since the start. In charge of mission goals, programming, candidate and planet alternatives, agent and body selection, all of it. We've seen our dreams, my dreams, evolve and come to fruition. Well, just about. So, naturally, you can understand why I might be a touch excited about whipping around this new body, which I developed, for the first time on Earth."

He's walking slowly but his stride is so long I feel like I'm running with him to keep up. Before our hike through nowhere exhausts me entirely I ask, "Where are you taking me? . . . and why have you finally decided to come here after so long? Is it because of the . . ." I struggle to formulate the word, ". . . *pregnancy*?"

Unstirred, he keeps walking until he speaks but still doesn't answer. "Careful, Hiro, the terrain begins to dip unexpectedly up ahead."

My frustration builds and builds. Lava nearly erupting from a furious, confused volcano. 'Just answer me, you oversized alien piece of shit,' I think but don't say.

"I'm sure at this point you must be growing annoyed, very much so I Imagine. Your low patience levels paired with your near maximum levels of anxiety and rage have you visibly livid."

"It's not like it used to be, you know . . . " I chime in. To my own amazement, I'm mildly boastful. "Depression may have blanketed the potential I've felt I'm supposed to have for every moment of my life so far, but that's done." So passionate and sincere and sure of myself. "Completely unable to control my emotions, a complete and constant spiraling wreck. Not anymore, not ever sin—"

"**YES**, young Hiro, after your accident we may have *somewhat* lost control *AT TIMES*. 'Dropped the ball' some of your kind may say. We've had more than one 'troubleshooting opportunity' in that sense, although, your particular case may be the most peculiar, and THAT is why I'm here after all this time."

As he finally begins giving me some amount of useful information, I take a step with my right foot where earth is supposed to be but isn't.

¡HRACK! Says my body at the end of my nostalgic descent.

"Fuck!" I yell from the ground, holding my newly twisted right ankle. I hear stones and sand and pieces of macadam sliding down the mean jerk path that just wiped me out.

"HA!" Banshee laughs out loud. "You ask and ask and ask but you don't listen; I **tooolllllld** you to watch your step."

'Way to rub it in,' I'm partially thinking but mostly I'm thinking 'OW OW OWW OWW OW, GODDAMN IT, OW.' Before I can even get to being annoyed about the former of the two thoughts, he's in front of me with his right hand extended towards me, if we can still call that thing a hand. It looks like what a regular person's hand would metamorphose into. Final form. I can't help but stare.

His giant black catcher's mitt of a hand is freshly manicured. I suppose maybe the body is too new to have scuffed anything up yet. I extend my hand as well. It looks comically small in comparison, almost engulfed by his as he practically tosses me into the air.

"Typical human behavior," he says as he plainly enjoys the sound of his own, new human voice, "to just wait for your turn to speak instead of actually listening or extending concern. *Ironic* for a species so full of sadness and supposed sympathy. So, if I tell you to be careful, it is for your sake, Hiro, not my own."

"Alright . . . **gotcha**." I spew with palpable attitude while I roll my eyes like I have with every teacher or other authority figure in my life. I throw my two thumbs up, but with the disrespectful nature of two middle fingers. He just smiles. I'm not sure how well he's picked up on some of our species sarcastic subtleties.

We continue walking at a steady pace. Every few steps forward somehow seems to make those odd aforementioned lights, now behind us, grow increasingly bright. I turn my head to see but only briefly. I'd prefer not to kiss dirt again so soon. When I turn my gaze back to directly in front of me, I notice two new lights of the same variety at my current 10 and 2. At first, they just flicker on and off.

ON OFF ON OFF ON OFF. ON OFF ON OFF.

But we keep inching forward without words, and as the lights behind us begin to return to their former starlike brilliance, their sister lights in front of us must receive the memo. Decibel by decibel, they mature to near blinding levels.

I try at first to pay the surrounding spotlights little mind, I really do. I just want to get back to why exactly our case, my case, is special. Of enough importance for head honcho over here to make a personal appearance. If it's because of the horrible mutant monster beginning to form in Arina's filthy fucking belly, then I have nothing to do with any of this. Nothing at all. And Blaire . . . less than nothing. Maybe get rid of me and leave her be. Turbulence again.

Four incredible, luminous blue lights suddenly appear from my 12, 3, 6, and 9 o'clocks to accompany or maybe even accentuate the four existing yellow lights at my 10, 2, 4, and 8. It overwhelms my eyes. I shut them and instinctively rub them with the near knuckle portions of my two pointer fingers.

With the insides of my eyelids acting as projector screens, I'm blessed with bursts of colors straight from my brain. My temporary blindness strikes me with nostalgia. I try to crack my eyes open just a touch, but I feel bombarded by red and yellow and blue fireworks. Primary color deja vu. I don't know why but I think of snakes.

My pecan-colored peepers begin to adjust, not enough to see *clearly,* but enough to see. I can't tell if it's just my eyesight understandably playing tricks or not but it *feels* like the surrounding lights are making their way closer, closing in on us. Closing in on me. Although I can't make out Banshee's facial expression, I can tell he's standing still, so I know it's just part of our little walk.

Every second brings my vision closer to homeostasis. About three of those life-altering seconds later I understand why it seems like those odd lights are verging on contact with us. It's because they are.

By the time I can operate my eyes normally, these hypnotic and mysterious sets of lights have created a perfect circle in the sky just a few feet above us.

My mind is void of thoughts outside of this very moment. There **is** nothing else. I think this is sort of what

IT STARTS WHEN YOU STOP

Tibetan monks spend lifetimes attempting to achieve—an impossible sensation to maintain.

They appear to be eight separate entities working in sync, slowly gliding into position. My zen moment dissipates as I think of the phrase 'in sync' and then of synchronized swimmers and then of snakes again. I can't shake the weird, random thought.

All of a sudden it feels like I'm being vacuumed up from the ground. A moment ago, the air was completely still and now I'm a dust bunny dead center in the middle of some sort of Middle Eastern Haboob dust storm blowing straight upwards. Against the resistance of *nature* or whatever this is, I attempt to make my way back down to the rocky dirt-covered Earth, seeking to grab something, anything, to hold on to.

Unsuccessfully, I flail my arms, gripping and grasping, fighting this mighty whirlwind. The feeling in your face when you're thrown down from the roller coaster's summit.

A purring sound surrounds us and surrounds the sound of the blustery, boisterous weather.

The hum . . .

Another noise I know I've heard.

As the presently indiscernible buzz grows in intensity, so does my inability to stay on the ground. All my muscles are actively working to remain on land while all my senses are being flooded. I make the mistake of looking at the blue light in my vision line. As soon as I do, it's over. Done. I lose control . . . of my muscles and mind and myself.

The light grows lighter in color but certainly not in magnitude. I feel my mind drift for just a second before I realize that my body is adrift as well. I mean, afloat, really. My senses awaken to an unsettling lack of bodily control. I force my eyes open enough to see my feet begin hovering from the ground. The cult of David Blaine. Bokor of flight. Dust and particles fly upwards into my eyes and nose and mouth but I don't care. I just fight and fight to swim back down. I wish I were fatter. Stupid slender young body.

I'm doggy paddling and breast-stroking, but it's like I'm on an escalator moving the opposite way. An activity that will definitely get you kicked out of most shopping malls, by the way.

Further and further, inch by inch I'm pulled away from the turf I'm fighting so vigorously to reach. Second after second, thought after thought, I'm understanding what this is. Believing what this is.

What this really is.

"Do not fear, Hiro. I've given you my word . . . my promised pinky!" He shouts over the noise, ". . . You are in no harm. Just allow yourself to become . . . tranquil."

He lifts his arms towards the sky, yoga style, slowly and reaches towards opposite directions until they're straight up, along with his chin and his gaze. He happily accepts the anti-gravity, and while I continue to do the exact opposite, he roars at me without looking in my direction, "Really! It's the safest form of transportation in the universe!"

The aesthetically pleasing and perfectly symmetrical glowing orbs have proved themselves to be interconnected. A unit. A team. They've organized and orchestrated their super-suction industrial vacuum system, and it sounds like it's time to depart.

"Seriously! Makes your human airplanes seem about

as safe as heated ice-skates!"

No more curiosity as to how he knew the way so well with no paths, never having been here before; he was just leading me to the landing pad, to directly below his . . . *vehicle,* right in the center.

Well, fuck it. No more fighting, I allow myself to become . . . tranquil. All aboard.

62

I'm suddenly inside of what looks somewhat like a hospital. Spacious and clean and full of rooms with doors. It smells like nostalgia and lemons, marginally familiar but not all the way there. A cleaning supply closet mixed with some sulfuric explosion I wasn't really present for but think of, that I couldn't have actually experienced but **feel** somehow.

The bulk of what I am looking at is on a color spectrum ranging from a shining white to a dazzling blue. It's mesmerizing, like we're inside of a crystal or a glacier, but at 68 degrees Fahrenheit, and with top-notch technology all over.

I get about one-third of the way through a visual scanning of the area before I see Dr. Banshee standing there with his arms crossed, looking sweetly at me. What I see would have surely surprised me weeks ago, probably several days ago, possibly several hours ago. But I think I can no longer be shocked.

Maybe not ever again.

Although his cufflinks, which no one wears anymore, remain perfectly intact, he appears to be missing most of his right shoulder. He's pixelated as if he's not real at all. I mean, he's not I guess, but this is still question-worthy.

"Uh, Dr. Banshee, what the fuck is happening with your upper body?"

He looks down and sees his bodily life-glitch occurring, but not an ounce of worry, just his pleasant African chuckle. He casually brushes where his shoulder **should** be. Nothing happens on this first attempt. He tries again with a bit more gusto and his shoulder pixels reappear, mostly at the same time, followed by some late bloomers popping in the succeeding seconds.

"Oh, don't worry, my young guest. This generic-line molecular teleporter offers several opportunities for improvement. For example, take a look down at where you'd typically locate your silly human sexual organ."

"Oh, fuck!" I can't help but cry out as I look to find that whole particularly important region of my body missing, just pixelated flashes of color teasing me. Also, my human sexual organ is really not that silly.

What's strange is I don't feel anxious, just surprised because, naturally, it's supposed to be there. I tap and brush the ol' package a few times until it returns to existence and my mind can move forward.

"Allow me to begin your tour, Hiro. Come." He gestures with his right hand for me to follow him, bringing his comically big fingers back and forth towards his palm. I do without question. I feel fearless.

As we walk through this college-campus-sized intergalactic vehicle, I'm fascinated by literally everything I see. It looks like a snow level of *Donkey Kong Country*, everything evenly coated in phosphorescent white and blue and purple. I'm feeling incredibly well.

"Coming up on the left you'll find a newly installed human restroom to specially accommodate you and your friends."

Pshh, friends. What friends are even left? Goat Feathers is certainly not my friend.

Banshee knows this, which makes me feel angry, but it's a different sort of anger than I'm used to. Less of an emotional angst and more a knowledge of being objectively wronged and needing to complete some sort of reciprocal action in order to feel content.

Something is up with me. Not in a bad way at all, but something.

We pass a sign signifying an enclosed restroom. Truly universal. Banshee continues his tour guide routine, "Ahh, the interesting stuff is just ahead."

Even amongst the vast array of beautiful everything, I see something on the left side of our narrow current hallway full of mystery doors. I don't know why, maybe instinctively, but I stealthily leap to the wall to pick up this mystery object.

While still moving forward, I grab it by what I'd guess is the center, although you never know when something around here is going to hover around and find friends and merge into a spaceship.

The object is roughly four inches in length and looks like two nails attached to each other at the dull ends, and then dipped in some sort of blue Topaz magic.

As Banshee turns his round, human-form face to make sure I'm still following, I cast my mental focus to meet his and I make a nearly closed fist. Clenched enough for this random contraband to not be visible, but not so tight for the two sharp, pointed edges to cause crimson to trickle from my pierced palm and fingers. Instead, they just creep out slightly past my pinky and pointer area, almost as if you were holding a double-ended space-pencil.

"What's behind these closed doors we're passing?" I ask.

Before he has a chance to provide an answer, I hear a gentle, yet firm, THUMP from the other side of one of those doors. It startles me enough to inadvertently squeeze too tightly the space-tool in my possession. One of the needle-like tips digs slightly into the back-left side of my right pointer finger. I cry out in pain, but only on the inside. On the outside, my calm face and demeanor play it off perfectly. Stress-free straight flush at the final table.

"Those doors? **Mmmoo**stly just small science rooms and offices, nothing to write home about, especially when we're on our way to the Science Community Headquarters. No worries . . . it's very nearby, Hiro. It's incredibly interesting."

¡**THUMP!** A similar THUMP from behind a different door, this one followed by a hardly audible HISS. An uncontrollable shiver takes over my whole body and I think of . . . I feel . . . snakes?

Snakes . . . again?

Again.

Snakes.

Before my train of thought begins to slither around too much, I hear Banshee's deep, exotic voice, "Come, come." He's not looking at me, he's facing forward with his left hand waving a bit in the air, fluttering his fingers to show his enthusiasm. Exactly what his foreign fervor means is yet to be seen.

The next room we come to, located on our left, isn't closed off and creepy like the previous ones we've passed. I mean, it's still creepy, for sure, but in its own unique manner. A large mirror, about 8-by-12 feet, separates the upcoming room and our current hallway prior to the door which actually allows entry. It's the same uniform ice-sculpture, transparent blue, with no doorknob. An identical window seems to be found on the other side of the room.

Once we're finally standing in front of the entry gate, Banshee looks to me as if he'd like me to begin leading the way all of a sudden. Lacking a usual self-doubt, I go for it. There's no pull option, so naturally I attempt to push the door open with my free hand.

As soon as my palm presses against the knob-less blue door, a light shock pulses from my fingers and wrist, then jolts through my arm and down my back. A visible wave of air or energy or imagination whooshes from the door directly towards my chest and nearly collapses it. Nearly collapses me.

"HA! Oh goodness! I forgot about your comprehensive unfamiliarity with our technology."

I'm surely giving him the dirtiest look possible as I nearly drop my new favorite toy, the one I found on this pristine floor. Well, it seems pristine, but I suppose it could just be the lustrous colors playing tricks.

He simply looks at the door . . . concentrates . . . then SHHHWWWIIHH, **it opens**. Incredible. Also, thanks for telling me, jerk.

He looks back at me and explains, "Our kind's thinking

has evolved well past yours, Hiro. Here, if you mindfully think something to be done, it is done, so long as you possess the physical ability to have done it. Understand?"

I don't feel upset about his action, or lack of action, which I interpret objectively as purposeful. There's just some more of that new, empirically straight-forward anger.

". . . Oh, yes. I see," I reply.

"Don't toil too intently if you're unable at first, the adjustments may simply take some time," he says before quickly walking forward into the massive science lab. Adjustments?

It looks like you could fit an entire second spaceship inside of this wildly large room. The ceilings are significantly higher than they were in the hallway—they must be 40 feet high. Honestly, I've never seen anything like it. It's beautiful.

I feel like I'm standing in an incredible extraterrestrial church, full of sculptures and elbowroom and intricate designs. I've always really loved the architecture and sheer aesthetic value of various houses of worship. It's just the ideas held inside of them I could do without.

"Allow me to show you around, Hiro." Despite his comment about adjustments seeming on the sketchier end of things, I feel . . . fine about it, just a bit curious is all. Plus, I know what about 0% of this surrounding equipment is, so that's holding a good amount of my attention at the moment. I'll come back to it.

"This is where countless hours of important, invaluable even, research has been conducted, on your species as well as many others." Everything looks shiny, like it's been laminated. "Here we have our most newly updated Brain Simulator Units."

They look like old-school arcade machines. Pac-man and Frogger and Dig-Dug all in aisles except they make innocent victims harmfully delusional or manically depressed. There are dozens upon dozens of them, a full 80's style mall arcade where you could hang out and smoke cigarettes. All of these rows of eating disorder and suicide RPG's, all of them empty.

Behind a dazzling set of blue beakers, I see complex silver scribbles, similar to those on the clothing of Goat Feathers, on a white-board dipped in glitter, but no one is here to fill and empty beakers or solve any mathematical equations. No aliens in their fraudulent, mixed-race, super-model or oversized African bodies. No little grey men with big black eyes or squirrel monsters or squid people or whatever they might actually look like. And at this moment, importantly, my mind is too occupied to involve any other thoughts.

63

The newly logical brain residing in my skull sees no reason not to continue following. Not at this point, what would it matter? But some secret squirrel in there provokes me to look once more at that machine, the one that looks the same as all the others but is out of order or off limits or is made of Legos. I've never been a handyman, no mister fixit, nor am I necessarily tech-savvy. There's just something.

Amidst the wintery Scandinavian landscape that surrounds this one problematic employee, a wave of yellow and blue and red glistens remarkably. Before I even have a second to appreciate it, it scurries back to its starting position, red and then blue and then yellow. Then once more: yellow, blue, red. Red, blue, yellow. My primary color conduit.

I suddenly feel as if my time is running out one hesitant footstep at a time. A shadow lifetime defining my path. A path the masses would surely deem unreasonable or silly or poopoo-brained.

"As a courtesy to all fellow passengers, please refrain from operating recreational Peligrosmoke machines until the smile icon returns to its flashing position."

I see Dr. Banshee while this squawk box intercom performs its announcement. I see him saying words, presumably in my respective language. I see his big stupid fraudulent body. I don't hear his sentiments or read his body language.

A ¡THUMP! and a ¡THUMP! and a definitive ¡HISS!

I need a moment to gather my scattered thoughts, wild little sheep I have to herd in order to find slumber. Sweet, confused creatures.

"Wait," I manage to say to Banshee, while my voice cracks embarrassingly, although there's really not much reason to be embarrassed anymore, no more school dances or sleepovers or job interviews to dread having to ever face.

"Before we keep on trucking," I continue as he makes a slightly confused foreigner face, "I have one question." As much as I'd prefer to never think on this subject, it may allow me to stall, reflect and make sure, just for a moment. My most recent slip-fall-combo had interrupted this line of questioning just moments ago. Or maybe it's been days. Tough to be certain.

"Well, Mr. Hiro," Banshee responds while I incidentally take notice of the perfect temperature in the room. "What is your question? Try to make it brief, as we've only a few minutes until our egress from this cluster."

"What about the . . . pregnancy? I mean, what'll happen to the baby? I don't even know how that works, if at all."

Even with a basically repaired brain, I'm still feeling flooded with emotions or rational thoughts or sharpened daggers. The best weather is the absence of weather. The best love is the absence of love.

I start remembering how quickly those seasons seemed to change that time with Shadow Me. Leaves metamorphosing and the rapidly varying precipitation and all of the dots in my mind connecting one by one yet all of a sudden. It wasn't nothing, not at all. It couldn't have been.

"HA!" Banshee cackles, "Oh right, that."

He grabbed **my** jaw for a reason. Something that didn't **REALLY** happen, but really **DID** leave a lasting physical ache in my body. I feel it, now, in the middle of what's objectively going on.

"Turns out, Hiro my boy, that there was no truth to that Goat's fable." He's giving me the precious particulars that I've desired yet can't truly focus on. "Not that that was the singular reason for our interjection in the project," Banshee continues.

Shadow Hiro made me know. I made me know. Talking about embracing destiny, my larger purpose. His and my Pez-style dynamite-teeth. I couldn't explain the self-sacrifice, not before. How could I? Not until all the pieces are there can you configure the puzzle fully. I think Goat Feathers said something eloquently obvious like that. If all goes accordingly, at least I'll know all of his dirty dick double-crosses were in vain. His puddle of burnt flesh will just be filled with slightly more bullshit. His burnt flesh that I'm going to create when I trigger the self-destruct component in my stolen brain.

"I won't lie and say we weren't a bit curious, but just a

predictable ploy from Mr. Feathers." Too many wheels turning to feel any semblance of relief. "The bodies in use on your planet aren't initially programmed with that capability, reproduction, but augmentation is always possible. Really, though, we just needed to see how much of our future is already in motion. Question him up and learn what we can before we dispose of him. For better or worse, he did enact our course of action, after all."

How strange it feels . . . being so familiar with the desire to make the majority of people just go away. Disappear. Easier that than them learning to understand me. Or me understand myself even. Always wishing I could simply become happy. Just some flick of a switch, and all of a sudden, no unwarranted angsty episodes.

"Anyway, Mr. Human Takafuji, that's that. From here on out we're going to be living very very well. You'll be helping us out a bit scientifically, sure, but you'll be well taken care of."

My golden chance for utopian paradise is here, but in a dark, twisty, sort of cinematic way. I'd hoped for something along the lines of sending the population to other dimensions, perhaps via magnetic wave handguns or tiki torch tarot card tricks, not necessarily dooming them to a lifetime of slow mental agony.

"I use my other pinky, though, to promise you of our very real upcoming departure, I'd estimate 45 yugs, ahh, roughly 3 minutes, that is. Time for about one more question that can't wait. Then I'll be forced to become stern." Banshee proclaims as his demeanor begins to intensify.

The miracle recipe for happiness is fully in my hands. I guess actually in my brain or blood or soul more likely.

Not only a contracted lifetime of sincere joy for myself, but the other two passengers in the seats surrounding me as well. Really the only two seats I'd ever care about in the slightest, this flight or any, at least altruistically.

"Right, my apologies, this one last reassurance before I'm void of questions and ready to get rolling," I say, fibbing through my teeth.

My single source of unconditional love throughout my existence, consistently stressed ever since my brain has been producing memories, she could have several decades with the volume so beautifully turned down. Those retina-damaging lights dimmed to let her seeing-vessels finally adjust.

"I don't want to sound rude, Dr. Banshee, I mean no disrespect," I say, formulating my final fragment of analyzation, "You take commands from no one else, right?" He looks mildly insulted, as I'd hoped.

On the other side of the uncomfortably tight armrests surrounding and restraining me sits a whole different type of love. The person that's showed me more genuine care and less judgement than anyone not connected by blood, even the completely overwhelming bulk of them.

Did she use me, in a sense, to accomplish a goal? Of course. I'm quite aware of my surroundings, real or fake or completely absurd. But she had to; we're all connected in this. We are. We're meant to. Cult talk. It's how she went about her task, how she went about knowing me, how she showed me the type of empathy you can't fake.

It'd be the three of us, and perchance others, shipped away to live together with a virtual inability to feel depressed.

"I only ask because I want to know if there's anyone

else I should expect to answer to on the totem pole," I continue before he has a chance for rebuttal or before I chicken out, "Or are you completely in charge?"

Banshee looks at me, proud and with certainty, "Oh, Hiro, there is surely no-one ranked higher than yours truly."

And there is my starting signal and my checkered flag all in one. Enough hope that if this inter-dimensional vehicle is destroyed, humankind may have a chance. As much as my human heart wants to see them once more, I can't risk a hug goodbye turning into a lost thought. A lost chance. A lost cause. I grasp my dually pointed new friend by its center and begin raising it up towards my face.

"Hiro, what is that you're holding? That looks like a ruptured machine fragment. Where did you find that?"

I do it with more certainty than I've ever had about anything. Courageous and confident but potentially still wildly irrational. I bring my new tool, my final puzzle piece inches below my eyes as I open my mouth wide.

"Hiro . . . Hiro, what are you doing? Give me that!" Banshee yells with indisputable worry developing in his voice.

I place the jagged double-dagger inside of my mouth, standing on its own against the roof and floor of my oral cavity. I feel the familiar earthquake returning underneath my feet, I feel the seasons changing again. One more look at Banshee before I close my eyes, one more breath, and I bite down as hard as I possibly can.

"Hiro! STOP! **NO!**"

The pain is incomparable to anything I've been forced to endure. An experience so gut-wrenchingly agonizing it borders hilarity. Comedic masochism to an eccentric degree.

The kickoff of this very brief but incredibly important maneuver begins as one may imagine. Horribly. An excruciating, but expected, skewer into the bottom of my mouth, along the border of my gums. This was anticipated; not what I felt next, though.

I watch Banshee run towards me to save himself and his precious project, but I hear nothing. Sweet slow motion. A pirate hero's prophecy. One final second of peaceful silence.

It's as if this nail has come to life and is slithering all throughout my body, snapping and shattering one rib at a time, breaking me apart bone by bone. Snakes.

It only takes another second to feel the route traveled by the top portion of my particularly pointy piece. Another devastating dart delivered. Right on target. Not a feeling of drowsy unease like when Goat Feathers caught us by surprise like the tootsie-pop-ding-a-ling he is.

A quick pinch and a fleeting moment of perfect bliss. A smile beginning to form before there are no more smiles, the snake suddenly standing between me and Banshee tells me this without words. It's just appeared for a last smooch goodbye before our plane comes to its inevitable crash. A closing hiss of venomous endearment before I finally decide it's time to kiss back.

ABOUT ATMOSPHERE PRESS

Atmosphere Press is an independent, full-service publisher for excellent books in all genres and for all audiences. Learn more about what we do at atmospherepress.com.

We encourage you to check out some of Atmosphere's latest releases, which are available at Amazon.com and via order from your local bookstore:

Tales of Little Egypt, a historical novel by James Gilbert
For a Better Life, a novel by Julia Reid Galosy
The Hidden Life, a novel by Robert Castle
Big Beasts, a novel by Patrick Scott
Alvarado, a novel by John W. Horton III
Nothing to Get Nostalgic About, a novel by Eddie Brophy
GROW: A Jack and Lake Creek Book, a novel by Chris S McGee
Home is Not This Body, a novel by Karahn Washington
Whose Mary Kate, a novel by Jane Leclere Doyle
Stuck and Drunk in Shadyside, young adult fiction by M. Byerly
These Things Happen, a novel by Chris Caldwell
Vanity: Murder in the Name of Sin, a novel by Rhiannon Garrard
Blood of the True Believer, a novel by Brandann R. Hill-Mann
The Dark Secrets of Barth and Williams College: A Comedy in Two Semesters, a novel by Glen Weissenberger

ABOUT THE AUTHOR

Johnny Abboud is a writer, artist, and avid reader. He lives in Allentown, Pennsylvania. This is his debut novel.

CPSIA information can be obtained
at www.ICGtesting.com
Printed in the USA
BVHW030316081220
594492BV00003B/12